I Am the Codyman

American Book Classics™
An imprint of American Book Publishing
325 East 2400 South, Salt Lake City, Utah 84115
www.american-book.com
Printed in the United States of America on acid-free paper.

I Am the Codyman

Designed by John Wik, design@american-book.com

Library of Congress Cataloging-in-Publication Data is available upon request.

ISBN 1-58982-023-1

Stubbs, Linda, I Am the Codyman

Special Sales

These books are available at special discounts for bulk purchases. Special editions, including personalized covers, excerpts of existing books, and corporate imprints, can be created in large quantities for special needs. For more information e-mail orders@american-book.com or call 1-800-296-1248.

I Am the Codyman

By Linda Stubbs

Dedication

Dedicated to the memory of Linda Boudreau, with whom I shared many a good book.

Chapter One

Never before in my two years of life did I want something so badly. If only I could talk.

Two days ago, my mother was taken away in a bed on wheels by men in blue trousers. They carried the weirdest suitcases I've ever seen, and I have seen a lot living in a hotel. I don't know why they left me behind—she takes me everywhere with her. It's been two days, and no one's taken me to see her.

Hopefully they'll bring me to her after this meeting. Michael Goodwin, my buddy and the concierge, said I had to come, so it must be about taking me to see my mother. Adam Park, my mother's lawyer, is here. So is Mr. Ellis, the hotel general manager. This must be important; I can feel it.

"Now then, Adam, what's this all about?" demanded Mr. Ellis. "Mrs. Haney's been dead for two days, and her suite still hasn't been cleared out."

Dead! No way. Those men in the blue trousers wheeled her away on a bed. Go find them, and you'll find her. Come on—let's go look.

"Michael, what's wrong with Cody?" Mr. Ellis spoke sharply. "Settle him down or get him out of here."

"Yes, sir. I'm sorry. I think he's beginning to understand what's going on. Cody, come sit with me and be good."

"Adam, get to the point."

"Mr. Ellis, since you are the hotel's general manager, I've come to you with a very interesting and strange proposal." Adam Park opened his briefcase. "I've brought with me the last will and testament of my client, Gertrude Haney. This was written six months ago, exactly one year after she moved into her suite here. I think it would be best if I read its contents and then we discuss the ramifications."

"Fine. Get on with it."

Adam took a deep breath. "The first part has a number of bequests, the last of which says,

"To Michael Goodwin, concierge of the hotel, I leave $50,000. This is to thank him for being a good friend, conscientious walker, and buddy to my love, Cody."

"Oh my God!" Michael exclaimed as he squeezed my neck.

Easy, man! It's just money. What's that compared to taking me out for a walk every day or playing fetch in the halls?

"Now, the section I had to see you about, Mr. Ellis," continued Adam.

"The remainder of my estate I leave in trust for the care of my faithful companion, Cody, my West Highland White Terrier. He has been like a child to me. He is the smartest, most loving dog I have ever had. He is no ordinary dog. Always living in the hotel—being exposed to so many things and so many people—has given him unique qualities. These are not the ramblings of an old lady. You will soon begin to see what I mean. Love him, and he will love you."

Oh, Mom, I understand, and I love you too.

"It is my desire that Cody continue to rent my suite at the hotel."

"Wait a minute!" Mr. Ellis exploded. "I never liked him being here in the first place."

"I know, I know, Mr. Ellis." Adam spoke calmly, like Mom did when I had to go to the groomer. "Let me finish reading, then we can discuss everything."

"We'll see about that."

Adam started to read again.

"I am reluctant to have him move elsewhere because he is familiar with the hotel, has many good friends who care for him, and has shown by his enthusiasm that he is happy here. Sufficient sums will be set aside each year for the cost of his suite, food, grooming, vet bills, and excursions.

"Because Cody likes so many people at the hotel, present and future employees will be given, on the day they retire, $2,000 for each year they have worked during Cody's life. In addition, Michael Goodwin will receive an additional $25,000 per year to continue his present duties as Cody's primary caregiver.

"I also bequeath $5,000 per year to any child of an employee who attends college during Cody's life.

"Now the challenge for Mr. Ellis. Cody is very sociable and has never been alone. Therefore it is my intention that he never sleep in his suite alone. Since he is paying for the room, you may offer free accommodation to any guest you deem suitable. If no guest can be found, perhaps a homeless person or persons might enjoy a warm room, hot bath, and a good meal."

"Good God! Is she nuts?" Mr. Ellis yelled. "This is no fleabag hotel that takes in just anybody off the street. I've had enough."

"Mr. Ellis, please." Adam held up his hand. "Just a little more."

I do not have fleas! I knew this guy never liked me; I could just feel it.

"Hurry up. I have a meeting in half an hour." Mr. Ellis was getting angrier every time he spoke.

"Now that I will no longer be around, Cody will have to be with people during the day. This can be with the staff or in the lobby with Michael or the guests."

Oh! Oh! Mr. Ellis' eyes might pop right out of his head. I think I'll try to catch them before they hit the floor.

"Cody, stay," Michael whispered.

"In addition, I would like Michael to occasionally take Cody on special weekend excursions to let him experience new things and enrich his life. Remember: great care should be taken for his safety."

All right, Mike! This is sounding good. If only Mom were around to enjoy it too.

"This whole arrangement is null and void if Cody dies of unnatural causes or suspiciously before his time, as determined by the City Center Veterinary Clinic.

"At the end of Cody's natural life, the remainder of my estate will be divided equally between the hotel and the children's hospital.

"If the hotel does not agree to these conditions, I direct my attorney, Mr. Adam Park, to approach two other hotels, mentioned below, with the understanding that Michael Goodwin also moves to these hotels."

Mom, don't be ridiculous. Of course the hotel will want me. Who wouldn't?

"If all these hotels decline, my next option is for Cody to live with Michael Goodwin for the sum of $150,000 per year, while the remainder of the estate would go to the children's hospital. Barring all this, Mr. Adam Park has agreed to care for Cody.

"Finally, please love my baby, for he has only known love, has only shown love, and can bring nothing but pleasure to the lives he will touch."

Adam leaned back into his chair as Mr. Ellis sprang to his feet.

"The woman was crazy! Do you think I'll rent out our prime suite to a dog, expect guests to stay with a dog, and let one hang around the lobby? I'll be the laughingstock of the industry. Good luck trying to get anyone else to be so stupid. Michael, go get that dog's things from the suite and pack him off with Mr. Park. I have a meeting to attend."

As Mr. Ellis blustered toward the door, Adam rose slowly and said, "Mr. Ellis, one last thing. My firm's accountants have done some preliminary figures. After fifteen years, adding inflation, investments, expenditures, and payouts, we're talking about somewhere around $225 million."

Oh, oh! I think Mr. Ellis just swallowed his tongue. Something big just went down his throat, and his eyes are getting big again. Why is he sitting down? I thought he was in such a rush. Now he looks like me— he wants to say something but can't.

Adam, with a slight smile on his face, looked at Michael and me. "Michael, why don't you take Cody out for a walk? I think Mr. Ellis and I have some talking to do. I'll meet you both in the lobby in a few hours. Shall we say 2:00?"

"Yes, sir," Michael replied. "Should I have Cody's things ready?"

Adam winked. "I don't think that will be necessary."

Thanks, Adam. A walk might be a good idea. I can't believe my mother is dead. I never gave her a kiss or said goodbye. A walk might help.

Mitchell, the doorman with the crooked grin, hurried to get the door when he saw us coming. "Morning, Michael. You two are late today. How's the little guy doing?"

Michael glanced down at me. "He knows something is wrong. He didn't eat much yesterday and wouldn't eat this morning. I think I'll take him down to the harbor and get him a hot dog from one of the vendors."

"What's going to happen to him now that Mrs. Haney has passed on?" Mitchell whispered.

Why do people whisper in front of a dog? Don't they know we can hear everything? Actually, come to think of it, I wish they'd whisper all the time. It would be a lot easier on my ears.

Michael picked me up and gave me a hug. "I think we'll know more this afternoon. See you later."

****

"Here, Cody. Maybe this will cheer you up—a hot dog with a little ketchup, just the way you like it."

Hold on to it for a minute. There's Dusty.

"Cody, slow down. Where are you going? I see. You want to share your lunch with Dusty."

Of course I do. You know he looks for food in the dumpster behind the hotel. I like to share.

"Hi, Cody." Dusty patted my head as I jumped onto his bench. "How are you doing today, fella? Hi, Michael."

"Hi, Dusty. He's been a little sad. I don't know if you heard. Mrs. Haney died two days ago, and Cody's been missing her."

Yeah, but I didn't know she was dead.

"Poor little fella. I guess he's homeless like me."

"Not quite. I think he'll be staying in the suite at the hotel."

"I'll be darned! A dog in a ritzy hotel like that!"

"I know. It doesn't seem fair when some people don't even have a roof over their head."

"Hey, don't feel sorry for me. You make your bed, and you have to lie in it. I get by okay, and I've got friends like you and Cody."

"Thanks, Dusty."

When we walked away, Michael picked me up again. I got the feeling he was a little sad too. "You know, Cody," he whispered in my neck, "I don't think we're always grateful for what we have."

Mitchell opened the door as we arrived. "Hey, Michael. I guess you know something. Mr. Ellis called a full staff meeting this afternoon. What's going on?"

"Can't say, but don't worry about it."

"Michael, we should talk." Adam immediately shepherded us into a nearby room. "Mr. Ellis has provided us with this office."

Good. If I hear all this again without Mr. Ellis interrupting, maybe I can get everything straight.

Adam settled back in the chair. "Michael, before we get started, tell me what you thought about the arrangements discussed this morning. Be perfectly honest."

"Well, sir," began Michael, "first, I hate to admit it, but...no, I don't hate to admit it. I am really fond of Cody. He's not like any dog I've ever known. He's very intelligent, and even though he's little, he acts like he's big. This may not seem too manly, but look at him—he's so cute. I never imagined I could like a small dog. I can't explain it."

Hey, what's to explain? Just look at me. Never mind; keep going. I love it.

"Before this morning, I was upset that Cody might be leaving and I'd never see him again. I even called your office yesterday to make an appointment. I wanted to know if there was any possibility that I could have Cody. Your secretary said you would see me today. You know, Mr. Park, I would have taken him for nothing. I didn't realize Mrs. Haney was so wealthy!"

"Thank you, Michael, for being so open about your feelings. And please, call me Adam. How do you think Cody will get along here at the hotel? And how do you feel about the responsibility you have been given to look after him?"

"I think he'll be fine. He knows a lot of the staff. Everybody likes him and talks to him. I think this can only get better once the staff is briefed this afternoon. He was used to being in the suite a lot during the day, so a move to the lobby will be different. I think he'll adjust as long as he finds a place for his afternoon nap. My biggest concern is the nights. I'd rather take him home than put him in a room with strangers every night. I'm afraid he might get kicked off the bed or yelled at. I feel uneasy about the whole situation."

"I know what you mean," replied Adam. "Mrs. Haney and I had many long discussions about this."

Not in front of me you didn't. Those must have been the times I had to stay in the limo with Jeffrey. I always wondered why I only went into his office sometimes.

Adam sighed. "She gave this a lot of thought, and she may be right. She felt Cody was used to a lot of people around, having been raised in the hotel. Many of these people like him and spend some time with him daily. She considered sending him home with you at night, but she didn't want him taken out of the suite and traveling every day. She felt the hotel would no longer be his home but just a place to hang out. I can see her reasoning. She also felt some people might benefit from spending the night with Cody."

Do I get a say in any of this?

"With this in mind, I have spoken to Laura at the front desk. It would be her job to identify possible candidates based on her feelings toward them. I think she has enough experience dealing with people to choose candidates who will not be cruel to Cody; however, the final decision will be left up to you.

"Mrs. Haney was not a snob as to whom should spend the night. Every effort should be made to find someone, but if you can't, you can take him home, or perhaps he will find his own place in the lobby after he's spent a few days there."

Yeah, right. Like anyone wouldn't want a free suite and an opportunity to spend the night with me. Attention! Look at this face!

Michael took a deep breath. "Okay, Adam. Let's give it a go. We can always look at it again in a month or so when we see how things work out. It certainly is an interesting proposal, and the hotel should improve because no one will want to lose their jobs with such a generous retirement bonus."

Adam laughed. "You know, I think that is exactly what Mrs. Haney was thinking. Very good, Michael, he's all yours. I won't interfere or check up on you, but you have my number if you need me. And one last thing—if you take him out on the weekend, please be careful. Bye, Cody. Be a good boy."

Have you ever heard about me not being a good boy? Sometimes I wonder how you ever got to be lawyer. Have you heard the one about the lawyer who...oh, never mind, that's not nice. I think I'll go over and give him a kiss so he knows I appreciate everything.

"Thanks, Cody. Good luck."

Let's go, Mike. We've got things to do and people to meet.

"Hi, Michael. Hi, Cody," greeted Colleen at the door to my suite. "We're just finishing up cleaning."

Uh oh! Something smells different in here. Not totally different, but something is missing. Let me into that bedroom. I can hardly smell my mother. Hey, where has all her stuff gone? It's not fair! First you take her away, and now you take all her stuff. I want my mother!

"Cody," demanded Michael, "stop running around. What are you smelling for? Do you want to go out? No? I get it. Colleen, let me see that bag for a second. Let's see...ah, here we go. Here, Cody."

Yes! Mom's slipper. Oh, Mike, you always know what I'm thinking. Thanks. This will be my favorite toy.

Chapter Two

Hey, put me down. Don't knock on that door. Give me a minute. Don't I get some time to prepare for my first guest?

Mrs. Semple, I know you. You've stayed here before.

"Hi, Cody." Mrs. Semple patted me on the head and gave me a biscuit. "Michael, I'm so glad I decided to stay here again, and the suite is so beautiful."

"You can thank Cody for that. And thank you for volunteering to be his first guest. He's been missing Mrs. Haney, and it's nice to have a friend for the first couple of nights. If you have any problems, call down to the front desk and Gordon will take care of it. He will be here at night to look after Cody, and I'll be back about 8:00 in the morning to take him out."

"Thank you, Michael. Could you arrange for a taxi to pick me up about 9:00 tomorrow morning?"

"No need for that," replied Michael. "While you are Cody's guest, his limousine will be at your service. Jeffrey will be waiting for you at 9:00 at the front door."

"My goodness!" exclaimed Mrs. Semple. "That's an unexpected treat. Thank you, Michael, and good night. Don't worry about Cody; we'll make out fine."

We'll see about that. I wonder if she knows how to play grr-toy. I'll get one and see what happens.

Here, try to take it. You missed. Missed again. Ha! There you go. Try to take it from me. "*Grr...grr.*" Shake it. That's right.

Okay, you've got it. Throw it. Throw it. Good.

Hey, you learn pretty quick.

"Come here, Cody," said Mrs. Semple. "Sit up with me in the chair. Good boy. You don't know how glad I am to be here with you. I don't have anyone in the city to talk to. My husband is in the hospital for his six-month heart check-up, and I think there might be a problem. He's been more short of breath than usual."

Hey, don't start crying. Just keep talking or think of happy thoughts. Here, try these: a ride in the car, a walk in the park, a piece of cheese—oh, oh, try this—sleeping in the sun. Here, I'll give you a big juicy kiss. That always helps.

"Thanks, Cody," she said. "That helps a lot."

I knew that. Let's go to bed.

"Why don't we go to bed? I have a long day tomorrow."

Man, she can read my mind. I better watch what I'm thinking.

****

"Come here, Cody. Why are you hiding? Didn't you like the shower running?"

Dumb question. Don't you like being hit by a car? Falling down the stairs?

Hey, there's Mike at the door. Let's go let him in.

"Good morning, Mrs. Semple. How did you and Cody make out?"

"Just wonderful! He's so funny! He spent half the night right under the covers. I do feel badly for him though. When I woke up this morning, he was lying on the floor with his head on an old slipper. I presume it belonged to Mrs. Haney. He must really miss her."

Of course I do. This is the second time I've lost a mother. I barely remember my real mother, but I remember snuggling into her, drinking warm milk, and being kissed all over. And my next mother was so wonderful. She loved me and taught me so many things. We had a lot of fun!

Now I'm on my own. I will never have a mother again. Wouldn't you miss the last mother you'll ever know?

"He'll get better," said Michael. "He was better yesterday than the day before. Come on, Cody. Let's go out. Good luck at the hospital,

Mrs. Semple. Jeffrey will be ready whenever you are. We'll see you this evening."

Bye, Mrs. Semple. Come on, Mike. I'll race you to the elevator.

Yes! I always win. Then again, I have four legs, and you only have two. But yours are bigger, so I guess more is better than bigger. I like the elevator—it tingles my insides.

****

Come on, Carter. Hurry up and get me out. Carter takes me out during the day to do my business. He's the bellhop. I'm not sure what that means, but he helps people with their suitcases. It's probably just another stupid word people use.

"Thanks, Carter," Michael said when we came back. "Since Cody will be spending his days in the lobby from now on, let's try him without a lead. Keep an eye on him today to make sure he's not bothering any of the guests or getting into trouble. My biggest concern is that he doesn't get out the front door."

This sounds promising. I have been wanting to give this place a good going-over, especially that big plant in the corner. It hasn't grown since I've been here…maybe I could help with the watering.

"Cody, heel." Michael turned and started walking away. "Let's go get your breakfast. You won't be eating in the suite anymore. I think I have found a spot by the kitchen door where you can eat and where we can leave your water."

Lead the way, Mike. Say the word food, and you've got my full attention. Smells like good food too. Open those doors and let me through!

Michael knelt down beside me. "These doors have to be kept shut, so we've had a little flap door installed in the bottom for you. This way you can go get your water anytime. Try it out. In you go."

Hey, don't push!

Where'd you go?

Mike, where are you? I hear you. Open this door and let's go. I don't think you'll fit through that door, so why are you trying? You want me to come back out. I wish you'd make up your mind. You just pushed me through, and now you want me out again. All right, I'll play your silly game.

Tada! Here I am.

"Good boy." Michael beamed. "Okay, through the door."

I don't believe it; the boy's confused today. All right, here I go. Why don't you try the big door?

Good boy, you made it, Mike. Never mind. The smells are getting stronger. Let's go. Another set of doors? Hey, where's the door for me? Mike, open up, man. I'm starving.

Great. Here it comes. I can tell by the way you're standing I'm in for a lecture. Don't be a pig; don't eat too much, you'll get sick. I've heard it all before—open this door!

"Cody, stay!" Michael got down on his knees again. "This is the kitchen, and you are not allowed in there due to health regulations."

Yeah. Yeah. I eat too much, and it's bad for my health. Don't worry. I won't eat too much. Since I know the way, I'll come back a lot and eat a little. It's always good to figure out the angle.

"Over here is your water, and your food will be put out at the regular times. Look at me talking as if you understand." Michael shook his head and smiled.

What's not to understand? There will always be water here, and there will be food after Carter takes me out in the morning and when the guy on TV says, "Good evening and welcome to the 6:00 news." Same thing for almost two years, just a different place. What, did someone paint a dummy sign on my back while I was sleeping? Open that door and I'll show you I know how to eat in moderation. Good, here comes someone. They'll open it.

"Cody, no! Stay!"

Whoa, cool it. I wasn't going to leave you. You're always welcome to go anywhere with me. Get off your knees and let's go. You can do it. Here, give me your pant leg, I'll help. Come on already. You're making me mad.

Never mind. I hear someone coming from behind the door. This is your last chance to come with me 'cause I'm gone.

"No!"

Well, you don't have to yell. I always obey the "no" word. I'm telling you, Mike, you've lost it today. You push me through a door that was specifically made for me to get to a door that you won't let me in! Sometimes you humans make absolutely no sense.

Here comes Jennifer, carrying a stack of plates. I might be able to get in since Mike probably will forget about me. Every time he sees Jennifer, he gets a weird look on his face. If he were a St. Bernard, he would drool.

"Hi, Jen," said Michael. "I wonder if you can take those dishes into the kitchen and then come back for a few minutes. I'm trying to teach Cody not to go into the kitchen and to stay out of the way of the door. I don't want him to get hit or someone to drop an order all over the place."

"Sure, I'll be right back."

This is rich. Does he think I can't hear someone coming? And that door's already been opened once. Am I yelping with pain from getting hit? I don't think so.

Here she comes. No, it's a slightly different step. Don't move. Hey, what do you have on those plates? Where are you going? That's the direction Jennifer came from. Mmm, I'll check that out when I get rid of Mike. I'll just mosey down for a drink, then follow the first guy with food.

"Jennifer, I want you to go in the right door and out the left door a few times. Just to get him used to that."

I get it. He's giving her a training session on the doors like he did for me.

"That's good," said Michael.

Ha ha, took you three times. It only took me twice. He should have pushed you the first time too.

"Thanks, Jen. Can you go in, hold the door open, and call Cody?"

Yes! Call me, and I'll be there in a flash.

"No," Mike whispered.

What? Make up your mind. Mike, you need serious help. Sorry, Jennifer, I think Dreamy-Eyes has lost his mind. Call all you want. I've been told "no," and there is nothing wrong with my mind.

"Good boy, Cody. What a smart dog you are." Michael beamed with pride.

That's true, but compared to you and Jennifer I'm beginning to think it's no contest.

"Can you help a minute longer, Jen? I want to teach him not to follow the waiters and waitresses. Get your next order, and take it to the dining room."

****

Five minutes of training Jennifer, and I'm still waiting for my meal. Finally, here comes Mike.

Hey, wait a minute! This is my regular old food. You can't bring me back here with all these smells, walk past with bacon and cheese omelets, and expect me to eat this! Get in there, and scrounge up some real food. Go! Go!

"Cody, don't push," said Michael. "Just because you're outside the kitchen doesn't mean your food is going to change. You need a healthy, well-balanced diet to live a long and healthy life."

Yeah, yeah, go on.

Mmm, I guess not. I suppose this is better than nothing.

"Does Cody want a piece of bacon?" Jennifer said on her way back from the dining room.

Yes, he does! Watch this. I'll sit up pretty. Does that answer your question?

"I'm not sure he should have one."

Not sure? Mike, I'm getting worried about you.

"I don't want him getting fat."

Hey, where there's a problem, there's always a solution. Just take me out for longer walks. Think about it.

"Come on, Michael, one piece isn't going to hurt him," pleaded Jennifer.

"Oh, all right. But just one and we can't make this a habit. I'm responsible for his care, and I don't want any problems."

Ho hum. Now give me that bacon. Yeah, oh man, this is living. How about another piece? Come on, Jennifer. How can you say no to this face?

"Please, Michael. He's so cute. How can you say no to that face?"

Ha ha, told you. Another conquest. I'm ready. Drop that bacon, right here. I'll catch it. Good idea! Let's play catch-the-bacon.

"Sorry, Jen. It's just like raising a child. If you give in to them because they are cute or demanding, you soon have more trouble than you can handle. You've seen some of the kids that have stayed here. It's not worth it. Thanks for your help. I have to get back to work. We're still on for tonight, right? I'll pick you up at seven? Come on, Cody. Time for you to hang out in the lobby."

Sounds good to me. I'm ready for a nap.

"Cody, you cannot lie around on all the lobby furniture," said Michael. "I've arranged this one chair for you to nap on."

Mmm…comfy.

"I don't want to see you on any other furniture."

I heard you the first time. Now go away, I'm sleepy. It sure is noisy in here compared to the suite.

I wonder why Mike wants to pick Jennifer up tonight? Why didn't he just pick her up then and get it over with? I've never seen him pick anybody else up except me.

****

This is what I call a perfect day for a walk. Hey, Mike, let's go this way. There's Angel, my black poodle friend. We haven't seen each other in months. Mike, are you listening? Never mind. Just follow my lead.

"Angel! Where have you been?"

"Cody, it's so good to see you. You won't believe what I've been doing—I've been going to dog shows."

"Dog shows? What's that? A special theater where you take your dog to watch a show?"

"No, silly."

"I've got it. You go and watch shows about dogs."

"Cody, you are so funny! No, all these people take their dogs to a big arena. They groom them all up and walk them in an area where a judge picks out the prettiest."

"That's not fair. All dogs can't be as pretty as you or me. Sounds boring."

"Actually I was thinking about you at the last show. There were obedience trials. You could win that easily. You're so smart!"

"Brains over beauty, huh? That could be interesting."

"There must be different levels because some dogs were on leads, some were off leads, some were picking up gloves and bringing them back, and some were jumping over walls. Some dogs did things without being told. All their owners did was move a hand, and the dog went and did something."

"Hold it, go back. Did you say some of these dogs were out in public without their leads?"

"Of course."

"Okay, Angel, think back. Were any of these terriers?"

"Sure, a few."

"And they didn't just put their heads down and take off?"

"No, silly."

"Aha, I knew it. Don't call me silly. That's what my mother said a terrier would do."

"Maybe. When they came out of the ring, the lead was put right back on them."

"Yes but—" Hey, Mike don't pull. I'm talkin' here. *"Gotta go, Angel. I'll see you again. Good luck!"*

"Cody, I heard my mom say one of the dog shows is on TV this weekend. Check it out."

"I'll try."

How am I going to see TV in the middle of the day in the lobby? Even if there were a TV there, I don't know how to work it.

Open that door, Mitchell. I've got things to do. I want to check out that plant. Not that I'd really water it. That could mean some serious discipline.

Something's wrong here. It smells like a squeaky toy. What does that mean? Is it just a big squeaky toy shaped like a tree? Who plays with a toy this big? I don't know, people have some strange ideas. No wonder it's never grown. Oh well, not my problem. I've got more places to explore.

What's in this room? It's awfully dark in here. Tables, chairs. It must be a dining room, but Mike didn't tell me to stay out of here. Boy, the floor sure stinks.

"Hi, Cody," greeted a young man. "Are you allowed in here?"

Think about it, and while you're at it, where is here? And who are you?

"I guess so. Mr. Ellis didn't mention it at the meeting. I'll check with Michael later. I'm Scottie, and this is the Black Knight Lounge, where our guests come for drinks."

Great. Someone else is reading my mind. Here we go again with weird words. The black makes sense. Not many lights are on, and most nights are black. The lounge part is stupid. I don't see anything for people to lounge on—no sofa, all chairs.

But people come in here to drink. That's what the stink is. No wonder the lights are so low. All the sloppy drinkers must come in here so no one sees them. Or maybe they miss their mouths 'cause the lights are so low. Interesting problem.

I think I'll see if this guy really reads my mind.

Hey, Scottie, I guess your mother really wanted a dog when you were born. Scottie dog—get it? We're almost cousins. Ha ha!

No change of expression. Just a lucky guesser.

Aha! A TV! Problem one solved. Now how to turn it on with the show I want. One training session coming up. Let's see what Scottie does if I stare at the TV and give a good bark.

"What do you want, Cody?"

Come on, Scottie, make a lucky guess.

"Do you want the TV on?"

I'll wag my tail. Everyone knows that's positive.

"Okay, here you go. It should have been on anyway."

I'll sit and watch awhile—positive reinforcement.

Phew. Ten minutes of watching this boring guy talk seems long enough.

"*Bark.*"

"What now? Is there something wrong with the TV?"

This guy's a little slow.

"*Bark.*"

"Want the channel changed? How will I know when to stop?"

Just turn it. I'll let you know. Not that one, keep going. Animals! I better sit and watch for a while.

"I guess this is the one. Sitting watching TV, that's great. Boy, I never met a dog as smart as you."

Of course not. I am the Codyman! Hey, I like that name.

"Sorry, Cody, I have a customer who wants the news on."

The 6:00 news? I'm out of here! Supper time.

Here it is, already waiting for me. It doesn't look like very much. Do I have more people to train?

I'll just sit here and see if any of the waiters go by. They'll give this cute face some real food.

"Hi, you must be Cody," said a passing waiter. "Do you want a little piece of steak?"

Oh yeah, I've got the touch.

Here comes another one.

Good, it worked again. This may be the best place in the hotel.

"Cody."

Uh oh! That's Carter. I don't want this gig busted. I better go and meet him.

"Come on, Cody. You have to go out, then you can go up to the suite with Mrs. Semple."

Sounds good. Someone to talk to!

****

"Good evening, Mrs. Semple," said Carter as she opened the door. "Here's Cody. Someone will be up at 9:30 to take him out before you go to bed."

"I've been sitting around the hospital all day. Could I take him for his walk?"

"Sure, that should be all right. He has a lead in the closet, or you can pick one up at the front desk. Good night. Good night, Cody. You've been a good boy today."

Wasn't I though?

Mrs. Semple patted me on the head. "Let's play a little fetch, then you come up and I'll tell you about my day."

If you need to play, let's make it quick. I've had a busy day too, and I need some rest.

There, that's enough. Move over and let me up. Okay, rub my back and tell me what's going on.

"Cody, I'm so scared. My husband is far worse off than we expected. I hope he doesn't need a new heart. I doubt he could get one at his age, and we won't know until tomorrow."

Please don't think like that. I've seen lots of people have a change of heart, and age didn't seem to make a difference.

"I don't know if I'll be able to sleep tonight."

Great, just what I need. I've still got a lot of exploring to do tomorrow, and I need my rest. Here, just rub me and relax.

"Cody, I'm so glad I have you to talk to. I feel a little better already."

Hey, what did I tell you?

****

"Good morning, Mrs. Semple." Michael smiled as she opened the door. "I trust you had a pleasant night."

"Yes I did, thank you. I didn't think I'd be able to sleep, but Cody is such a comfort. I just find it very relaxing rubbing his back and talking to him."

Yeah, yeah, I'm a joy. Let's go! I need to go out, and I am hungry.

"Okay, Cody," said Michael. "Once we're downstairs, you're on your own. Go get your food."

I'm gone! You don't have to say food to me more than once.

Boy, it's slim pickins today. Half a piece of bacon and one toast crust. I wonder what's happening in the lobby?

Hey, I think I'll go outside.

Mitchell stepped in front of me and crossed his arms.

"No you don't. Not by yourself."

Busted.

All right, I have to think about this. I have to make my move when Mitchell's attention is elsewhere.

Ah, here comes a woman with a carriage. I'll just follow along behind her.

So far so good. Mitchell's opening the door. Here I go!

Hey, Mitchell! Put me down!

New plan, coming up. I think I'll sit behind the plant and watch for a while.

That's it! Mitchell always helps with the regular doors but never with that big round door. If I wait for a lot of people to go out different doors, I could jump into a section of the round door and get out.

I'd better study this a little bit more; I might only get one chance.

Hey, mister, use the round door. Good. Okay, he steps in a section, pushes the handle and all the sections move. So if I get in the one behind him, I'm free.

Yes! I'm in!

Hey, let me out of here! You didn't push it far enough.

Good. Here it goes. I smell the fresh air.

Put me down! No, Mitchell, don't put me back inside.

Hmm. Not a bad plan. I need someone who walks faster and pushes harder, but I'd better leave this for today. Mitchell is on to me. At least there's still plenty of lobby to explore.

What's over there? Holy....Moving stairs. Why would they make moving stairs? Strange people, again! The hotel puts in an exercise room, then puts in elevators and moving stairs so people won't get any exercise climbing the stairs. Does this make sense?

I think I've figured out how it works. Long step on, hop off. I don't like the way the steps disappear into the floor. What if my fur gets stuck in there? I could get skinned. What if the top isn't the same as the bottom?

I'm really shaking here. I don't think I can do it.

Yeah, right. Was that all talk to Mrs. Semple last night? Face your fears aaand...jump. I'm on! Up, up I go. I'm almost there, and yes, the same jump. Yahoo! Good dog, Codyman.

I wonder what's up here. More elevators and big rooms full of chairs and some tables. Sounds like someone is in that one down the hall. This must be where all those convention people meet. Boring.

I'm going back downstairs. Ready, jump. Boy, you're smart! Where have I heard that before?

Off! Think I'll try it again. This could become a daily routine.

"Cody, no!" Michael came running across the lobby. "I'm so stupid. I forgot about the escalators. You could get seriously hurt on these. I'd better teach you to stay off them."

Ha ha! Too late. I guess what you don't know won't hurt you. They don't go anywhere anyway.

"While we're at it, Cody, let's go look at the dining room and keep you out of there."

Why? We did that yesterday.

Hey, Mike, you're going the wrong way. Down the hall, remember? It should be funny when he realizes his mistake. Ah, a different door to the dining room. Actually, no door at all.

I know. Stay. Do not enter. Out of bounds.

Man, all those waiters talked to me yesterday. They even gave me food. They won't even look at me now. This must really be serious. Maybe some of the guests will see me sitting here and feel sorry for a poor starving creature. I'll try that when Michael's not around.

Enough already. I need a nap. Ah, the paws that refreshes. Get it?

****

I wonder why Mrs. Semple is so early. I hope nothing happened to her husband.

"Mrs. Semple," said Michael, "is everything all right?"

"I don't know what to do. I was supposed to leave tomorrow, but my husband's tests show some serious damage to his heart. The doctors want to operate. Then he has to stay in the hospital for another week after that. I'm afraid I'll have to move to a cheaper hotel."

"Don't you worry about a thing. You stay with Cody as long as you need to. We have to have someone with him and not necessarily someone different every night. Besides, you'll be helping us out. We won't be in a panic to find someone else. I think you two are getting along great, so it also makes it easier for Cody. He won't have to get used to someone new."

You mean I don't have to train anyone else.

"Michael, thank you."

"There, there, no need for tears. It is our pleasure to have you here."

I hate seeing tears. They make me sad too. Here, I'll jump on your leg to take your mind of them.

Mrs. Semple reached down to pat my head. "I would have found it very difficult to leave Cody. It's been so wonderful to have his company."

Thanks! I'm sarcastic at times, but I really do like to see people happy, and I'm glad to be able to help.

****

"Hi, Cody," said Morgan, the weekend concierge. "How have you been getting along this week? I bet it's been rough!"

Uh oh! It's Saturday. Gotta go.

Hey, Scottie! Change the channel. There's a dog show on. Not that one, go, go, stop. That's it.

"How did you know that was on?"

Wouldn't you like to know? Chalk it up to smart.

Oh my gosh, will you look at that. Hair all fluffed up, walkin' around nice and pretty. La-dee-dah. This is so phony. At least it's good for a laugh. Think I'll watch for a while.

Pick the Lab! Pick the Lab! Yes, two for two. Hey, there's Angel! Hi, Angel!

"Cody, no. You can't bark."

All right, all right, but that's my friend. Come on, Angel, go. Come on, Angel. Too bad.

"Cody, look at those dogs in obedience. I bet you could do all that."

You know it!

****

"Richard, this is Cody," said Mrs. Semple.

"Hi, little fellow. I hear I owe you a big thank you for looking after Martha," Mr. Semple said.

"He's just like an angel. God must have sent me to this hotel because his littlest angel was working here. He'll want to play fetch for a while, then we should get you to bed early."

****

I knew it. Two people, two showers. I think I'll sit up with Mr. Semple instead of hiding under the bed. He's so nice, it's no wonder Mrs. Semple was so worried about him.

"A little nervous of the shower, are you? Look, it can't get out of that room, and if you stay out here, I don't see the problem."

He's got a point there. Maybe if I sit at the door of the living room and keep an eye on the shower room door, it might work out. I could always duck for cover if that door starts to open. Thanks, Mr. Semple.

As Mrs. Semple came out of the bathroom, Mr. Semple went over and put his arms around her. "Honey, why don't we look into getting a dog when we get home? Petting a dog is so relaxing, and taking it for a walk is just the exercise the doctor ordered."

"You know, Richard, I always wanted a dog—now more than ever. Please, let's call it Cody in honor of the little fellow who gave me such strength these past two weeks."

"That sounds perfect."

Yeah, that would be great! I think this is a real honor. Still, I hope everyone that stays here doesn't run home, buy a dog, and call it Cody. I like having a unique name.

That must be Michael at the door.

"Good morning, everyone. Jeffrey is downstairs to take you to the airport. How did Cody get along with two people in the room?"

"No problem," said Mrs. Semple. "He started the night on the floor, but when I awoke, he was square in the middle of the bed. I don't think you should worry about letting a couple spend a night here."

Hey, it was a little crowded.

"Michael, dear," Mrs. Semple said with tears in her eyes, "can I give you a hug?"

Michael stepped forward, opened his arms, and kissed her on the forehead.

"Thank you for everything—especially the privilege of sharing my life with Cody. He is one remarkable dog. Come here, Cody. Hugs and kisses and thank you. I'll never forget how you helped me. We'll drop by next time we are in town. Bye, sweetie."

Ah, stop it. You're going to make me cry. Take care.

Chapter Three

"Cody, do you want to go in the car?" Michael asked.

I wonder why Mike asks such dumb questions. Can't he tell by the way I turn around in circles and keep running to the door?

I wish I could go every day; this once a week is a drag. Mind you, I'm not complaining. Once a week is better than nothing. I wonder where we are going today. The park is my favorite. Sometimes Mike and I go for a run or just walk the trails.

Mmm? No! Mike, no! You tricked me. It's times like this that our friendship is tested. Cathy's! I like her, but I hate what she does to me. Why do people bathe their dogs anyway? You don't see them bathing their cats or birds or guinea pigs.

I'm not going willingly. You want me in there, you'll have to drag me or carry me. What will it be today?

"Hi, Michael. Hi, Cody. How's my little honey today?" Cathy stepped forward to take my lead.

What do you think? Don't the tail between my legs and the ears back give you a clue?

"You know what is interesting, Michael? I know Cody doesn't like his bath or the hair blower or even his nails being cut, but he is the best dog I have coming in here. He never fights me, never tries to get away or nip at me. He just sits and shivers. I can't think of many people who would go through something that terrified them as much and never say boo."

Please, give me some credit. I know, no matter what I do, I'll still end up having to have a bath. At least this way I don't get hurt putting up a fight. I figure the better I am, the quicker I get it over with. Plus, Cathy likes me better, so I get extra hugs and treats. I've never been accused of being stupid.

Go on, Mike, get out of here. The sooner you leave, the sooner I get this over with.

Come on, Cathy, brush me first. It's the only good part. Ah! Think I'll drop off for a few minutes. Done already? This is like the calm before the storm. Check that water temperature, or you'll see a new Cody.

I just thought of something. I bet they do this to those show dogs all the time. I shouldn't have been laughing at them. I should have been filled with pity. Not too short on the nails. Good job. Final step, brush me up, back-comb my hair, give me a treat, and I'm out of here.

Hey, where's Mike? No way I'm hanging around here. Let me out!

"Just a minute, honey. Michael should be here in a minute. He's cute, isn't he? He's so tall and handsome with that blonde hair and big blue eyes. I wonder if he has a girlfriend."

Uh oh! That's the look Mike gets when he talks about Jennifer. I wonder what this is all about? I guess Cathy wants to pick Michael up. This I've gotta see. She's so little compared to him.

"How'd he get along?" Michael asked over the jingle of the bells on the door.

"Good as ever. I just love him."

"Thanks, Cathy. We'll see you in a couple of months. Come on, Cody, let's go get an ice cream."

Yahoo! I love ice cream. I'm a plain old vanilla freak.

Get the triple-decker, Mike.

Rats, a baby cone. I was hoping he'd read my mind like he usually does. Hold it steady 'cause the Codyman's ready.

Mmm. Good.

"Jeffrey, will you pull over to that waste can? I'd better get rid of the rest of this ice cream. This wasn't such a good idea right after his grooming. It's all over his face."

Who cares? That's my cone!

"Michael, I always have the baby wipes for Cody's feet on muddy days. Would you like one for his face?"

Yeah right, now you tell him, after the cone is already in the garbage. Hey, go get it out. Stop the car, get the cone. See what I mean about wishing I could really talk?

****

Michael sat down on the chair next to mine. His shoulders sagged. "We don't have a guest to stay with you tonight. It was bound to happen sometime. Maybe we'd better start looking earlier in the day. I can't stay any later to give my approval. I have a date with Jen at 7:00."

Yeah right, what am I supposed to do? I'm not staying in the suite alone. And don't think I don't know what a date is. I watched all those afternoon soaps with my mother. All that face-kissing, taking off clothes, rubbing against each other, and showering. Then you go find another girl and do it all over again and make Jennifer cry. I've seen it all a hundred times. I don't think this is the way to find happiness. Why don't you just go back to picking her up? At least your eyes sparkled.

"You are going to spend the night in the lobby. You know Krista and Gordon at the front desk. They will look after you."

This doesn't sound too bad. I spend most of the day here anyway. I have my comfy chair, and I can go down and see what is cooking in the kitchen at night. This might turn out to be pretty good.

I think I'll go watch TV for a while with Scottie. Maybe some of those dark-room drinkers would like to pet a dog for a while. I might get lucky, and they'll share their pretzels.

****

Help! Run for your life! I don't know what it is, I don't want to know what it is, and I don't care what it is! I'm out of here. Aaah! Better get down the hall to my food corner.

Phew! What was that? Okay, so I do want to know. Some guy was pushing a big noisy thing in front of him and dragging something behind him. It's coming down the hall. I'm trapped! Help!

I never thought it would end in a dark hallway, swallowed by the ultimate dog-eater. What can I do?

The dining room! Sorry, Mike, I have to. From there I'll go out the other door to the lobby.

Uh oh, the doors are opening! Here it comes! I'm gone.

I forgot—no Cody-sized door in this one. All right, all right. Stop. Think. The way is blocked behind me. Cody, you can do this. Stand up and push. Put your nose on it. Push. Come on. That thing is getting closer. Dig those paws in, slow steady push. Come on, you can do it. You're the Codyman!

Yahoo! I'm out! And through the dining room so fast, no one will ever know...I hope. There's my blanket under the front desk, nicely protected on two sides.

****

It's about time you got here, Mike. I'm so mad at you.

"Hey Cody, what's wrong? You're acting like I left you in the car alone. Sit! What's the matter? Are you angry with me?"

Can you find a stronger word? If you can, use it. I thought you cared for me. How dare you leave me in the lobby at night to be terrorized? This thing was after me all night. I don't think whatever it was wanted to be there either. This guy kept dragging and pushing it around. No wonder it was mad!

"Krista, Cody seems awfully upset. Did something happen to him last night?"

"I don't know. About 3:00 he came running across the lobby, ran under the front desk, and hid under his blanket. He didn't move until about 7:00."

"Did anything unusual happen?"

"I don't think so. Nothing that doesn't happen every night—a few check-ins, Mario did the late-night cleaning."

"Was he vacuuming?"

"Of course."

"That's got to be it. I don't know if Cody's ever seen a vacuum before. We usually went for a walk when the suite was being cleaned. I know he hates the hair dryer; imagine what the noise of a vacuum would sound like to him."

Yeah! Now you're catching on. Is this thing living or not? I want to know if it can come after me by itself. I hope this will be the end of my nights in the lobby.

"Cody, how about we go to the park today?" Michael asked. "Maybe that will help you forget last night. Spring is finally here, and a walk will be good for both of us."

Don't even try. I'll never forget last night. But that doesn't mean I'll turn down the park. Plus I want to check with some of my friends to see what they know about this vacuum cleaner thing.

****

Mike, doesn't this smell great! I feel frisky. Stop for a minute. I want to talk to Angel.

"Hi, Angel. Listen, what can you tell me about vacuum cleaners?"

"It's not a good thing. When I hear it coming, I take off to the bedroom. When it gets to the bedroom, I take off to the living room."

"You mean you go right past it?"

"Sure, no choice. It goes over the whole house. I have to run past it or meet it face on. No options really. I just run by fast. I think they are slow; it's never caught me yet. Actually it hasn't even made a move toward me, but I'm not taking a chance. Why? Did you have a run-in with one?"

"Oh no. I just saw one for the first time last night. I was just wondering about it."

"Were you scared?"

"No, I just stayed away from it 'cause I didn't know what it was."

"I think it could suck little guys like us right in."

Great, that's all I need to hear.

"Don't worry, Angel, I'll keep my distance. At least I have a big lobby to move around in. I'll never have to go near it."

"You're lucky, Cody."

"Yeah, I guess so. See you around."

****

"Michael," said Laura, "I have a guest for Cody tonight. Do you remember Mr. Jackson? I think he might be down on his luck. He usually asks for an executive room, but this time he just wanted a single. He looked kind of sad. I thought Cody might cheer him up. He hesitated at first, but I think I convinced him. He's in the lounge if you want to check him out."

"Okay. Come on, Cody. Let's go see how you feel about him."

Hey, I'll take anyone after the night I had last night. Nothing could be that bad.

"Mr. Jackson? Hello, I'm Michael Goodwin, the concierge, and this is Cody. I understand you are willing to be Cody's guest in his suite."

My goodness, what a sad man. Nothing bad about him, just very sad.

"Hi, Cody, Mr. Goodwin. I don't know if staying with Cody is such a good idea."

"He certainly seems to like you, and he doesn't take to everyone. Why don't you give it a try and if things don't work out, we'll move you to another room?"

"All right. I have to go out late this afternoon, and I should be back about 9:00."

"Perfect," said Michael. "Cody usually goes out about that time. We will bring him up to the suite around 9:30. Call down to Krista at the front desk if you have any problems. Thanks. You will really be helping us out."

Man, I can't wait to hear what his problem is. I hope he doesn't decide to move to another room. That would mean back to the lobby for me, and I don't feel like showing that vacuum cleaner who's the boss tonight.

Chapter Four

Oh, great! He's not falling-down drunk, but he's not feeling any pain. I shouldn't say that. He has plenty of pain, but it's all emotional. Come on, Mr. Jackson, let's play grr-toy. That cheers everyone up.

"No, I'm sorry, Cody. I don't feel like playing tonight. Come on up here, and I'll tell you a sad story."

I knew it! This is what I was waiting for. Lay it on me.

"Two years ago, my partner Bill and I had a successful real estate business. We made good money and had millions of dollars of property. Then I found out Bill had a serious gambling problem. He had leveraged all our properties, cleaned out our accounts, and stolen from the trust accounts. We had to sell everything to clear his debt. On top of that I had to spend hundreds of thousands of dollars in legal fees—my own money—just to clear my name."

Okay, so start all over again.

"This was just the beginning of my problems."

The beginning? Ouch.

"Just as I was considering starting another business, my wife filed for divorce. I thought we had a pretty good marriage, but she said she didn't want to start all over again. She just wanted half my savings and investments, and she'd be out of there. This broke my heart—not just losing my wife, but also my son, Daniel Jr... Danny. He's nine. I coach his little league team in the summer and his basketball team in the winter. Once a year we go on a big camping and fishing trip. Or we used to.

"A month after they left, I found out that my wife had a boyfriend. Apparently this started before we separated. No wonder she was so ready to leave. From everything I've heard, this guy is a real bum. He drinks too much and has a foul mouth. He blew the settlement money from the divorce on booze—a quarter of a million dollars that should be helping my son. At least my wife won't marry him because she doesn't want to lose her alimony.

"At this point, I hardly care what happens to Joyce, but Danny....The courts gave my wife primary custody with weekend visits for me. Danny started changing. He began talking back to me and demanding things. He no longer wanted me to hug him.

"I tried to win back primary custody, but no luck. That's when my wife started making excuses to keep my son from seeing me. Danny would be sick or going to a friend's. When I called, they wouldn't let me talk to him or said he wasn't there, or in the bath, or sleeping, or some other lame explanation. I can't even remember all the excuses she made. In the past three months I've seen my son once.

"I've tried to go back to court, but the wait is so long. Finally, I took my lawyer with me and went to the house two weeks ago. They were gone."

No wonder you're so sad. I feel awful, too. Here, I'll kiss your cheek. What can we do about this?

"Now comes the worst part."

Worst? How can it get worse? I don't know if I can stand any more, and it isn't even my life.

"A week ago the police came to tell me I was being investigated for child abuse. I nearly died. My lawyer can't even track down Joyce to question her. The police say she is in hiding, and they won't reveal her location. I hope she is just doing this to keep me away from my son."

Are you nuts? Why would you hope that?

"What if my son has been abused and they are looking at the wrong guy? I know it's not me, so that person will continue hurting him."

I see what you mean. Maybe their investigation will clear your name, like it did for your business problem.

"Yesterday, I was formally charged. That's what I'm doing here. I just can't take any more. Life without my son is not worth living, and to be accused of such a horrendous crime is unbearable. I've come here to end it all."

Good idea. But I don't think this is the place to put an end to all these ridiculous lies. You need to be out looking for your son. He is old enough to speak for himself.

"Don't worry. It won't be messy or noisy for you, little fella. I'm just going to take some pills, then we'll go to sleep, and I'll never wake up."

What! You're going to kill yourself? Daniel, think about this.

"I know people will think I'm guilty as charged, but I'm going to leave a note saying I couldn't stand being falsely accused. If I've lost my son, then I don't want to live.

"I went to see my lawyer this afternoon to arrange all my finances. I've set up a trust fund to continue Danny's child support. The rest of my money has been set aside for his college education, with the balance going to him when he graduates. This should give him a good start in life."

This is so stupid. The money won't mean anything to him if he doesn't have his father.

"I'm going to leave him a letter, explaining everything. He'll understand why I had to do this."

Yeah, right! He won't understand any more than I do. He may think you've abandoned him, but he knows you didn't abuse him. Daniel, think! He probably doesn't even know what's going on. You've got to fight for him.

"I'm leaving a letter to the authorities explaining everything. I know I'm innocent, but I also know how the justice system treats fathers. I don't have a chance. Even if I win, people will still think I got away with it. And I know I'll never see Danny again."

For Pete's sake, Daniel, fight this. Go find your son. Explain everything. Help him.

"Do you want to know how logical I've been? The reason I came here to the hotel was so my house wouldn't lose any value because I died in it. That is part of Danny's inheritance."

Inheritance isn't money and possessions. It's family and good memories. What memories is your son going to have? A father who didn't love him enough to fight?

Oh man, what am I going to do? He's writing the letter!

"What are you barking at? Do you want to go out?"

I'd better stop. He'll call down to the front desk, and they will take me out of here.

"You just want to sit on my lap? Okay, come on up. I only need to sign this one."

Write slower. I need time to think.

"There, done. Next, my letter to Danny. This is going to be really tough. Hey, come back here with that."

You wish! I'm not going to make this easy.

"Come out from under that bed."

Okay.

"Look what you've done, torn it all apart. Now I have to write it again."

Maybe I could do this all night. He has his plans so well made, he won't want to change them.

"This time I'm putting it in the drawer so you can't get it. I thought you were well-behaved. You wouldn't think the hotel would put guests with a dog who would destroy their property."

You thought—that's a laugh. You haven't thought all evening, or at least not the right thoughts.

"Now what do you want? No, I'm not playing. I have to write my letter to Danny."

Think, think! What can I do? Maybe I can get hold of this one. Only this time I won't destroy it. I'll just run around and keep it from him. If he catches me, I'll chew it up so he has to write it again. I just have to keep going 'til the morning. Things are always worse at night. Maybe he'll change his mind. I hope I can keep going that long. I'm already tired...

"There, finished." The desk drawer slammed.

Rats. I fell asleep. It's too late to get the letter. The pills—that's my last chance.

"Okay, Cody, let's go to bed."

Thank goodness. He must have changed his mind while he was writing to Danny. Of course, how could you write such a letter and not realize what you are doing?

"I'll be right back. I'm going into the bathroom for a minute."

Oh no you don't. I'm coming with you. Why does he need two glasses of water? I'd better stay close and alert. No more dozing off.

"It's 3:00, Cody. I can't wait much longer. I've shared everything else with you. Do you want to hear my letter to Danny? No, stay. I don't have to go get it. I pretty well have it memorized."

Too bad. I was hoping for another chance to snatch it.

Dear Danny,

I love you more than anything on this Earth. These past two years have been the most difficult of my life. Not seeing you every day has been agony. My heart began to break when we started missing our weekends together. Now this latest allegation is too much for me to bare. Please, Danny, do not believe what others tell you or let them convince you to believe a lie. You know I never hurt you and that I never could hurt you. I'm sorry, Danny. I just have no more fight left in me. The legal system and your mother have drained me dry.

Please try to live a good, honest life. Get a college education and make something worthwhile out of this mess. When you have children of your own, love them dearly, as I have loved you, because after everything is said and done, that's the only thing that matters.

At least you know that your father loved you until the day he died. Goodbye, son. I will always be watching over you. Make me proud.

Your loving father

If I could cry, I'd be bawling. No wonder you were so sad. But please think this over. Once you die, you never come back. Just like my mother. You can't change your mind. What about everyone you leave behind? Think how bad Danny will feel. He'll blame himself for missing those weekends and letting his mother take him away. Daniel, please!

Hey, where did those pills come from? Give me those.

"Cody look what you have done. You spilled the pills all over the floor."

I sure did, and I'm not done yet.

"Cody, no! Bad dog! Don't push those pills under the bed. Give them to me."

Drastic times call for drastic measures.

"Ouch! You bit me."

Yup, first bite of my life. Sorry.

"I'll just move the bed. And when I get hold of you, you'll be sorry."

Maybe, maybe not.

"Damn, the stupid thing is bolted to the floor."

Thank goodness. He had me worried.

"This isn't the end of it. I'll just take the mattress off and get you that way."

Oh no! What am I going to do? I can't eat these pills. That would be good though—"Dog Dies to Save Man's Life."

"Damn. Whoever heard of a box spring being permanently attached to a bed frame? This can't be happening. It's like that dog knows what I had planned."

That's it, Daniel, you just sit down there and cry. Mike should be coming soon to take me out. When he finds me under the bed with all these pills, he'll know what you were trying to do and he'll help you. He's a concierge, and it's his job to help people.

Good, the phone. Is that you, Mike?

"Hello?...How did you find me?...Where is he? Is he all right?...Really! Are they in custody?...Of course. I'll be there in about an hour. David, you just don't know....Never mind, maybe some day."

This sounds promising. But why is he sobbing?

"You saved my life. How can I ever repay you?"

You can start by not squeezing me so tight.

"The police arrived at my wife's home yesterday afternoon with more questions. Her boyfriend had gone out, and she broke down. Apparently, she and my son have been living in terror of this guy. He forced them both to lie about me. My wife and he are both in custody until everything is straightened out. I have to go pick up Danny. My lawyer thinks I'll have a good chance of getting custody on a permanent basis."

That all sounds great.

"When I think of how close I came to taking my own life, it makes me sick to my stomach. I owe you so much. When everything settles down, I'll be back to thank you properly. I'll tell the front desk on my way out that you are here alone."

Don't bother. A little peace would be nice. I'm exhausted. I need some sleep.

****

Hey, Mike! Good thing you're noisy. I was sound asleep near the bedroom door.

"Cody, are you driving your guests out early? What's all over the bedroom?"

I wouldn't go in there if I were you.

"Man, what a mess! What was going on in here last night? Are you all right? Come here. Let me check you over. "

Ah, feels good. Check my back again and behind my ears.

"You seem to be all right. I don't know what happened, but I guess we made a poor choice in guests."

You sure didn't. I was exactly what Daniel needed. It makes me shiver to think what would have happened if he had stayed in another room. At least no one will ever know.

Uh oh! I forgot about the pills under the bed. Someone will find them. Wait—I know exactly what will happen. The vacuum cleaner will eat them and die. Yahoo!

Chapter Five

Mike led the way down the hall toward my food. "Let's go out the back door, I have a surprise for you."

After the past two months, there isn't much that will surprise me.

What—no leash? Hey, this *is* a surprise. I'd better get out fast before he changes his mind. This is heaven, full run, and breeze in my face!

Oops! Fence.

"Cody, come!"

I'd better go, and fast. I want to prove a terrier doesn't just take off.

"I guess I don't have to ask you if you like it. We thought you might enjoy getting out more often."

Thank goodness. I hate people standing and waiting for me to go. Such pressure! But what's the catch?

"I bet you get bored in the lobby between your naps. I'll come back in about half an hour. I don't want you to think we've abandoned you."

Don't worry about me. I want to go exploring, and there is no way you'd abandon me. I'm the center of your life. I'd better start watering a few spots so everyone knows this is the property of the Codyman.

I bet this is like the backyards some of my friends have told me about. Angel's owner just opens the door and lets her out. I always envied her; but no more, now I have my own backyard.

****

"Cody."

Half an hour already?

"Come on, you have a visitor."

A visitor? Everyone who comes to the hotel is a visitor.

Daniel! I wondered what had happened to you.

"Here he is, Mr. Jackson. We just put a new yard in for him, and he was checking it out."

"Hi, Cody. Come on over and sit on this sofa. I have someone I want you to meet."

I'm not allowed up on the sofas, but I've heard the guest is always right.

"Cody, this is Danny. Danny, this is Cody."

"Hi, Cody. My dad says you really helped him with a problem."

Problem? More like a catastrophe. But he probably didn't tell you everything, and he shouldn't. Besides, it all happened because he loves you so much.

"He sure did," said Daniel. "Cody, I told you I'd be back to thank you properly. Danny, pass me that bag Cody's been smelling."

He caught me! I was trying to be so sneaky.

"We barbecued an extra steak last night to bring to you today. I hope you like it."

"We cut it up into little pieces for you and everything. Look, Dad, he loves it! He's barely chewing it."

Here comes Mike. I'm in trouble.

"Cody, what are you doing up on the sofa?"

Daniel stood, raising one hand. "Wait, that's my fault. I put him up here."

"I'm just teasing. It's all right. Steak, too?"

Daniel sighed deeply. "You see, when I stayed here last month, Cody really made a difference in my life. I really don't want to get into it, but I think you should know what a special dog he is. I'm telling you, I swear he understands English. Not only that, but he translates it into logical, analytical action."

"Mr. Jackson, please, I know he is exceptionally smart as far as dogs go, but I wouldn't credit him with much beyond that."

"Don't underestimate him. He might just take over this hotel."

"Too late for that; I sometimes think he already has."

"By the way, I've been wondering—why are the bed and box spring bolted to the floor in Cody's suite?"

"His previous owner was raised in California. She was scared to death of earthquakes. She never wanted her bed moving around the room if one struck. Why? Did you lose something under there?"

"Let's just say I *found* something under there. I don't want to elaborate, but don't ever unbolt it. Please trust me on this."

"Actually, we scheduled workers to take care of it this week."

"Okay, look at it this way. You put strangers in a room for the night with this wonderful dog. I'm sure you must worry sometimes. I know for a fact that Cody knows he's safe under the bed. So why don't you just leave it for him?"

"You've got a good point. Thanks, I'll cancel the work order."

Thank goodness, I was worried for a second. Thanks, Daniel. Now you've really paid me back although you didn't have to. Why don't you buy a dog? Then you'll have some one to look after both you and Danny?

"Cody, come here. I need a hug. We have to go. Danny and I are going to pick up our new puppy."

Okay, so you're one step ahead of me.

"I was going to get a Westie, like you, but I decided to totally leave that part of my life behind me. We bought a new house with a big backyard, perfect for a dog. We're getting a Springer Spaniel. I think it will help Danny and me. If the dog turns out to be half as smart as you, we'll be lucky. Thanks, Cody. I'll think of you every day. I thank God he put me in your suite every time I look at Danny. See ya, buddy."

"Bye, Cody," called Danny as he ran off to join his dad.

"Cody, I don't know what goes on in that suite, but we've had more people thanking us for letting them stay with you. Every one of them offered to give you a home."

Oh no! Don't even think it! I'm happy right where I am.

"Come on. You've got an appointment. Let's go in the car."

****

Man, there's a lot of dog smells at this place. Everybody must be coming here to mark their territory. Why bother? Why not go find a fresh spot?

Whoa! Put on the brakes. I remember this place.

"So, you do remember Dr. Cameron's. I was wondering if you would. It's been a year since your last visit. Come here, I'll carry you….Hi, this is Cody to see Dr. Cameron."

"Hi, Cody," said the girl behind the front desk. "Have a seat. He'll be with you in a minute."

Don't put me down! Can't you feel me shaking? It stinks in here. The overwhelming smell of fear. Good thing I emptied my bladder before we came in here.

Hey, what's that on the counter? It moved! Oh great. Just what I need, a stupid gray cat with white paws. I know, I know. Some people really love their cats, and I have friends who live with cats and say they're all right. But I just can't stand them.

Lucky me, it jumped down. Let me go, Mike. I've got to defend myself. Hold me back!

"You better stay back."

"Hey, big fella."

"Don't big fella me. You come any closer, and you'll wish you never jumped off that counter."

"Now, now, what's your problem?"

"You're my problem. I hate cats."

"Why?"

"I just do."

"That's a good reason. Not too bright, huh?"

"What are you talking about?"

"You say you hate cats, but you don't even have a reason. I call that stupid."

"I can give you a reason—plenty of 'em."

"I'm waiting."

"Well, you just keep waiting. I hate cats so much, I'm not even going to talk to you."

"Ha! I knew it! You can't come up with a single reason."

"I don't need a reason. What are you doing here anyway?"

"I live here."

Chapter Five

"What is this stinking place?"

"I knew you weren't too bright. This is the veterinary clinic. I can tell by the look on your face you haven't got a clue. This is where they bring dogs to torture them. A doctor is going to come and get you soon. You'll be taken into a room where you will be poked, prodded, and have things stuck in you. They even take some dogs into the back room and cut them open."

Mike, help me! Please get me out of here.

What's wrong, Cody? It's all right. Here comes the doctor."

"Cody."

I'm not Cody. Hey, is there a Cody here?

"That's you, big fella. I hope you get out alive."

Mike picked me up. "Okay, I'll carry you."

"Hi, Michael. Put him up on the table."

Don't do it, Mike. I've been good. I won't go on the sofa again.

"Cody, no! I'll stay right here beside you. It's okay."

Yeah, sure. You're not the one who is going to be poked and stuck.

"Sorry, Dr. Cameron, I've never seen him so nervous. He hasn't been here for almost a year. I didn't think he'd remember."

"I don't think we can know what dogs really remember or think. Okay, let's give him a good going over, then we'll give him his shots."

At least he's going to give me something.

This isn't so bad. He's just feeling all my parts and listening to my insides. I'm going to say something and see if he hears me. *"Doctor, what time is it?"*

"He's in good health; everything is fine. How has he been since Mrs. Haney's death?"

"He's great. I think he was looking for her for about a week, especially when we went into the suite, but he's fine now."

It would help if you didn't bring her up.

"My only concern is his weight. He feels a bit fat to me."

Hey, Doc, speak for yourself. I'm nothing but pure muscle. I'm a lean, mean, fightin' machine. I am the Codyman.

"I think he should go on a diet."

"We don't put that much food out for him, and he's quite active. We go for a walk everyday. I don't know why he'd be...ooh, yes I do. He eats down by the kitchen. I bet he's been begging from the waiters."

Busted.

"I'll put a stop to that and see that he gets more exercise. How overweight is he?"

"Let's put him on the scale and see."

Think light. I'm a Pomeranian.

"Twenty-three pounds. Let's aim for twenty-one. Two pounds doesn't sound like much, but remember it's about ten percent of his body weight."

"When you put it that way, it sounds pretty bad."

Sounds even worse to me. All those weeks of training the waiters down the drain. Maybe they still won't be able to say no to me. I'll just have to develop a new plan.

"Lift him back up here, and we'll give him his shots."

Yeah, give me my shots. I never had a treat called a shot before.

Ow! What was that?

"It's okay, Cody." Michael patted my head.

It's not okay. It hurt.

"There, he should be all set for another year. If you have any problems, just bring him in. You know, I use to have Westies, and Cody's a wonderful specimen of the breed. If he ever has puppies, I'd love to have one."

What! You call this a doctor? He doesn't even know I'm a boy. Get me out of here.

"Hey, big fella. I heard you yell. I guess I should call you big yeller."

"Oh, go stick your tongue in a socket."

****

"Here we are, Cody. Home sweet home."

Thank goodness. I need a nap. Hey, I smell a dog! One must have checked in while we were out.

There it is—a Lab. Oh man! She must be a mean one. She's got a suitcase handle for a lead. I guess if she's that mean, her owner needs to have a good grip on her. It should be safe to get a little closer. Why is she ignoring me?

"Hi, I'm Cody. Why are you wearing a suitcase handle?"

"I'm Emmy. I can't talk to you right now; I'm working."

"What do you mean you're working? You're just walking to the elevators."

"That's right. That's my job, to get my mother from place to place without her bumping into anything."

"Is she blind or something?"

"That's right, seeing-impaired. I'm her eyes. I'm called a seeing eye dog."

"Wow! A dog with a job. That's cool. Your job is more important than some people's jobs."

"My mother certainly thinks so. Listen, I can't talk any more now. Maybe I'll see you when we come down for dinner. I'll be able to talk better then."

"That will be great."

I've got to find out more about this. She can sit outside the dining room with me while her mother eats. I think I'll go get a snack while I wait.

"Hi, Cody," Scottie said. "I hear you were at the vet's today."

Don't remind me.

"I guess I can't give you any more cheezies. Michael sent a memo out to everyone telling us not to give you treats. Absolutely nothing, at least until you drop a couple of pounds, and then only from Jennifer. Sorry, guy."

You're sorry? Imagine how I feel. I'm not giving in easily.

****

Six o'clock news—dinner time. Let's check this out.

Okay, so far so good. There's my food. Looks like the regular amount. I'd better eat it fast before it gets cut back.

Now, to check the begging.

"Sorry, Cody. I'm not allowed."

"Sorry, Cody, new orders."

"Sorry, Cody. No can do."

Sorry, Cody. Sorry, Cody. If I hear that one more time I'm going to scream. Listen, guys, these orders are from a demented doctor who can't tell a boy dog from a girl dog. You can't do anything a guy like that says. If he got my sex wrong, he probably got my weight wrong. Come on. Give me a break. Look at this face. Does it look fat?

Ah, good old Jennifer, she's the one allowed to feed me.

"Sorry, Cody."

Ahhhhhh!

****

"Wait, Emmy! You can't go in the dining room."

"Why not?"

"You're a dog. We're not allowed in."

"I'm allowed to go anywhere my mother goes. Remember, I have to help her."

"But I thought you said we could talk while she eats. Will you be back out?"

"No. I have to lie at her side. I thought you could come in and we would talk. I don't have to look out for her, but I can't leave."

"Bummer. I really wanted to talk to you."

This has been one of the worst days of my life. I just have to talk to someone.

"Hey, Emmy."

"Where are you, Cody?"

"Over here, under the chair."

"I can't see you very well through all the legs."

"Good. That's what I was hoping. Can you hear me all right?"

"Sure. You know how well we can hear."

"Just checking. There are a lot of other noises in here."

"I know, but we'll just have to concentrate on each other. I learned how to block things out during my training. How did you get in here anyway?"

"I waited 'til the hostess took some diners to their table, then I snuck in. I'm really interested in your job and how you got it."

"It was difficult. Not just the training but the emotional stress. I was born in a special facility that produces lots of seeing eye dogs. When I was a little puppy, I was tested to see how smart I was. They also checked to see if I was brave and curious."

"How did they do that?"

"Mostly through playing. Hiding things under towels, flipping open umbrellas, things like that. Anyway, I passed all those tests and was sent to a family to live for a year. I really liked it there, especially the two kids. My training really started with them. Just the regular stuff most dogs get. You know—walking on the lead, heeling, sitting. I thought this was my home until the day they took me to a new facility and left me."

"Oh, Emmy. That must have been awful."

"It was. I was very sad for a while, but I was given a new trainer called Tony. He was great! We spent every day together. I learned to walk on this big harness. Then I learned to walk around obstacles without my trainer banging into them. The next step was to go out on the streets and learn about stopping at crosswalks, waiting for cars to pass. You know, stuff like that. The final step was a major test in the big city. That was the craziest, but I did well."

"Boy, Emmy, that sounds hard."

"It was, but Tony made it fun."

"Sounds like you liked him a lot."

"Yeah, I did. But then it was time to put all my training to good use. One day I was taken to a room to meet my new mother, Heidi. I liked her right away but didn't want to go with her. I kept going back to Tony. We had to train Heidi to walk with me and learn what I was saying through my movements.

"I began to understand how much she needed me. I didn't realize up 'til then what all my training had been for. With my help, she could go out in the world and have a certain amount of freedom. I felt bad about leaving Tony, but it dawned on me that I had finally found a permanent home with Heidi. I wouldn't be torn away from another companion and put somewhere else."

"Emmy, this is so sad."

"Don't feel bad; I don't. When we get home, the harness comes off, and I'm just like any other pet. As a matter of fact, it's a great home."

"You seem happy now, so I guess it was worth it all. I think it's neat a dog has a job."

"Lots of dogs have jobs."

"Are there a lot of seeing eye dogs?"

"Sure, but I mean other jobs."

"*What do you mean?*"

"*There are drug-sniffing dogs, produce-sniffing dogs at big airports, tracking dogs for lost people, rescue dogs in disasters, guard dogs, police dogs, dogs who look after people in wheelchairs. Lots of things.*"

"*I never realized we did so much work.*"

"*I'll tell you, it may not be considered working, but I think most dogs have a job.*"

"*How do you figure that?*"

"*I think most dogs' job is to bring joy and love into their owners' lives. Many people would be very lonely without their dogs. No matter what kind of day the person has had, their dog is always glad to see them. You see what I'm getting at?*"

"*Yeah, I do, and I think you're right. Just this morning a guy who stayed with me a month ago brought in a steak to thank me for helping him.*"

"*Boy, you must have really helped him. How come he was staying with you? Where is your owner?*"

"*It's a long story, but the short version is my owner died and arranged for me to stay here. I have a suite of my own, and nearly every night I have someone different staying with me.*"

"*Now that's sad. No one to love you.*"

"*No, you've got it all wrong. I love hearing their different stories. Sometimes I can help them, but mostly they just want someone to listen to them. Besides, Mike, the concierge, is kind of like an owner. He's around all day. We go in the car, running in the park—you know, good stuff like that. He really likes me, and I love him. He just put a backyard in for me. So you see, I really do have it good.*"

"*You sure do. So why did you really need to talk to me?*"

"*I had a bad day! Mike took me to the vet's.*"

"*Say no more! Poked, prodded, and stuck with needles, right?*"

"*It was awful.*"

"*It won't get any better, so you'll just have to bite the bullet.*"

"*Huh? What's that supposed to mean?*"

"*I'm not sure, but I've heard lots of folks say it to someone who doesn't want to do something but has to.*"

"I have one more problem. I hope you can help with this one. The vet said I was too heavy, so Mike has told everyone who works in the hotel not to give me any more snacks. The best part of the day was seeing how many snacks I could get."

"But, Cody, look where that got you. Fat!"

"So what? I feel good, and I think I look good."

"But being overweight isn't good for your heart. You probably won't live as long as you should, and in a few years your hips will likely start hurting. Then you won't be going for walks or running in the park with Mike. I bet you've been sleeping more lately."

"Yeah, I have. How did you know?"

"The heavier you are, the less energy you have. So you sleep more. It will only get worse if you continue snacking."

"But I love all the special foods. Bacon, pretzels, chips, and especially cheezies."

"I know, I know. This will be the hardiest thing you ever go through. It won't be like biting the bullet to go into the vet's office once. It's long-term and every day. You'll smell everything and want everything. It will be difficult."

"You sound like you've been through this?"

"Yep. Six months, snack-free. I get an occasional treat now and then. And you know what? It tastes twice as good, and I appreciate it a lot more. At least we have an advantage over people who are trying to lose weight."

"How's that?"

"Think about it. You won't be snacking because no one will give you anything. People can get all the food they want. They really have to bite the bullet to stick to their diets."

"You're right there."

"I think the best way to get through a diet is to have a really good reason for doing it. I wanted to be around for as long as possible to help Heidi. You enjoy helping people with their problems. Think about all the people you could help if you stayed around longer."

"You're right again. Plus if I'm not so tired, I can listen longer at night up in the suite. I still might try for the odd treat or two. Thanks, Emmy. God must have sent your mother to this hotel so you could help me."

"Do you think there is a God?"

"I guess so. Mrs. Haney use to watch the church services on TV every Sunday, so I know a little bit. I didn't pay too much attention, but I think lots of people do though. Many of the guests who have stayed with me say things like, 'Thank God you were here,' or, 'God must have sent me here to you, Cody.' Some people even think I'm an angel who was sent to help them. I don't know, but look how you appeared just when I needed someone to talk to. If it wasn't God, then I'm just plain lucky."

"Who knows, maybe a little of both. Nice talking to you, Cody. Good luck on your diet, and keep up the good work here. Maybe we'll be back some day."

"Bye, Emmy. Thanks for everything. Heidi is lucky to have you."

I'd better get out of here before I get into trouble.

Chapter Six

"Breakfast all gone?" Carter asked.

This is the first day of my diet. Do you think I'd leave anything in my bowl?

"Come on. I'll put you out for a while."

Maybe someone will come along and give me something to eat.

Now, now, I can't think like that. I have to remember everything Emmy told me. I have to bite the bullet. I like that saying.

What a nice day! I'm going to lie down by the fence and watch the world go by.

"Yo, Buster."

"You scared me. I didn't see you out there behind the bush. My name's not Buster; it's Cody. Who are you?"

"Is this your private lot?"

"I guess so. No one else has been in here yet."

"Well, ain't you special!"

"I guess, but probably no more than you are to your owners."

"I ain't got no owners. I'm my own man."

"Okay, nobody owns you. I mean the people who look after you and feed you."

"No such people."

"Sure there are."

"Are ya deaf or just plain stupid? I got no owners, don't live in no house, and no one feeds me."

"How do you survive?"

"I get by. I sleep where I want and find food where I can. I'm free. Better than you, locked up in that little space."

"I'm only here a little bit each day, and I enjoy it."

"Sure, just like all the other sissy dogs I've talked to. You wouldn't last a week in the real world."

"I can't say I'd even want to try. We're supposed to live in a house with real people. Did you ever live with people?"

"A long time ago when I was a pup. Then they moved away and left me behind. I'm glad they did. I can do whatever I want."

"I don't believe that. I bet you haven't eaten for days."

"Wrong, I had a piece of bread yesterday. Out back of every restaurant and hotel is a big garbage dumpster. People are always droppin' something. If I get there first, it's mine."

"Who would get there before you? Are there other dogs who live like you?"

"A couple, but mostly cats, rats, and birds."

"Do you remember when you lived in your house? Did they call you anything?"

"I think it was Jake."

"Why don't I call you Jake?"

"Suit yourself."

"I like it. Okay, Jake, what kind of dog are you?"

"I've heard people call me a Heinz 57. Guess that's what I am."

"Good enough. I haven't heard of that breed before, but I learn new things every day. Jake, I don't care how tough you are. I bet you'd like a nice warm house, regular food, and someone to pet you."

"Maybe."

"I knew it. Why don't you go make friends with someone and maybe they will take you home?"

"Are you nuts? I can't go near no people. They kick at me and shoo me away."

"Jake, I hate to admit this, but you really do need a bath and a good grooming."

"What's that?"

"Well, you get into a tub, have water put all over you, then they put soap on and rub it all in. Then they rinse it off and dry you. Finally they *brush out all the knots in your coat. You look better, smell better, and people want to pet you more."*

"That don't sound too bad."

I hope I never run into him after he's had his first bath!

"Will it get rid of fleas?"

"Sure, a special soap will do that."

"Fleas are the worst part of livin' out here. They drive me crazy!"

"I don't think I can help with that, Jake. This is one more time I wish people could understand us. I'd talk to Mike. I know he'd help out."

"That's okay, little buddy. I'll be all right. I gotta go. It's just about time for the restaurant to be throwin' out breakfast. Maybe I'll come back sometime. I hang out around the waterfront a lot if you're ever down that way."

"Sure. Bye, Jake."

That's sad. I'm moaning because I can't have treats, and here's Jake who doesn't even get one decent meal a day. I guess I should be happy with what I've got.

"Cody, come. Sorry, boy, I forgot about you."

No problem, I'm glad you did. Jake probably would have run away if he saw you.

****

Michael looked down as we entered the park.

"I hope you don't mind walking longer today? We have to get you slimmed down."

The longer the better.

Good, there's Dusty. I haven't seen him for ages.

"Hi, Cody. Long time no see. How about a little treat?"

"Sorry, Dusty. Cody's on a diet. The vet says he has to lose a couple of pounds."

"I bet he's not happy about that."

No, I'm not, but I'm getting used to it. What a nice man. He has no home or regular food, but he always has something for me.

"I think he's adjusting. Sorry we can't stay and talk. I have to give Cody more exercise than usual. Take care."

"Sure. Bye, Cody. Bye, Michael."

See you, Dusty. He's so nice. I wonder why he lives on the streets. I don't think he likes to talk about it. He's never said anything. Wait! That's it!

Mike, stop. I want to go back.

"Oh no you don't. We're not going back to the hotel already. You need some more exercise."

No, not to the hotel, I have to go back to the harbor. Come on.

"Cody. No. Heel."

Yeah, yeah.

****

"Cody, what's been wrong with you this past week?" asked Michael. "Ever since you've been on your diet, you've been acting weird. You never want to walk anywhere but the harbor. We haven't been to the public gardens for over a week. Carter says you bark at the back door to get out, and he has to pick you up to get you in. It's as if you are looking for something."

If you must know, I am. Get this lead off. I can't stand it any more. I've got to get out of here.

All right, no more sneaky moves. I'm going to sit behind this plant. As soon as that door opens, I'm going, and going fast.

Here we go! Now!

Yes! I made it!

"Cody, no! Stay!"

Sorry, Mitchell, no can do. I'd better hurry. Mike will be hot on my heels. I'm going to be in serious trouble when I get back, but I just have to find Jake.

Screech! Screech!

Wow, that was close. I've got to pay more attention. What did Emmy say? Stop at the crosswalks and wait for cars. I'll just pretend I'm heeling. If people are waiting, I'll wait. When they go, I'll go. I can run between the corners.

I won't get lost. I've been to the harbor hundreds of times. Besides I was bred to hunt rodents. I'll just follow my scent home.

"Jake, where are you?"

He's nowhere around the places I'm familiar with. I guess I'll have to go further up the harbor. I might just have to check in both directions. I'll start this way because it's behind the hotel. If he was up at the hotel, maybe he'll be down here somewhere.

"Jake?"

Maybe he's here. I smell a dumpster.

"Well, well, a pretty boy."

"Hello, cat. Have you seen—ouch! You cut my nose!"

"That's nothing compared to what's going to happen to you if you come close again."

"Sorry, I'm just looking for a friend. He's a dog named Jake."

"We don't use names down here. Now take off."

"All right, I'm going."

This is one more good reason to hate cats.

Boy, I'm getting tired. I've been out for ages. Mike will be worried. I'd better head back and try again tomorrow.

Oh no! My tracks are crossing each other. I thought I was so smart, and now I'm lost. Great, a dead end. I don't think I like that term right at the moment.

"I told you not to come back."

Uh oh! I might as well turn around and face her. *"Look I was just..."* Six of them! Now what? I can't fight. I can't even run. By the time I make it out, I'll be torn to shreds.

"This is the pretty boy I was telling you guys about. The one who hates cats."

"I didn't say that."

"You didn't have to. I could tell by your body language. What do you say, fellas? Want to change his coat from white to red?"

"Sounds good to me," said the biggest of the bunch. *"I haven't had any fun lately."*

"Wait. You've got it all wrong. I love cats. One of my best friends is a cat who lives in the vet's clinic."

"Maybe he's telling the truth," said the oldest cat. *"I know a cat like that."*

"Who's your vet?"

"Dr. Cameron."

"What color is the cat?"

"*Gray with white paws.*"

"*Yup, same one. What's her name?*"

Rats! Caught.

"*Uh, I forget.*"

"*I knew it!*" said the first cat. "*He's lying to save his skin.*"

"*Wait! It's Boots.*"

"*That's right,*" the older cat said.

Wow, lucky guess. People are so predictable.

"*I don't care. I don't like this guy. I told him to stay out of here, and he came back anyway. Are you guys with me or not?*"

"*Let's do it,*" they all yelled.

"*Hold it,*" growled an intruder.

"*Let's get out of here—it's Terror!*"

"*That you, Code?*"

"*Jake! I'm sure glad to see you.*"

"*What are you doin' out here so late?*"

"*I was looking for you. Why did they call you Terror?*"

"*That's the name I use on the street. I didn't want to frighten you when we met so I pretended not to have a name. But call me Jake; I like it better.*"

"*Jake, I owe you big time. You saved my life.*"

"*What're friends for? Why were ya lookin' for me? It musta been important for ya to come out at night by yourself. Ya musta busted out.*"

"*I did break out, but it wasn't dark yet. I've been looking for you for hours. Listen. I think I have a solution to your problem.*"

"*What problem?*"

"*Oh, come on, Jake. You know what I mean. Your lifestyle.*"

"*I'm happy.*"

"*Look, I don't want to change everything. Just some. Hear me out. Wait 'til I'm finished. If you don't like it, I won't bother you again.*"

"*I'll give ya two minutes.*"

"*Good. I know this man who is exactly like you. He lives on the street, finds food where he can, and has no one to care for him. I think if he had a friend like you, it would help him a lot. Here's how I see it helping you. You'll get the pats I know you miss, you'll have someone to care about you, and best of all this guy is a man. He can open the dumpsters and get way more food for you. He also goes to a shelter sometimes, so he could get food there for you too. What do you think?"*

"I think it's a stupid idea. Why would he want me anyway?"

"I know this guy. He always has a treat for me. I think he would like company. He's all alone, just like you. Come on, Jake, give it a try. If you don't like him or he doesn't like you, then just walk away and come back to this. But think of the advantages if you like each other!"

"Fine. I still think this is dumb, but since ya went to so much trouble, I'll go along with ya. At least we can't explain why we're there."

"That's right, but if you like him, then follow him wherever he goes. That way he'll get the idea you want to be with him. If he doesn't tell you to get lost, you'll know he agrees. Now let's go. Do you know the hot dog stand with the big wheels and red and white cover? The one by the park entrance."

"Sure, but it won't be there at night."

"It doesn't matter. Just take me to where it usually is."

"Okay, this way."

Dusty jumped to his feet.

"Cody, am I glad to see you! Michael's been by five times hoping you'd show up here. He's frantic. Come here, fellow. He left a lead in case you did. I'll take you back to the hotel."

No way. Not 'til you've met Jake.

"Jake, get out of those shadows and come meet Dusty."

"Well now, Cody, who's this? Found a friend, have you?"

"Come on, Jake. Let's get closer to him."

"Okay. He don't seem too bad."

"See—I told you."

"You want me to meet your friend?"

That's right.

"Hello, friend. What's your name?"

"Bark."

"No sense barking. I don't know what that means. Cody, look at him. He looks as bad as I do. Here, boy, want something to eat?"

"Wow, Code, he's already givin' me food."

"I told you he was nice."

At that moment, Michael came running over and dropped to his knees.

"Cody! Thank God! You had me scared to death. What happened to your nose?"

Hi, Mike. I'm glad to see you too. I hurt my nose when I beat up some cats.

"Jake, this is Mike. Remember, I told you about him?"

"Sure. He's really frightened. Can't you feel it?"

"Yeah, I can. I sure feel bad, but I just had to find you. I've been looking for a week. I just couldn't wait any longer."

"I might be glad you didn't wait. We'll see."

"Michael, don't be too mad at him. You're going to think I've totally lost it, but I swear to God I think Cody went and found this dog for me. Look at him—he's as dirty as me, and he's so thin. I bet he's homeless too."

"Dusty, that's ridiculous."

"Maybe, but you tell me why Cody was gone for hours and then he shows up here with this mutt. He knows how to get to the hotel from here. Why didn't he go there instead of coming here? You said he dragged you down this way all week long, and he'd sit out the back for hours. Maybe he was looking for the dog to bring to me."

"I don't know, Dusty. He can't be that smart. Can he?"

"Maybe he is."

"Hey, Code, even I'm beginnin' to think you're smarter than most dogs I met."

"Thanks, Jake."

"So what are you going to do? "

"I really believe Cody wanted me to meet this dog. You take Cody home. He must be exhausted. I'll let this dog stay with me if he wants. I can't make him, but I know I'd enjoy the company."

"Yes! Okay, Jake, this is your chance. If you like him, give it a go. I'll be back whenever I can. See ya."

"Bye, Code. Even if it don't work out, thanks for tryin'."

"My pleasure. Thanks for saving me from those cats, too."

"Cody," said Mike, "you didn't really...nah! Come on, let's go home."

"Thank goodness you found him," said Mitchell as he opened the door.

"Yes, we're going to have to keep a closer eye on him."

"I'm telling you, Michael, except for the first day, he's never tried to get out. I swear it was like he had to get somewhere today. He just went flying out the door."

"I'm beginning to think that maybe he did. Come on, Cody, you missed your dinner. Let's get you something to eat and get you settled down for the night."

Sounds good to me. I'm exhausted.

"By the way, when you disappeared, we didn't have time to find a guest for you. So you'll be in the lobby tonight."

Aaaahh!

Chapter Seven

"Wow, Jake, you look great!"

"Thanks, Code. I ain't got no more fleas bothering me. Dusty swapped work at the animal shelter in exchange for a bath and groomin' for me."

Uh oh, here it comes.

"It was great. I'm the bomb now."

"You mean the bath *was great?"*

"Sure. It rocked."

He must be losing touch with reality.

"Umm, one other thing, Code. I got a new name. Dusty calls me Bud."

"Bud. I like that. How do you feel about it?"

"It's okay. Thanks for settin' us up, Code. It's workin' pretty good! I ain't never ate so good, and look at me! Clean as a whistle."

"I'm so happy for the two of you. Do you want me to call you Bud?"

"Yeah, whatever. I don't mind startin' a new life."

Dusty patted the bench beside him.

"Cody, aren't you going to come sit beside me anymore? Come on."

"Is it okay, Bud?"

"You don't got to ask me."

"Don't worry," Dusty continued. "You'll always be my little buddy, but now I also have a big Buddy. I hope that's okay?"

Sure, Dusty, I'm happy you're happy.

"You know, I still swear you brought Bud to me because we were both alone. I have no idea where you found him, but thanks. It was a two-week-early birthday present."

You're welcome.

"Hey, Jake—I mean Bud. What's Dusty's story?"

"I don't know. He don't talk much about that. Once this fancy car went by, and he said, 'I used to have a car like that.'"

"Sounds like he used to have a lot of money."

"He might talk more later. I ain't seen him talk much to people besides you and Mike."

"Mike wants to go. See you, Bud."

On the way back to the hotel, Mike said, "You know, Cody, I'd like to do something for Dusty."

I already found him a dog. What more could someone want?

"I don't know anything about him, but I can tell he's well-educated. He doesn't seem to drink—at least not like a lot of guys on the street."

What does the way he drinks have anything to do with it?

"I've offered help before, but he's always very politely said he gets along fine and he's exactly where he belongs. It makes you wonder, doesn't it? No one 'belongs' on the street."

I never really understood what that meant until I met Bud. What can we do?

"Dusty said it's his birthday next week. Why don't we have a party for him?"

Yes! I love parties—lots of snacks. Yeah right, probably not for me.

"He can stay with you in your suite."

Super.

"Jen and I can go shopping this week. He's about the same size as I am."

Wait a minute. My suite, my friend—I want to go shopping.

"Do you want to go in the car with us when we go? I know, dumb question."

My feelings exactly.

"Come on, let's go tell Jen."

****

Jennifer hugged Michael. "That's a wonderful idea. You're so thoughtful."

Yeah, yeah.

"I don't know Dusty, but I've heard so much about him. I'd like to come to the party if that's all right?"

"Of course."

Not! This is an all-boy party. Who wants a girl around? Especially one who won't give me treats anymore.

"I only work the morning tomorrow. Can we go shopping in the afternoon?"

"Sure. Meet us in the lobby at 1:00. Maybe we can take Cody for a walk in the park afterwards."

"That sounds wonderful."

That sounds wonderful.

"Come on, Cody. I'll put you out back for a while," Michael said.

Hooray! Two walks, and time outside. Plus, I like rolling in the grass without anyone telling me I'm going to get dirty.

"Hi, little dog."

Well, hi, little boy. Where did you come from?

"What's your name? I'm Andy. I live down over there."

You're awfully small to be out in the city by yourself.

"I'm five. How old are you?"

Two.

"You live in some big apartment building. My mother and I live in an apartment. It isn't very big, and it doesn't look as nice as yours. Do you go to school? I'm in kindergarten. I can already read a whole book. I learned to read from Elmo on Sesame Street. He's my favorite, except maybe Big Bird. Do you watch that TV show?"

No, but I'll check it out.

"Cody! Come on in."

"Your name is Cody?"

Yup. Sorry I have to go.

"Hey, Cody. Do you want to be my friend?"

Sure, Andy.

****

Michael had on his silly Jennifer grin. "Jen, are you ready? Cody certainly is!"

Hey, car, shopping, park. This is great. I never went shopping before.

"Where are we going, Michael?"

"The mall, I guess. There's more variety there."

Sounds good to me, whatever a mall is.

Hey, why are we going in the elevators if we're going in the car? I've been tricked again. Wait a minute, we're going down. I never go down from the lobby. What's down here?

Wow, look at all the cars. Is Jeffrey down here? Is this where he keeps the limo?

Michael opened the door to a red car. "Here, Cody. The Camaro is mine."

Wow, Mike's car.

"In the back, Cody."

No way. It's too small. Shove over, you two. I'm going to sit right up here on this thing between you. I can't wait to see the elevator that fits this car.

"What are you going to buy for Dusty, Michael?"

"I guess new clothes. I doubt he can use anything else. I phoned Cody's lawyer, and he said to buy him an inexpensive watch from Cody. Not that Mr. Park is cheap, but he thinks an expensive watch might get stolen."

"That's a good idea. Do you think it would be all right if I bought him a wallet? I don't want to make him feel bad about not having any money."

"Nah, that's a good idea. He might have some ID or pictures or something, and he must have money sometimes. Besides, I've seen the outline of a wallet in his back pocket."

Sounds like I'm giving him the best gift. Proper thing.

"Here we are. Let's go, Jen."

Jen? What about me? Let me out! You said we were going shopping. You lied again!

"Cody, no. Sorry, pal. They don't let dogs in stores."

Then why did you bring me?

"That's a good boy. We won't be long."

You better not be.

****

It feels good to stretch my legs. I've been stuck in that car for hours. Poor Mike can't be having much fun.. He has to hold on to me with one hand and to Jennifer with the other. Can't she walk by herself either? Look, there's Angel. Let's go.

"Angel, I haven't seen you for ages. Wait up. I saw you on TV. Wait, what's wrong with you?"

"Nothing."

"Oh wow! What's that smell?"

"You know exactly what it is. Now get back."

Man, what is that? I feel tingly all over. I have to get closer.

"Come here, Angel. Look how pretty I'm standing."

Now why did I kick that dirt up? I'm not myself.

"Hi, Michael," Angel's owner said. "I think you'd better keep Cody back; Angel's in heat."

"So that's what he's prancing about. Thanks, we'll see you again."

In heat? Is that why she smells so good? Because she's too hot? How am I going to check this out?

****

"Come here, Cody. I'll show you Dusty's presents before we wrap them. Here's the waterproof watch you're giving him."

That's good, since he lives outside.

"I bought him these clothes. Everything from underwear to a jacket. Mr. Park bought Dusty a new pair of walking shoes for being so kind to you. What paper do you want your gift wrapped in?"

This one with the little puppies on it.

"Good choice. Don't wrinkle it."

Here, wrap this!

"No, Cody, I don't want to play. Get that rawhide bone out of here. I have to finish wrapping these gifts."

I don't want to play. Wrap it up!

"Cody, no."

I'm not listening. Here!

"Oh, all right." Michael took the bone and threw it across the room.

Mike, look. Follow the bone. Under the paper. Think.

"Do you want me to wrap this up?"

"*Bark!*"

"Dusty will get a kick out of this."

Michael, Michael…sometimes you're so dense.

****

When I went out in the afternoon, Andy was sitting outside my fence.

"Hi, Cody, I've been waiting for you. Do you always come out at this time? I hope so because this is when I finish school, and my mother doesn't want me to go right home because she's sleeping. I can stay for a while before I have to go home and get supper ready."

What do you mean, get supper ready? You're just a little boy.

"I think we'll have peanut butter sandwiches tonight."

I think you got lunch and supper mixed up.

"I hope there's some bread left. We don't have much food right now. Do you run out of food at your place?"

Are you kidding? We have so much food we throw it out. Maybe you could find some like Bud. No, that's not right. It's bad enough that dogs and men like Dusty live off the streets.

"I hope you don't mind me talking to you. I'm not allowed to talk to people about my mother or my life. My mom says if I talk about it, I'll be taken away from her. That would be awful because I love my mother."

I understand that.

"We get one check a month, and Mom goes out with lots of men who give her money. The trouble is she has to buy more drugs than food. Do you have drugs in your building?"

Not that I know of.

"Mom tried to quit once, but she got so sick I had to look after her for three days. She couldn't even get out of bed. Finally, she got me to go out and find Harold, and he came over and gave her some stuff, and she got better."

How can one little boy deal with so much.

"She does the best she can. When the check comes, we pay the rent, and then we go shopping for food. We try to get enough to last. We do pretty good. The hardest thing for me is at night. I'm afraid sometimes when I'm alone."

I know what you mean. I don't even stay in my suite alone.

"Don't ever tell anyone. People would think I'm a baby. I hate it the most when there's a storm outside or I hear people fighting in the next apartment."

"Cody," Carter called. "Come on in."

"I guess you have to go. Bye, Cody. I'll be back tomorrow."

Bye, Andy. I'll be here.

****

Come on, Mike, I'll race you to the suite.

Yes! Another victory. Hurry up and knock on the door. I've had a long day, and I'm tired.

Uh oh! I'm out of here.

"Cody," Michael spoke sternly, "come here. Just a minute, Mr. Jennings. I'll go get him. Here, I'll just get one of his leads."

Stay back, Mike. I'm not going in.

"Cody, stop pulling back. What's wrong with you?"

No. Put me down. I'm not going in there. He's a very nasty man. Can't you feel it?

"Here he is, Mr. Jennings. I guess he just wanted to play some games."

I don't think so.

"Cody, no. Stop growling," demanded Michael.

"Hey, I didn't agree to stay with some vicious little mutt who wants to attack me. What kind of place is this anyway?"

"I'm sorry, Mr. Jennings. I don't know what's wrong with him. He's never acted like this before. I'm afraid we'll have to find you another room."

Jennings put his hands on his hips. "Damn right you will. I'm not staying with that thing. I hate dogs anyway."

"Then why did you agree to Cody's suite in the first place?" asked Michael in his I'm-sounding-polite-because-I-have-to voice.

"Who wouldn't want a free suite? He'd be happy enough in the living room."

"I'm sorry, sir. Didn't Laura explain Cody had to sleep on the bed with you?"

"Sure, but what difference would it make to a dumb dog?"

Hey, who are you calling dumb? I was smart enough to figure you out!

"I don't think dogs are as dumb as we think they are. Certainly not Cody. After all, he could tell right away that you didn't like him."

"Don't give me that. He's just a typical nasty little dog."

"I'm going to go down to the front desk and arrange for another complimentary room for you. I'll send a bell hop up to help with your bags."

"Why can't the dog get bumped?"

"I'm sorry. This is Cody's suite."

Yeah, it's mine. Now get out.

"What do you mean, *his* suite?"

Michael hesitated. "Well, he has a permanent booking."

"He must be loaded!" Jennings exclaimed.

"Not really. Come on, Cody. Let's go."

Thanks, Mike. That guy's so mean he almost caught my paw in the door when he slammed it!

"Cody, I'm awfully glad I worked late tonight. I'd better speak to Krista and Gord about this kind of thing since one of them usually takes you up. I'll speak to Laura tomorrow. I think you should meet everyone before we ask them to stay with you."

Good idea. I never want to go through that again, and I don't want that smell of nastiness in my suite.

"Now we have a problem. You have no one to stay with you."

No, not the lobby two nights in a row. Mind you, I didn't hear the vacuum cleaner last night. I guess eating up Daniel's pills really did make it die.

"How would you like to go home with me tonight?"

Chapter Seven

Yes! Double yes!

****

"Come on in, Cody. I hope you like it. I just bought this townhouse last month. It needs some fixing up, but I wanted something close to the hotel, so I could get there quickly if you needed me. Come on, I'll show you around."

Not bad. I wonder if he has a backyard. Open the door.

"Do you want to go out? Good boy. Out you go."

This seems nice. I'll have to check it out in the morning when it's not so dark.

"Grr. What are you doing here?"

"I'm spending the night with Mike."

"Get back in the house, then. I don't like you."

"You don't even know me."

"And I don't want to. Now get!"

"You're mean."

"I'm a Doberman. I was born mean."

"All Dobermans aren't like you."

"I'm a guard dog. My owners want me to be mean."

"Can't you be a good guard dog and not be mean?"

"Stop asking so many questions. I'm sick of it. My job is to keep people away. How do I do that without growling and barking? I'm coming over there and tearing you apart."

Man, this is one unfriendly dog. Well, he can't scare me. I'm going to give it right back to him.

"Cody, come."

Sure thing. I hate acting tough, but at least I'm not backing down from any bully.

"Yeah, that's right. You better go running."

"I'm not running away from you. I always come when I'm called."

"I'm not surprised, you little wimp. I don't cower to anyone."

"Butch, get in here," a man yelled from next door.

"Hey, Butchy, at least I don't go running with my tail down."

"I'll see you later, squirt. You're mine."

"Not if I see you first."

"Cody, what was that all about? I've never seen you acting so ferocious."

I've never run up against a dog like that before. I had to stick up for myself. It sure does take the pleasure out of your backyard, though. Thank goodness the fence was there.

"Come on, it's getting late. Let's go to bed."

****

The next morning we walked to the hotel. Mitchell rushed over to open the door. "Hi, Michael. Hi, Cody. You guys must have been out early today; I didn't see you leave."

"No, Cody spent the night with me."

"I bet he liked that."

"I think so, but he had a run-in with the Doberman next door."

"Is he all right?"

"Who? Cody or the Doberman?" Michael started laughing as he bent down to take off my lead. "You should have seen this little guy. It's a good thing there was a fence between them. You wouldn't have known our sweet little Cody. He was ready to give that Doberman a real fight. He thinks he's a big dog in a small body."

Mr. Ellis came storming into the lobby. "Michael, I want to see you in my office. Now."

Uh oh. Sounds like Mike's in trouble.

****

Michael returned a short time later. His shoulders sagged and his head was bent.

"Michael, what's wrong?" Jennifer laid her hand on his shoulder.

"You won't believe this. Last night we made a mistake in choosing a guest for the suite. When I took Cody up, he wouldn't go in. He just growled and barked and tried to get away. After I offered to get Mr. Jennings another complimentary room, he admitted he hated dogs. I guess Cody could sense that."

"So what's the problem?"

"Mr. Jennings came down this morning and asked to speak to Mr. Ellis. He's threatening to sue the hotel and Cody for mental anguish and physical peril. He says Cody attacked him."

See, Mike, I was right about that Jennings guy. Just like I'm right about that Doberman.

"Michael, that's terrible. Did you explain what really happened?"

"Yes, but it doesn't matter. You know our policy with our guests."

"Don't worry. Everything will come out in court. You can explain what happened, and if you take Cody, the judge will see how ridiculous this all is."

Michael sank down onto a chair. "I'm afraid not. Mr. Park and Mr. Ellis want to settle. They don't want the hotel's name all over the papers. Can you imagine the field day the media would have with a dog living in a hotel suite? If all this gets out, we could have all kinds of crackpots putting in phony claims. Jennings is a lawyer, so he's representing himself. He's agreed to stay away from the hotel and not discuss any of this with the media in exchange for $100,000."

"$100,000?" Jennifer put her hands to her mouth. "Michael, this isn't right."

"I know, but I have to agree for Cody's sake. I shouldn't even be telling you this. Please don't mention it to anyone. Mr. Ellis doesn't want this getting out."

"Of course not, darling. What happens now?"

"After last night, I'd already decided that Cody would be introduced to any prospective guests before we asked them to stay. He'll let us know how he feels. He tends to shy away from people he doesn't like."

"That's a good idea. What did Mr. Ellis say to that?"

"He agreed to go along for the time being, but he won't stomach one more incident."

Chapter Eight

"Come on, Cody. Jen and I are going up to decorate the suite for Dusty's party."

Goody! Are we putting the treats out now?

"Jen, I hope we're not overdoing this. I'm really worried that I might offend Dusty. I don't want him to think this is charity."

"Do you feel like it's charity?"

"No, I just like him. We've kind of been friends for a year now. We've never discussed his past life, but we've sat around and talked about current affairs and life in general. He's cool and, I think, well-educated. I wonder what brought him so low."

"Maybe some day he'll tell you. In the meantime, just enjoy what you two share right now."

"You're right. Planning for the future is wonderful, but nothing will ever happen if you don't take care of business today. Besides, this place looks great."

"Now we just need to get Dusty here. Do you know where he will be?"

"He's usually at the edge of the small park by the harbor. Cody and I are going to look for him on our walk. Wouldn't it be awful if we don't find him today? Or if we find him and he won't come? I don't even want to think about it. I'll ask him to be in the lobby at 7:00. You're free, right?"

"Yes, I'm off at 4:00. Why don't you ask him to come back with you and we can order room service? I bet he'd like a nice supper. After all, it is his birthday."

"Great idea, and it's covered under the terms of Mrs. Haney's will. Even if it weren't, I'd still do it. Thanks, Jen. Why don't you go up to the suite after work and you can yell surprise when we come in? I'll tell Laura to give you a key."

"This will be fun! Good luck. See you later."

"Okay, Cody, let's go find Dusty."

I'm ready. Isn't this great? Dusty and Bud are spending the night in my suite.

****

"Now what? He's not here. Let's go look around the waterfront. He must be here somewhere. I guess he's usually here a lot earlier than this. I feel so bad; I don't even know where he spends the rest of his time."

Don't feel bad, Mike. We'll find them.

"We've been looking for half an hour. Let's go back to his bench and look again. We can decide what to do from there."

Michael sat down with his head in his hands.

"Cody, come sit up here. Look at me. This is turning into a disaster; you have to help. I know you're not a tracking dog, but can you find Dusty? Smell around and see if you can find Dusty's scent. Find Dusty. Thatta boy. Find Dusty."

Okay, okay, be quiet and let me work. Hey—work, just like Emmy. Well, not just like Emmy, but like some of those other dogs she told me about.

Wow, so many smells. I never really noticed before. I smell Dusty and Bud all over the place. Ah, smells like this tree is Bud's favorite place to leave his mark. Maybe I should concentrate on finding Bud, and that should lead to Dusty.

Come on, Mike, I'm going to follow the strongest scent. It should be the newest.

"Cody, do you know what you're doing? I don't think Dusty would be walking around the bushes like this. You're all over the place. I think you're just wandering around."

Just follow me. I think I'm on to something. The trail is getting stronger.

"Come on, Cody. This is useless."

Oh no you don't. Don't ask me to do something and then stop me halfway through because you can't figure out what I'm doing. Come on. I don't want to be dragging you along. It hurts my neck.

"All right, a little bit longer. Then we'll go back to the hotel and chalk this up to poor planning."

They weren't my plans.

"Hey, Cody, look. I think that's Dusty up ahead in that crowd. Come on, let's run."

Yes! I am the Codyman!

"Dusty, wait."

"Hi, Michael. What are you two doing out so late?"

"Looking for you."

"Hey, Code. What's up?"

"Just listen. You'll find out."

"Listen, Dusty. I need a favor from you."

"Sure, what can I do for you?"

I knew it would be easy.

Michael spoke slowly, as if he was trying to decide what to say. "I'm in a bind. You know one of my jobs is to find someone to stay with Cody. Well, for the past couple of days I've been having some problems. Last night we had someone who gave him quite a fright, so tonight I'd really like to have someone I know likes him and will be kind to him."

Dusty looked away. "I'm sorry, Michael, but I don't think so."

Dusty, why not? You like me.

"Dusty, please. You'd really be helping us out. Especially Cody."

Dusty looked back, stepped forward, and opened his jacket. "Look, Michael. I know how I look. Who'd want to see me walking through the lobby of a swanky hotel like yours?"

"I understand."

Don't you quit now, Mike.

"What if we went in the back door and up the service elevator. Would that help?"

"I suppose, but I can't leave Bud. He and I have become pretty tight."

Of course you're not leaving Bud. He's half the reason I'm excited about you coming.

"Oh, I'm sorry, Dusty. I forgot about Bud."

Mike, look at me. See, Bud and I are friends. I've never heard another dog couldn't be in my suite, and they are certainly allowed in the hotel.

Michael smiled. "If that's your only excuse, then bring him along. He and Cody certainly shouldn't have any problems."

"All right. But only because you're in a bind, mind you. We'll be at the kitchen door around 8:00. We have to find supper."

"Dusty, if it's all right, I'd like to buy you supper to thank you for finding Cody a couple of weeks ago when he ran away."

"You know as well as I do that I didn't find Cody. He found me and gave me a special gift."

"But you had his lead and would have brought him back. At least he had someone to go to. I'm grateful for that."

"You shouldn't be grateful. I still think I'm the reason he ran off in the first place."

"Dusty, humor me. Come up to Cody's suite, and let me buy you supper."

"Fine. You win."

Yes! Good job, Mike!

"What do you think, Bud? We're going to have a good time."

"I don't know, Code."

"What do you mean, you don't know? What's wrong?"

"Nothin'."

"Nothing? If there's nothing wrong, then how come you look scared?"

"I ain't scared of nothin'. I saved you from those cats, didn't I?"

"Yes, you did. Come on, you'll love it."

"How did you find us?" Dusty asked.

"Luck, I think. When you weren't on your bench, I asked Cody to find you. I know that was stupid, but it was my last hope. We'd been looking for half an hour. Anyway, I thought he was following your scent. He smelled for a while then started across the park, but I think he was just wandering around. He was all over the place. There's no way you'd be walking where he took me. Around bushes, back and forth across the path. What are you laughing at?"

"He wasn't following me. He was following Bud. It must have been a stronger scent, and he knew if he found Bud, he'd find me."

"Well, I'll be! I think you're right."

"Maybe now you'll start believing just how smart he is."

We all headed off to the hotel with Mike and me leading the way. When we got to the door, Mike took out his key. "Come on in, guys."

"What's wrong, Bud?" Dusty stopped and went over to him. "Come here, boy. Michael, I don't think he wants to come in. I bet he hasn't been inside for a long time. He's always been free to run away. He's frightened. When I bathed him at the shelter, I had to carry him and he was shaking like a leaf. I'm sorry. I can't leave him, and I'm certainly not going to make him go inside."

Just hold on. I'll talk to him.

"Bud, this is where I live. Nothing will happen to you here."

"Code, I can't help it. I'm afraid."

"Bud, you're the Terror. Remember? You're not afraid of anything."

"I hate buildings. Every time I've gone near a door, someone's thrown somethin' at me or kicked me. Now I just stay away."

"Bud, listen, I know this place. Mike has asked you and Dusty to come, so no one will do those things to you."

"I don't know, Code."

"Look. Mike and I will go first. You'll see it will be okay. Come on. You've got to bite the bullet and overcome your fears. Trust me, it will be worth it."

"I'll try."

"Good. Stay right beside me, and I'll explain everything."

"Okay…"

"Hmm," Dusty said, "looks like Bud changed his mind."

Michael started laughing. "Yeah, Cody probably talked him into it."

What are you two laughing about? That's exactly what happened.

"Bud, listen. Everything is okay. My suite is at the top of the building, so we have to get in an elevator. Don't be scared, it's safe. It's like a big box with doors and moves up and down. Actually it kind of feels neat on your stomach. Just follow me."

"I don't like being shut up in here."

"I know, but Dusty, Mike, and I are here."

"Aahh!"

"It's okay. We're just going up. It won't take long. Try and enjoy it."

"I guess it ain't too bad. It does feel kind of funny."

"Here we are. Come on. Let's run ahead to my suite."

Come on, Mike, open the door. I can't wait.

"Surprise!"

"Oh my gosh. I don't believe it. How did you know it was my birthday?"

"You mentioned it last week," Michael said. "Remember when you said Bud was an early birthday present? We didn't know the exact day, just lucky I guess. Dusty, this is my girlfriend, Jennifer."

"Hello, Dusty. I've heard such wonderful things about you."

Dusty took a step back and put a hand up to his mouth.

"Dusty, you all right?" Michael asked.

"Oh sure, sorry," he said as he shook his head. "So you didn't really need me, and Cody didn't really have a bad experience last night, did he?"

"Yes he did. But we didn't really look for a guest for him because we were hoping you would agree to come. We wanted to have a little party for you. But after the night Cody had, I'm even more glad we had planned this for today."

"It doesn't matter. I'm pleased you thought of me. And I'm glad we came. Look—decorations and everything. I feel like a kid again."

"Jen, will you run in the bedroom and get Dusty's presents?"

"That's going too far. The room and dinner are more than enough."

"What would a birthday be without presents?" Jennifer called from the next room.

"What would you like to do first, open your presents or order dinner?" Michael asked.

Chapter Eight

Jennifer returned with her arms full of presents. "I have a good idea. Why doesn't he open your presents now and save the rest for after dinner?"

"Sounds good to me." Dusty smiled and took the gifts. "All those are from you, Michael?"

"It's not much."

"You're going to help, are you, Cody?"

"I forgot," said Michael. "He loves opening gifts. At Christmas he has his head stuck in everyone's presents trying to help. Get out of there, Cody."

"Leave him alone. He's fine."

Thanks, Dusty.

"Come on, Bud. Help."

"No, it's okay. I'll just sit here and watch."

"Michael, thank you. A whole new wardrobe from top to bottom. I sure needed these."

"I'm glad you like them."

Dusty turned to Jennifer. He had a small smile on his face. "Now, young lady, did you want me to open these because you thought I might take a shower and change?"

Jennifer's face turned red. "No, Dusty, please don't think that. I'm sorry."

"Well, I happen to think you're right. Would it be all right if I showered before dinner?"

Shower! Dusty, this is a party. Don't ruin it!

"Are there any shaving supplies in the bathroom, Michael?"

"Sure. The place is always stocked."

"Thanks. I'll be back in a minute."

"Hey, Code, you're spookin' me. Why are you sitting way over by that door? Are you scared of somethin'? Should we get outta here?"

"No, no. I'm just thinking."

Jennifer sank down onto the couch. "I'm so embarrassed. I did hope he might want to put on his new clothes, but I didn't think about how it would make him feel."

"Don't worry about it. I think he was teasing you. He has quite the sense of humor. Just wait until he comes back, and we'll see how things are."

"So what do you think?" Dusty sashayed out of the bedroom.

"Wow, you look great!" declared Michael.

"And so handsome," Jennifer added.

Dusty started laughing. "That's me, a regular Prince Charming. These clothes fit perfectly. If it's all right, though, I'd like to keep my other ones. I know a couple of guys who might like to have them."

"Of course, they're your clothes. Would you like to have them sent down to the laundry? They'd be ready in the morning."

Dusty chuckled. "I can just hear the comments from the workers. 'Boy, this guy must have been on the road for a while,' or ragging each other, 'Hey, Joe, you bringin' your own laundry in now?'"

Michael joined in the laughter. "That would be good. Let's get the laundry bags and put it out for pick up."

"I hope they don't mistake it for garbage."

Michael continued laughing as he handed Dusty a menu. "Let's order dinner."

"I don't even have to look. I haven't had a steak for years. Order me the biggest sirloin on the menu, medium rare."

"Are you sure you don't want a filet mignon?"

"No way. It wouldn't be big enough."

"Why don't we order two extra steaks for the dogs?" Jennifer suggested.

Yes, Jennifer! Now, you're talkin'. I might not mind you hanging around Mike and me so much.

"Did you hear that, Bud? A steak!"

"Sounds good, but Mike ain't answered yet."

"Okay," Michael said. "Why not? It *is* a party. Besides, Cody hasn't had a treat for two months. He might even be looking a little thin."

Thin! Look again, I'm gaunt.

"Hey, Code, this Mike seems like an all right guy."

"Yeah, he is, Bud."

****

Dusty leaned back, and patted his stomach. "Man, that really hit the spot. Good thing you suggested we wait to order dessert."

Michael smiled. "It was good, and the dogs sure enjoyed their steaks."

Well, of course.

Jennifer got up from the table. "Why don't we take our coffee into the living room and open the rest of the presents?"

Yeah, come on, Dusty. I want you to open my gift.

Michael passed a gift to Dusty. "This is from Cody's lawyer. Just a thank you for your kindness to Cody."

"I'm not even going to debate with you. It's all just been too wonderful." Dusty held up his new shoes, then turned them over. "Oh no, no holes. Don't look so shocked. I'm just joking. If you can't laugh at yourself, how can you enjoy anything else?"

"Here, Dusty. This is from me," Jennifer said, smiling.

"And what's your excuse for buying me a present?"

"You always bring a present when you're invited to a birthday party," Jennifer replied quickly, beginning to catch on to Dusty's humor.

"Jennifer, it's lovely, exactly what I need. My poor old wallet is just about shot. Thank you, my dear."

"You're welcome."

Yeah yeah! Get to my present.

"Look, Bud, this is the best. It's from me."

"Here, Cody, take this to Dusty," Michael said.

"Sure, now he thinks I'm smart."

"Code, you're always complainin' 'cause ya think Mike don't think you're smart. Then you mock him when he asks ya to do somethin' easy."

"You're right, Bud. I do tend to be sarcastic at times. I didn't mean it."

Here, Dusty.

"I wonder what could this be? I can't think of anything else I need."

Just great. We made a mistake. He doesn't want it.

"Wow, Cody, a new watch! This is wonderful. It even glows in the dark. I love it. Come up here, and get a hug."

Michael picked up the last gift. "One more. I saved this until last because I think it's the cutest thing Cody's done yet. When we were wrapping your presents, he went and picked this out of his stuff. I thought he wanted to play. So I threw it across the room. He went and got it and put it under a piece of wrapping paper. When I started wrapping it, he sat and watched. He looked at me as if to say, 'It took you long enough.' I guess he just wanted to pick out his own gift. Here, Cody, take this to Dusty."

I don't think so.

"Here, Bud, this is for you."

"Really?"

"Cody, no, take it to Dusty."

"Wait a minute, Michael." Dusty put his hand on his chin. "Maybe it's going exactly where he wants it to."

"But…man, this is getting crazy."

"It is, isn't it? Do you realize how much he had to understand just from your conversations? Then he had to know Bud was coming, and then make a conscious choice to wrap him a present. After today, Michael, you should never be surprised by anything he does."

You tell him, Dusty.

"Hey, Bud, open your present."

"I ain't never opened a present."

"Really? Here, I'll show you. Put one foot on it and grab the paper in your teeth and pull. Here you go. A rawhide bone."

"Smells good. Do I eat it?"

"No. Well, eventually. You mostly chew on it. If pieces come off, then you can eat them. It's mostly just good chewing."

"Thanks for thinkin' about me."

"Isn't that cute," Jennifer said. "Cody helped Bud open his present. I agree with it being scary. Cody's a lot smarter than some people I know."

"A lot of people I know," laughed Dusty.

Who's that knocking at my door?

Jennifer jumped up. "I'll get it."

"Happy birthday to you. Happy birthday to you. Happy birthday dear Dusty. Happy birthday to you."

"Doesn't this just top it all? A birthday cake, too. No wonder you suggested we wait for dessert. I must be getting dense. It never dawned on me."

Chapter Eight

Michael placed the cake on the coffee table in front of Dusty. "We didn't know how old you were, so we just put on a bunch of candles."

"If the truth be known, today is my 49th birthday. I bet you thought I was a lot older. Didn't you?"

"Maybe just a little," admitted Jennifer.

"I can't say my lifestyle has been very good for my health. Speaking of which, it's getting late, and I'm really looking forward to a good night's sleep. I can't tell you how much this party has meant to me. Thank you both."

Hey, what about me?

****

"Thanks for taking the dogs out, Mike. Good night, and thanks again for the party. Did you have a good run, boys?"

Sure did. I got more exercise than I do when I go out alone.

"Why don't you chew your bone, Bud?"

"I think I will."

What are you doing, Dusty?

"I think I'll switch things over to my new wallet. It's nice, isn't it? Thanks for inviting us tonight. It's nice to see where you live. Not bad for a dog."

Look, Dusty, you dropped this picture. Who's the little girl? Why do you look so sad?

"Thanks, Cody. This is my daughter. Isn't she beautiful? She's ten in this picture. I haven't seen her for sixteen years."

Oh, Dusty, I'm sorry. Here, I'll get up with you. Do you want to keep talking? Lots of people say I'm easy to talk to.

"Since I started looking out for Bud, I've been thinking a lot about my daughter. I guess it's because I'm responsible for someone again, and someone cares for me. Tonight's party and all the kindness Michael and Jennifer have shown me have just made it worse.

"I guess it's time I take a good look at my past. Everything I've done and everything that's happened has been entirely my fault. That's why I've been homeless these past seven years. I ended up exactly where I deserve."

Nobody deserves to be on the street.

"You may not think so, but if you hear the whole story, you'd agree. My older brother died in Vietnam when I was a freshman in high school. My parents were devastated. I buried myself in my books. My parents had been so disappointed when David hadn't gone to college. I was determined to make them proud of me.

"I was accepted at Harvard on a full scholarship. It was there I was first introduced to computers. It was instant love. I used to make money on the side by helping other students feed in their computer cards so they wouldn't disable the machines and shut down the system. The university even hired me to fix the computers and work out the glitches. It made me laugh. Here I was—twenty years old, in college, and making more than my father."

Dusty sighed. "That year, 1974, was a big one for me. I was finishing up my undergraduate degree; I met my wife, Sara; and the microcomputer was introduced. I was ecstatic—a computer that could sit on a table. Oh, the possibilities!

"Sara wouldn't finish her degree for another year, so I stayed for my masters. I had free access to all the computers, I was being paid to teach undergraduate computer courses, and I was making money on the side both from the university and businesses that wanted to start using computers effectively.

"Sara and I were married in early 1975. Six months later, she was pregnant. I was furious; I didn't want that kind of responsibility. Of course, that changed the minute Janey was born. She was so tiny and so beautiful. She had a mop of black hair and big blue eyes. I have to admit, this was the first time I truly, fully loved another human being. I cut back my workload to spend time with her. Sara and I decided I should get my doctorate. I didn't teach and only did consulting work to provide for my family. I made enough that Sara could stay home with Janey. I was happy.

"In '78 I graduated. Dr. James Elliott Kronby. That's right, Cody. Dusty is not my real name. I started using that shortly after I ended up on the street because that first summer I always felt so hot and dusty.

"Anyway, when I graduated, I started a computer consulting firm. Soon I was busy enough to hire three associates. Life was good, money was pouring in. Sara and I built a beautiful house in the suburbs. I wanted Janey to have everything money could buy, I loved her so much."

Dusty started talking so quietly, I had to scoot onto his lap to hear him.

"I think life started to change a few years later, but I didn't realize it at the time. In 1981, the year the IBM PC was first introduced, I opened my first retail store. Not only was I running the store, I was still running my consulting business, which had grown to twenty associates. I also was writing programs to help my business clients.

"Sara began to complain that I was too busy, that she and Janey never saw me. I tried to explain I was doing all this for them, but as I look back, I was just caught up in the excitement of the expanding technology. I was determined to be the biggest and the best.

"I just forgot about everything but work. In the next three years, I opened forty retail stores and five consulting firms all over the Eastern seaboard. Sara didn't care; she asked for a separation, said she couldn't continue living like this. I thought she had everything. She had a huge house, servants, memberships in all the best clubs. She said all she wanted was a husband and a father for Janey that she could depend on."

I think she was right, Dusty.

"I tried to change, but I couldn't. I had just turned 30 and was on my way to making millions. Six months later, Sara filed for divorce. I cried for the first time since my brother's death. I insisted on joint custody but was denied because I was on the road so much. I was just too difficult to find if an emergency should arise. I tried to make weekend visits enough, but I even started to miss those. I didn't want to, but something else was always coming up. Finally Sara said she had had enough. She was sick of consoling Janey because her father had canceled one more weekend because of business—or even worse, just plain forgot.

"When Janey was 10, she and Sara moved back to Sara's parents' home in Chicago. I kept in touch for a while by phone, but I started feeling so guilty that I even quit that. I figured I didn't deserve to have such a wonderful person in my life. I set up a trust fund with my lawyer to look after them both and then I walked away.

"Now I really started to expand—100 retail stores throughout the country, 25 consulting firms. Hours and hours a week just keeping up with the developing technology. After five years of this, I started falling apart. I began to drink heavily and decided to live the life of a wealthy bachelor. I bought expensive toys that I never used. I made frequent trips to Las Vegas. I lost heavily at the tables, but I didn't care. I wanted my little girl, but I knew it was too late.

"Needless to say, my business began to fall apart. My best men left to start their own companies. My stores began to lose out to competitors. I no longer kept up with the newest developments. The final blow came in the fall of 1993. My father died of a massive stroke. I hadn't seen him in three years because I was too busy or too ashamed of what I was becoming. I went on a bender that night that lasted two weeks. When I came to, I realized I had missed my father's funeral. It was then that I wished it had been me who died in Vietnam all those years ago."

A tear rolled down Dusty's cheek. "Four months later I met with my lawyers, accountants, and business managers to shut everything down. They said I'd be lucky to come out with two million dollars. I said, 'Fine. Send eighty percent of what's left to my daughter and the rest to the Harvard Business School.' It was then that they told me that my daughter and Sara had disappeared. Apparently Sara's parents had died four years earlier in a car accident. Some time after that Sara and Janey had moved to another city. Access to the trust account was through her lawyer in Chicago, and he would not say where they were."

Dusty's body sagged. "That was the day I walked away from everything I had known. I was the lowest person on Earth, so I went to the lowest place I knew—the streets. At times I thought about ending it all but never had the courage. So here I am, seven years later, still exactly where I deserve to be, on the street."

Oh, Dusty. That is so sad. You had it all, and you never realized that you only needed love.

"Bud, what do you think?"

"What? Oh, sorry, Code. I was chewin' on this rawhide bone and musta fallen asleep. What'd ya say?"

"Didn't you hear anything?"

"I heard he had a daughter and a brother who was killed. What else?"

"Never mind. Go back to sleep."

"You know, Cody, just telling you my story out loud has helped a little. I've been hiding things for so long that I was beginning to lose all feeling. I cut back on my drinking a long time ago, about the time you and Michael started coming by. I started reading the papers again and even occasionally going to the library to look at the latest computer books. I can't believe the advances in these past seven years.

"And ever since I've gotten Bud, I've begun to feel a sense of responsibility. I actually care for that old mutt, and that surprises me. Besides, there's no sense in moping about the past. I made choices in my life, and I have to live with the consequences. I'm just lucky to have found new friends in you, Michael, and Jennifer. I was shocked when I met Jennifer this evening; I bet my daughter looks a lot like her. I just hope she turned out as nice. That might have been hard after being abandoned by her father. I wish she knew I loved her, but I doubt she'll ever believe that. I chose money and power over her. I think I pretended to myself that I was doing all that because I loved her. And where did that get me? A broken man whose best friend is a dog."

Hey, don't knock it. Some people don't even have that.

"Thanks for listening, Cody. You know, I think you understood everything I said. You're even licking my face as if you know I'm done. Unlike Bud and pretty much any other dog, you never fell asleep, and even I'm only half-awake at this point. Let's get to bed."

"Ready, Bud?"

"I'm already sleepin'."

"No, not out here. Come on in the bedroom and get up on the bed."

"What's that?"

"Just follow me."

"Sleeping up on the bed with me, are you? Hey, Cody, are you going right under the covers?"

Darn right. Best place in town.

"Good night, guys."

Good night, Dusty, have a good night's sleep. You deserve it.

"Hey, Bud, are you asleep?"

"I'm tryin'."

"Can I ask you a question?"

"Sure. But I'm not talkin' to you while you're under the covers. Come out."

"Okay. Listen, the other day in the park I met my friend Angel. I started feeling things I'd never felt before. Her owner said she was in heat. Do you know what that means and why I was feeling like that? Hey, why are you laughing?"

"Come on over. Have I got some things to tell you."

****

Michael knocked and entered the suite.

"Good morning, Dusty. Sleep well?"

"The best sleep I've had for years, and it wasn't just the bed. I want to thank you for asking us here and for the party. It meant a lot to me. You know all those things people say after they spend a night with Cody? I understand now. Whatever they've said, double it for me."

"Would you like to spend another night?"

"No thank you, Michael. It's about time I got on with my life."

"Okay. Here's the laundry we sent down last night."

"Great, thank you. Let's hit the road, Bud. Bye, Cody, and thanks for everything."

"Bud, is that stuff you were telling me last night really true or were you just teasing?"

"I wouldn't lie to you. We're tight. Believe me, it's true. And you know it is just from the way you were feelin'. Good luck, little buddy. Next chance you get, don't hesitate. You'll love it. Bye."

Chapter Nine

"Michael, have you seen Dusty yet?" Jennifer asked.

"No. He wasn't at his usual places. It's as if he's vanished off the face of the Earth. Cody and I went up to the men's shelter today, and they haven't seen him for over a week. I hope nothing's happened to him. I'm phoning the hospitals tomorrow and maybe checking with the police. But if he doesn't want to be found, he won't be."

Jennifer gave Michael a quick hug. "I'm sure he's fine."

I sure hope he didn't run off because he was embarrassed he told me his story. I thought it might do him good, but now he's vanished. Poor Dusty. I hope he took Bud.

"Thanks, Jen. Come on, Cody. Laura has someone she wants you to meet."

We headed across the lobby to his desk.

"Good morning, Mrs. Boudreau. Hi, Rachel. I'm Michael, and this is Cody."

Cool. A chair with wheels on it. I'm going to check this out.

"Mom, look! He looks just like P.J. Come here, boy. Come on up."

Sure, why not. I'll check out the world from a new level. Good view!

"Mrs. Boudreau, Laura told you about Cody's suite. Are you interested?"

"Yes, of course. We have an appointment this afternoon, but should be back by supper."

"Mom, Michael, can I take Cody for a ride around the lobby before we go?"

Mike put his hand on Rachel's shoulder. "Sure, Rachel. He likes new things. If he doesn't, he'll let you know."

Hey, don't volunteer me so quickly. Wait, this is neat. I can see all sorts of new things. Not just feet and legs.

A few minutes later Mrs. Boudreau came over to get us. "Come on, honey. We have to go. We shouldn't be late."

Rachel turned away from her and crossed her arms over her chest. "I don't want to go."

"Rachel, we've been all over this. I don't want to hear any more of this foolishness. Down you get, Cody."

Before I could jump down, Rachel gave me a hug and whispered in my ear, "Cody, I need to talk to you. I'll see you later."

This is interesting. People don't usually *need* to talk to me. They just do.

****

Rachel came wheeling across the lobby with her mother running after her.

"Leave me alone. I'm not talking to you."

"Rachel, please. We need to talk."

"No! I want to go to the room alone. Please. Just give me the key, and leave me alone for a while."

"Honey, I can't."

"Mom, please."

"Okay, okay. One hour. Then we need to talk." Mrs. Boudreau handed over the key.

"Thanks." Rachel took the key and wheeled away.

Michael came over with a concerned look on his face.

"Is everything okay, Mrs. Boudreau?"

She shook her head and slumped down onto a sofa.

"No. It's not. Rachel just stormed off to the suite. This afternoon we went to a training center to look at companion dogs. They're trained to give assistance to people in wheelchairs. Rachel was totally obnoxious. She loves dogs but wouldn't even look at them. I was really hoping she would fall in love with one. I know she's only ten, but a dog could help her be more independent. I would feel a lot better if she had a dog to look out for her, but I just know she'll have nothing to do with it."

Michael sat down beside her. "If she loves dogs, what's the problem?"

"Did you see how her face lit up when she saw Cody? Our Westie, P.J., died six months ago. Ever since then it's Westie, Westie, Westie. That's all she wants. But I want her to have a dog that can do things for her."

"Maybe when she settles down you can convince her a companion dog would be better."

Mrs. Boudreau wiped a tear from her eye. "After this afternoon's debacle, I don't know if she'll ever talk to me again."

Michael took a deep breath and let it out slowly. "Mrs. Boudreau, you're going to think I'm crazy, but I think we should send Cody up to help Rachel. I don't know what he does, but many of his guests have said he's been a great help. I think mostly people just talk to him, and they feel better."

"Rachel will talk to him. She was always talking to P.J. I don't see how her venting her anger will make her all of a sudden want a different dog, but if you send Cody up, at least I'll know she's not alone. How should we handle this?"

"Why don't I call up and ask her to open the door, that Cody is on his way up? We'll just put him on the elevator and push his floor. He'll get there all right."

"All right, I'll try anything."

"Hello, Rachel? This is Michael down in the lobby. Would it be okay if Cody came up?...Good, can you open the door for him?...Okay, I'll put him on the elevator. He'll be there in about one minute. Leave the phone off the hook. When he gets in the suite, come back and tell me he's made it....Okay, Cody, let's go. You're going up in the elevator by yourself. You'll be fine."

I know, I've done this hundreds of times. Just push the button.

"There you go. Go to the suite."

Well, where else would I go? I love this. I'd ride the elevators all day if I could reach any of the buttons.

Good girl, Rachel. You've already got the door open.

"Hello, Michael? He's here. Thanks for sending him….Could you ask my mother to stay away for another hour or so?…I don't care. I just want to talk to Cody."

What's new?

"Cody, I'm so glad you're here. Nobody understands. I don't want another dog; I just want P.J. He was my friend. I told him everything. He encouraged me to do my exercises so I'd get stronger."

I wonder how he did that?

"I miss him so much. I just want him back. What should I do?"

Don't look at me. I mostly just listen. That's all most people expect.

"What's wrong? Can't you talk?"

"*Bark, bark.*"

"I don't mean speak. I mean really talk."

"*What, like this?*"

"Exactly!"

Oh my God. Am I imagining things? I've got to test this out.

"*Hello.*"

"Hello, Cody."

"*Can you hear me?*"

"Of course I can."

"*How?*"

"I don't know. A gift, I guess. Hasn't anyone ever heard you before?"

"*Not that I know of. I've never really tried it before. I just assumed people couldn't. Besides, no one has ever asked me a question and waited for an answer. Wow! I don't believe this. Ask me something else.*"

"Why do you live in the hotel?"

"*My owner died and arranged for me to stay here.*"

"Are you lonely?"

"*Oh, never. I have lots of friends in the hotel who look after me, and lots of different guests stay up here with me.*"

"Don't you miss your owner?"

"*Yes, but I know she isn't coming back, so I learned to accept life without her. Lots of people love me, so it's pretty good. And I've been able to help lots of guests with their problems. I even helped a homeless friend find a dog, so neither one would be alone. It worked out great.*"

I think.

"Maybe you can help me?"

"I'll try. Your mother filled Mike and me in a little. Can I ask you some questions?"

"Okay."

"How did you hurt your legs?"

"They aren't hurt. They just don't work anymore. When I was six, I dove into the shallow end of our swimming pool—I really loved swimming. I broke my back. I knew I wasn't supposed to dive there, but I did it anyway. I'm lucky I can still use my arms."

"Do you swim anymore?"

"No, Mom's too scared something might happen. I miss it though. I could go in with a life jacket on."

"What's that?"

"It's a coat you put on that makes you float. I think it would be good exercise."

"Did P.J. go swimming with you?"

"Are you kidding? He hated the water. He wouldn't even come to the side of the pool. He use to hide under the bed when it was time for his bath!"

Why am I not surprised.

"Do you like water, Cody?"

"Not one bit."

"Why not?"

"Dunno. Was P.J. your dog?"

"Not really. Mom had him before she was married."

"Did he sleep on your bed?"

"No, he slept on the floor beside my mother's bed. Dad didn't like him on the bed. Mostly he laid beside Mom wherever she was, even during the day. I asked him to once, but he said he just didn't feel right not sleeping beside Mom."

"When did you and P.J. start talking?"

"After my accident."

"Did he become more your dog then?"

"A little bit. He used to ride on my lap in the wheelchair and make me go further than I wanted too. When I lifted my weights, he always made me do more than the day before. The doctors were surprised that

I got strong so quick. I told them P.J. helped me. He told me I'd get stronger quicker if I did a little more every day. They didn't believe me, so I dropped it."

"Did you tell other people that P.J spoke to you?"

"Sure, Mom and Dad. But they just smiled and said, 'That's nice, honey.' I knew they didn't believe me."

"Anybody else?"

"Some kids at school. But they laughed and made fun of me. So I never mentioned it again."

"That was probably smart. Did he spend more time with you after that?"

"Yes, but he wasn't always happy, and he was always looking for my mom."

"What happened to him?"

"He just laid down one day and died. The vet said his heart just stopped."

"Was your mom okay?"

"She cried. I've never seen her so sad, not even when I got hurt. She cried for about a week."

"How did you feel?"

"I was sad too. I missed having someone to talk to. I could say anything to P.J., and he never laughed at me. He always believed me."

"So you want a Westie again so everything will be the same?"

"Yeah, I guess so."

"One last question. Do you hear all dogs now?"

"Yes."

"Okay. Listen. Wait until I'm finished before you say anything. It might not be fun to hear, but it's all true. P.J. is gone, and you can never get him back. I think you want a Westie so you can pretend that it is P.J. That's not fair to the new dog. Every dog wants to be special. This new dog would feel like he's a stand-in.

"And don't you think having another Westie would be hard on your mother? Everyday she saw him, she would think of P.J. Think how sad that would be for her. Does all this make sense?"

"I guess."

"Now, let's look at the advantages of getting one of the trained dogs from the center. I learned about trained dogs from a seeing eye dog.

They can pick up things you drop and things you can't reach from your wheelchair. They can turn lights on and off. They can open doors. Think how wonderful that would be!"

"I want a puppy who won't be attached to anyone else."

"I know, Rachel, but the dog should be specially trained. I've spoken to working dogs. They love their jobs and love to help their owners. They form a special relationship with them."

"But, Cody, I can talk to dogs. I could train the dog myself. None of those things you mentioned seem too hard."

"I never thought of that. It would be easy."

"So what kind of dog do you think I should get?"

"A Lab. They're kind of cute; they are intelligent; they are big enough to reach the light switch; and best of all, they love the water. He could go in the pool with you."

"Oh, Cody, that's perfect. But how am I going to convince my mom?"

"I think she'll be happy that you want any dog other than a Westie. Tell her everything I've told you. She'll probably figure they can have the dog trained professionally later. Now listen, make sure you *pick the puppy out. Ask them questions. Don't just pick the cutest. Make sure it's the smartest and the friendliest."*

"Yes, I will. I love you."

Hey, you're hurting my neck. Oh well, squeeze away.

Just then Mrs. B. quietly knocked as she opened the bedroom door. "Hi, honey, can I come in?"

"Sure, Mom. Cody and I were talking. I'm sorry about everything. I've changed my mind about wanting a Westie. I've decided I want a Lab, but not one from the center. I want a puppy, so it will truly be mine."

"But, honey…"

"I know. Let me finish. A Lab is big enough to do everything the center trains them for. They're smart, and they love water."

"What's that got to do with it?"

"Mom, don't you see? I want to get back in the pool. I could wear a life jacket, and the Lab could come in to look after me. If I got stuck, he could drag me to the side. Please, Mom. I need this."

"Well…we can talk about the details later. I'm just glad you want any dog."

Yes! One more for the Codyman.

"Thank you, Mom. Let's go get a puppy next week."

"I don't know if we can do it that quickly, but we'll try. Cody, I guess Michael was right. You are a special dog."

"Mom, if you only knew. Thanks, Cody."

"You're welcome."

Chapter Ten

Mr. Ellis strode across the lobby. "Laura, has everything been arranged for Cody's care this week? I don't want any problems."

"No, sir, there won't be. Michael looked after everything before he left."

Left! What do you mean, left? Michael, where are you? Please don't joke like this.

"Why is Cody running around the lobby?"

"I'm not sure, sir."

"Go get him and settle him down."

"Yes, sir. Cody, come. Come here, honey. What's the matter?"

What's the matter? Are you nuts? Michael is gone. Isn't anybody else around here upset? Am I the only one who loves him?

Carter hurried over to help. "Laura, why don't I take him out for a walk? Maybe he just needs some exercise. Come on, Cody."

I'm not going with you. I want Michael. We've been looking for Dusty. All right, stop pulling. I'm coming. But I'm looking for Michael and Dusty. Maybe they're together.

****

"Hi Cody."

"Hi, Angel."

"What's wrong? You sound so sad."

"Mike's gone."

"What do you mean, gone? Is he dead, or has he just left?"

"I don't know. Maybe he's just gone away because he made plans for my care. Maybe he made plans like an old dog, and he's gone away to die."

"Oh Cody, don't be so dramatic. You know how much he loved you. He'd never leave you."

"See, you said it yourself. Loved. Past tense."

"That was just a slip of the tongue. I mean loves."

"Sure, you're just saying that. If he left, why didn't he take me? I go everywhere with him. He just couldn't face me with the truth. He's gone for good. I'm so sad."

"Cody, I'm so sorry. It will be all right."

"No it won't. Nothing will ever be all right again."

****

When we got back to the hotel, Laura was waiting to introduce me to a guest. "Cody, this is Miss Joyce."

I don't want to meet anyone. I want Michael. Wait a minute.

"Hello."

"Hello, Cody."

She hears me! Maybe she can ask about Michael.

"How long will you be staying?"

"He's so cute." Miss Joyce squatted to pat my head.

"Miss Joyce, do you like dogs?"

"Is he timid?" she asked.

Humph. Just a lucky hello. I'm not sitting around my suite listening to other people's problems. I've got enough of my own. See ya.

****

"Laura, I think we should take Cody to the vet," suggested Carter. "He's hardly eaten anything in four days, and he won't go for his walks. When I put him in his yard, he just sits at the far end and looks out the fence. I have to go out and pick him up to bring him in."

"I know. He's spent every night in the lobby because he's rejected every guest. I have an appointment for him this afternoon."

Just great. I'm looking for sympathy, and you make it worse by taking me to the vet to be tortured. Well, I'm not going.

****

Laura walked into the lounge. "Scottie, have you seen Cody?"

"He was at the door a minute ago. Just a sec. I'll look around."

"How can you see in here?"

"You get used to it. Come here. Look."

"Cody, I see you. Come out from under there. Could you find a darker corner?"

Nope, I tried. You've got me now, but I'm still not going.

"Fine. I'll carry you."

That's right. The whole way.

****

"Well, big fella, you back again so soon?"

"Be quiet, Boots."

"How do you know my name?"

"I ran into some of your family on the docks."

"I'll have you know I come from upper-class breeding."

"Yeah sure, dirt bag."

"My, my, aren't we in a foul mood."

"Cody," called Dr. Cameron.

"Hi, Doctor. I'm Laura."

"What seems to be the problem with Cody?"

He can't fix what's wrong with me. I've got a broken heart.

"I'm not sure. He hasn't eaten much for four days. He's sleeping a lot, and he isn't friendly with any of the guests. He doesn't want to go for walks and has turned down all rides in the car. He's usually jumping at the front door to get a car ride. I gave the front desk a stool sample in case he had worms."

"Okay. Let me take a look. He seems all right, and his temperature is normal. His chart says that my assistant checked the sample, and it's clear. Tell me, has there been any major change in his routine?"

Finally.

"No, everything has been the same, except he hasn't spent a night in his suite since Michael left."

"Michael's left?"

Yeah, isn't it awful?

"No, no. He's just on vacation. He'll be back Monday."

What! Monday? Why didn't anybody tell me?

"Michael is his primary caregiver, correct?"

"Yes. The two of them are quite close."

"There's your answer. He's pining for Michael. Dogs will often go off their food and become lethargic when their owners leave them. You see it at the kennels all the time. I wouldn't worry. Why don't you try a little bacon fat or Parmesan cheese on his food?"

"What about his diet?"

"He's lost three pounds since he was here last—a pound more than needed. Spice up his food, and I don't see the problem in giving him the occasional snack. But don't overdo it like before."

Yes! Bacon, cheese, snacks. This guy isn't all bad.

****

Jeffrey got out to open the limo door. "Is he all right, Laura?"

"Yes, thank goodness. The doctor thinks he's missing Michael."

"Stupid. We should have thought of that. I've missed taking him for his rides. In fact, he looks more alert already."

"I was thinking that, too. I don't know why he would be."

Because Michael's coming back! Aren't you happy? I thought he was gone for good.

****

Andy! I haven't seen you for a week.

"Hi, Cody. I'm sorry I haven't been around for a while. I've been sick. I had some kind of infection."

Did you have to go to the vet's?

"My mother couldn't pay for a doctor, so I just had to get better by myself. She says we don't need anybody sticking their nose into our lives."

Chapter Ten

I'm beginning to think a child's business is everyone's business.
Look how thin you're getting.

"Cody, who's your little friend?" Carter came out the door and
walked across my yard.

Andy.

"Hi, I'm Andy."

"You come to visit Cody a lot."

"Yes, he's my best friend."

"Where do you live?"

"Uh, just down the hill. I have to go now, my mother will have my
supper ready. Bye-bye, Cody."

Bye, Andy.

****

I'd better start looking for a guest, or I'll be stuck down here again.
This guy looks all right, but he sure is nervous about something.

"Hello, little dog. Where did you come from?"

Heaven.

Laura hurried over. "Mr. Delnegro, I'm sorry. This is Cody. He
doesn't usually jump up on our guests."

"It's okay. He's cute."

Come on, Laura. Look at me. I like him.

"I think he might be trying to tell me something," Laura said.

Yes! She's explaining it all to him; I knew I could do it.

"Wow. I've never stayed in a suite. Heck, I've never even seen one
before. Sure, I think I'd like company tonight anyway. It might take my
mind off a big presentation I have to give tomorrow. Thank you."

"You're welcome. We'll bring him up after his last outing about
9:00."

"Would it be all right if he came up earlier? Say around 7:00? I'll
bring him back down at 9:00 to go out."

"That should be fine. We'll see you later." Laura knelt beside me.
"Well now, Cody, I see you're not going to wait for introductions
anymore. You're just going to decide for yourself."

Hey, I was desperate. I was afraid you were going to wait 'til Michael got back. I need some guests to help pass the time.

****

Krista took me up to the suite. "Good evening, Mr. Delnegro. Here's Cody. When he's ready to go out again, just bring him to the front desk and someone will show you where he goes out. Have a good night. Be good, Cody."

Yeah right, have you ever had any complaints about me? I don't think so.

"This is a beautiful suite you have here, Cody. A separate dining room and living room. Even two bathrooms. I'm impressed. This is bigger than my apartment. Look at all the toys you have! Can you play fetch?"

Can I play fetch? Do cats stink? "*Grr, grr.*"

"So you like a tug-of-war. Grr…grr…"

Hey, I like you. You get right down and growl along with me.

Fifteen minutes of grr-toy? I quit. I'm tired. You must be really trying to keep your mind off something to play that long. Here, rub my back and tell me your worries.

"Thanks, Cody. That took my mind off tomorrow for a while. I'm really nervous—it's so important, and I hate talking in public.

"Tomorrow I have to give a presentation to a group of venture capitalists. I'm on the verge of a great discovery, but I need a lot of money to continue research. I'm great in the lab, but I'm awful when I have to speak. I stammer, hem and haw, and skip over whole passages. I wrote up my report last week and I think it's good, but I haven't looked at it since. I'm afraid I won't like it, and then I'll start making changes. I just know I'm going to blow it."

Do something about it. Is this your report on the desk? Here, read it to me. I'll sit up on the chair and be your audience.

"Cody, what do you want me to do with this?"

Read it.

"I can't look at it."

"*Bark! Bark!*"

"What do you want?"

"*Bark.*"

"Do you want me to read this out loud?"

"*Bark!*"

"This is crazy. What the heck—I feel crazy enough talking to a dog."

Ouch. Just listening to this stammering is painful. And who knew presentations went for so long?

"That was awful. I'm going to read it again."

That's better. You're getting there.

"One more time."

Phew. What a difference!

"Thanks, Cody. You were right. It got better every time. I might be able to get through this tomorrow without looking like a total fool. Oh my goodness. It's 10:30. I bet you have to go out."

You were on a roll, I didn't want to interrupt you.

****

Laura came up in the morning. "Good morning, Mr. Delnegro. How did you two make out?"

"Terrific. I think this little fellow might have saved my whole career. I'll let you know later today."

"Are you spending another night with us? You're certainly welcome to."

"Oops. With all my nervousness, I forgot. I'll phone. That's one smart dog you've got there. Thanks, Cody. Wish me luck."

Good luck. But I don't think luck will have anything to do with it. You've worked hard, and your paper is great. I think.

****

Let me in this door. This has been the longest week of my life. Look out, I'm coming through.

There he is, sitting at his desk. Move over, I'm coming up.

"Hey, Cody. Hi, fella. Stop licking me, that tickles."

You left me. You never told me. You scared me.

"I know, I know. I missed you too."

I'm mad at you. Let me down. I'm going to ignore you. See how you like it.

"Come here, Cody. Cody, come. So you're going to ignore me. I know you're mad I left you. I heard you had a bad week. I'm sorry. I had vacation time, and I went to visit my mother in Bradenton. Come on, Cody, I won't do that again."

Beg all you want. I'm not giving in. I'm mad, mad, mad.

"All right, I'll leave you alone for a while."

Hey, you can't do that! You owe me. I can't do this. I'm really glad to see you. Here, rub me.

"Am I forgiven? Thanks. Look—I brought you back a new toy."

Wow! You *were* thinking about me.

****

Oh my gosh! Michael, come here. It's Dusty and Bud!

"Dusty, am I glad to see you! Cody and I have been everywhere looking for you. Have you been all right?"

Dusty lowered his head. "I'm sorry, Michael. It never dawned on me you'd be worried. I should have called. Can we sit down for a minute?"

"Sure. Come on over here."

"Hi, Bud. I'm glad to see you. I was worried."

"Hi, Code. I thought you might be, but I couldn't tell Dusty. I wasn't sure where we were, so I couldn't come myself."

"That's all right. I'm just glad you're both okay."

"Do you want me to get us some coffee?" Michael asked.

"That would be great. Come here, Cody. Sit up here. I missed our visits in the park."

Yeah, sure. You missed them so much you stayed away.

Michael returned with the coffee and sat down opposite Dusty. "I'm all ears."

"Let me first say that the birthday party you and Jennifer had for me was the beginning of all this. That, and my friendship with Bud."

Don't forget me.

"After the party that night, for some reason I told my whole story to Cody. It made me take a closer look at my life. I decided there are probably some things I can't change, but maybe I should start to work on those things that I can. My whole life before the streets was centered around money and power. Something that happened a long time ago made me realize that maybe there is more to life. No, not maybe, there *is*. I have a twenty-six-year-old daughter whom I haven't seen in sixteen years."

"Jeez, Dusty, I'm sorry."

"Don't be sorry. It's my own fault. I made decisions in my life and tried to fool myself into believing it was because I loved her. I mean, I did and do love her, but the decisions I made were not for that reason. When I started losing her, I didn't do anything about it. I imagine it's too late to make amends, and I don't even know if I'll try."

Michael leaned forward. "Dusty, that's not fair to your daughter. Even if she rejects you, that's her right. Listen, my dad ran off when I was seven. I would have given anything to have him back. Even today I would love to see him. Sometimes I think the wondering must be worse than what I might find out."

"I don't have to worry about rejection right now. I don't even know where she is. Before I could start to look, I felt I had to clean up my life. You remember I told you I worked at the animal shelter for a couple of days in exchange for a bath and grooming for Bud?"

I sure remember. Bud liked it!

"While I was there, I noticed their computer wasn't working. They couldn't afford to have it fixed. I used to be quite the computer whiz in my day. Anyway, I went back and offered to take a look at it. It took me awhile because that model came out since I've been on the streets. Between the manuals and my background, though, I fixed it up. I rearranged their programs and suggested ways to use them better. When I was finished, they recommended me to an auto repair business next door. This led to another referral. Seems like most small businesses can afford the computers but not the expense of maintaining them or paying someone to train them to use them. The funny thing is, most problems are simple. The programs aren't installed right, or the employees screw up a setting, and the machine's always crashing. Simple problems, but expensive to get someone to look at. I figured I should start out with pretty cheap rates, and I've been really busy. I got enough money for a small apartment and a phone with an answering machine. Now clients can leave a message. I even got cards printed up. Look—'Dusty's Computer Services, Repairs and Instruction.'"

Dusty smiled. "Almost all my work is just teaching people how to use their computers and their programs. And I set it up so that Bud goes everywhere with me. He's great, he just lies beside me."

"Dusty, that's terrific!"

"It sure is. I have a roof over my head, hot food every night, a great dog, and I just got an old car. Still, I want to know if my daughter is all right, even if I don't speak to her. There was a time when she was the only thing that meant anything to me."

"Dusty, you have to do more than that. You can't just find her and not speak to her."

"No. I couldn't. What if she tells me she doesn't ever want to see me again?"

"What if she does? She's earned the right to reject you. But, Dusty, what if she doesn't?"

"I don't know…"

"Dusty, you have to talk to her or you'll never know. If she rejects you, you won't feel any worse than you do already. And if she doesn't reject you, think of the possibilities. You're a young man. You've got years to make things up to her."

"You might be right, Michael. She does have a right to know what happened to me, and I suppose she has a right to tell me to get lost."

Michael relaxed back into his chair. "Now what?"

"I'm not sure. I have a few more contracts to finish up. Then I'll start scheduling time to search. I'll keep in touch."

"Wait! What's her name, and what do you know? Maybe I can help."

"Jane Ellen Kronby. Her mother's name is Sara. They left Chicago in 1989, destination unknown. She closed out her trust account five years ago when she turned twenty-one. She was in Washington. That's all I know."

"Do you mind if I pass this by some friends?"

"Whatever you think might help."

"Thanks, Dusty. Good luck. I'm glad you came by. At least I can stop looking for you."

"Sorry about that. Thanks for your help. Come on, Bud."

"Well, Cody, what do you think of that?"
I think he needs a whole pile of luck.

Chapter Eleven

"Michael, a letter came this morning for Cody, care of you." Laura smiled as she handed him the letter.

All right—my own mail!

Michael opened the letter. "It's from Rachel. Remember the little girl in the wheelchair? Listen to this."

Dear Michael,

I know this sounds crazy, but will you please read this letter to Cody? Don't laugh, please. I'm trusting you to read it to him.

Of course he will read it to me.

"You aren't going to, are you?"

He sure is.

"Why not? If she ever stays here again and asks me, I won't have to lie. What harm can it do, other than looking foolish? Come on, Cody, we might as well get comfortable."

"Can I listen?" Laura asked.

Yeah right. She doesn't want him to read it to me, and then she wants to hear it.

"Sure. Here, Cody. Sit up beside me. This is a letter to you from Rachel."

I know.

Dear Cody,

I got my puppy. The week after I saw you we went to a breeder who had ten Lab puppies—black and yellow. They were eight weeks old. I wanted a yellow one, but I remembered what you said—to pick the smartest. I had a little problem because none of them spoke very much.

Rats! I forgot they wouldn't know many words.

Three blacks and one yellow knew more than the others. So I only looked at them.

I asked the owner if I could see each of them by themselves. I rolled a ball. They all ran after it, but only one black and the yellow brought it back. So I only looked at them. I hid the ball under a blanket, and they both found it. I thought this was pretty good since they were so young. I couldn't think of anything else, so I asked to hold them. They both licked me, but when I started to wheel around, one got nervous and wanted off. The other one laid down and went to sleep in my lap. I was so happy—it was the yellow one, a boy. I hope you don't mind, I called him Cody.

Hey, you and everybody else.

He's three months old now and is really smart. Maybe even as smart as you. He does everything I ask him, usually. You know how puppies are. And you were right, he loves the pool. If we leave the back door open, he heads right for it. Best of all, I have been in the pool. Mom finally gave up and let me in. I told her one day, "Hey Mom, at least you don't have to worry about me diving in and breaking my neck." I thought she was going to faint. Then she started laughing. She bought me a really cool life jacket. Cody and I play for hours.

I just wanted to let you know. Thanks for the advice.

Love, Rachel

P.S. Cody sleeps on my bed and lies beside me when I watch TV.

Way to go, Rachel!

"Isn't that sweet," Laura said.

Michael chuckled. "Don't you just love a child's imagination?"

She's not imagining anything. She really got a puppy.

"I know. Pretending Cody gave her advice."

That's right, I did. Oh well, I guess from their point of view it is a little far-fetched. Hey, that's punny.

"Have you heard from Dusty lately, Michael?"

"Not for a couple of weeks. He tracked his daughter to D.C. She graduated from Georgetown University two months ago. You'll never guess what she graduated in—computer science. But the university doesn't know where she is now. He thinks he's hit a dead end."

"It's so sad, isn't it? You know, if she's into computers, maybe Dusty could find her on the Internet somehow. I have lots of friends who are always surfing the 'Net. Maybe they can help."

"That would be great. I'll call him now. He just got back into computers, so he might not know too much about the Internet…Hmm, I got his machine….Hi, Dusty. It's Michael. I'm just on my way out, but could you give Laura a buzz? She's got an idea that might help you find Jane. Talk to ya later. Bye….Laura, when he calls back, you can tell him about your suggestion and get the information you need."

Isn't it nice to see people trying to help other people?

"Come on, Cody. Let's go for a run in the park."

It's too hot to go running.

****

"Michael, can I see you for a minute?" Carter asked as we came back inside.

"Sure, what's up?"

"I'm not sure, probably nothing. Nearly every day, Cody meets a little boy at the back fence. His name is Andy. I've tried to talk to him a couple of times, but he always says he has to go. He looks about five, a cute little thing, but uncared for and malnourished. I thought you might like to check it out."

I don't think Andy will like this.

"I will. What time does he usually arrive?"

"Cody usually goes out about this time, so he's probably there now. Why don't you go around the building so the fence won't be between you?"

That's a bad idea. You might scare him.

"Good idea. You put Cody out, and I'll sneak up behind him."

Carter led me down the back hall and opened the door. I ran as fast as I could to warn Andy.

"Hi, Cody."

Andy, run! Mike's going to sneak up behind you. He might tell someone about your mother, and they'll take you away. I don't want to lose a friend. Look behind you, Andy. Run! "*Bark, bark!*"

"Cody, why did you do that?" Michael demanded. "I wasn't going to hurt him."

I know, but other people might. His mother is his only family in the whole world.

"You know, Cody, now you've really piqued my interest. I won't give up this easily."

Oh great. Now what have I done?

****

The next morning Laura walked toward us wearing a big grin.

"Hi, Michael. Last night my friend Morgan and I brought a laptop over to Dusty's. It was pretty neat. We got all the telephone listings and e-mail addresses for every J.E. Kronby in the United States. Dusty started with the e-mail addresses because it's cheaper, but Morgan doesn't think everyone will answer. The e-mail asks for the J.E. Kronby who graduated from Georgetown this spring. Morgan thinks we should get back later to everyone who didn't reply with a reason for asking. If we find her, Dusty will handle it from there."

I hope he finds her.

"That's great, Laura. Thanks for helping. Cody, why don't you go out now. I have some work to do."

Good. I hope Andy wasn't scared away for good. Hurry up. Open the door.

Hooray! Andy!

"Hi, Cody. Thanks for warning me yesterday. I can't stay long because Mom's really sick and I have to stay home with her 'til she gets better. I'm sad, she looks so bad."

It's okay, Andy. I'm sure she'll be fine.

Michael, no!

"*Bark, bark, bark!*"

"Hey, put me down!"

"Ouch!" yelled Michael. "Don't kick!"

Andy, no. He won't hurt you. Michael, how could you?

"I hate you, Cody. You told on me. Why didn't you warn me?"

"Andy, settle down. I just want to talk. I'm not going to hurt you. Cody didn't tell on you. How could he? And he didn't see me coming. I snuck along the wall. He didn't see me until the last second. He tried to bark. You heard him."

"How do you know my name, mister?"

"The man who puts Cody in and out, Carter, he told me. My name is Michael, and I look after Cody. I just wanted to meet his friend."

"I have to go, my mother is sick. Let me go."

"I will let you go if you promise not to run away. I promise I won't keep you more than two minutes. I just like to know who Cody is playing with. You know, to make sure they're okay for Cody. Deal?"

"Two minutes and that's it and I'm an okay person. I wouldn't hurt Cody. He's my best friend."

"Why don't you tell me about yourself?"

"My name is Andy, and I'm five years old. I live with my mom down there in that apartment building. I'm a good reader."

"That sounds pretty good. I take it you like dogs."

"They're okay. But I really like Cody."

"Why?"

"I can talk to him, and he listens."

"Don't people listen to you?"

"I don't talk to them."

"Why not?"

"I don't know. I just don't. I have to go. Mom's sick."

"Instead of visiting Cody out here, would you like to come in to play with him?"

What a great idea!

"In his apartment?"

"Actually, this isn't an apartment building. It's a hotel."

"What's a hotel?"

"It's something like an apartment building, but we only have rooms, not apartments. When people come to town, they need a place to sleep, so they pay us to stay in one of our rooms."

"How do they eat if they just have a room?"

"We have a dining room where they can buy their meals."

"Boy, that's a good scam. Charge them double."

"It's not exactly like that." Michael laughed.

"How come Cody lives here and not in a real house?"

"His owner died several months ago and left him in our care."

"Do you like Cody?"

He sure does.

"Of course. We have a good time together."

"Then why don't you take him home to live with you?"

"I would, but I'm not allowed."

"So where does he live in the hotel?"

"The truth is he has a whole suite of rooms. It's bigger than some apartments."

"That's not fair."

"What isn't?"

"That he lives alone in all those rooms."

"No, no. He's never alone. Every night we try to find a guest to stay with him. He's met lots of different people, and he's been a big help to many of them."

"How do you know they won't hurt him?"

"Cody gives his approval first."

"But he can't really talk, you know."

"I know, but if he doesn't like someone, he just walks away. If he likes them, he sits beside them or stands up on their leg to get his ear scratched."

"He's smart, huh?"

"Yes, he's very smart. Would you like to come into the hotel to see Cody sometimes, if your mother says it's okay?"

"I don't know. I have to go."

"Okay. I'll check with you again. It's been nice to meet you, Andy."

"Thanks. I'm sorry I kicked you."

"That's all right. You *should* kick and yell if a stranger grabs you. You did the right thing. I hope I didn't scare you too badly."

"You didn't scare me. I'm not afraid of anything."

Andy, you shouldn't lie.

"Bye, Andy."

"Bye....He's nice, isn't he, Cody?"

Yup. Unless he goes on vacation and leaves you behind.

"I have to go. I'll be back when Mom gets better. I'll see you later. Bye."

Bye, Andy.

Chapter Twelve

"Cody, I have another vacation coming next week."

No, Mike. I can't stand it.

"Would you like to go with me?"

Would I? Yes! And I'd get to meet your mother.

"Why don't we go camping for a week? I think you'll like it. I spoke to Mr. Park, and he agrees."

Camping? If everyone agrees, then I probably will like it. Then again, you guys all like showers. Maybe I'd better just wait and decide for myself.

****

Michael started putting my lead on.

"Come on, Cody. We have to leave early in the morning, so you can spend the night with me."

Oh good! Camping *and* another night alone with Mike. I'll face that Doberman any day for that.

"We're home," Michael called from the front door.

Aaah, Mike, you live alone.

"I'm here. I'll be right out."

Jennifer came out of the kitchen drying her hands.

Hey, what's she doing here?

"Hi, Cody. I'm glad you're spending the night with us."

Us! What do you mean, us? There's you, Mike, and me. The only us in those three is Mike and me.

Come to think of it, this place does have a strong smell of Jennifer around. She must be coming over a lot.

Mike, I thought we had to get up early. Send Jennifer home, and let's go to bed.

"Cody, I just checked out the backyard," Michael said. "The Doberman isn't there. Why don't you go out, then we'll get to bed."

He must be going to say goodnight to Jennifer while I'm out. Bye, Jennifer, see you in a week.

Ah, it's nice to be out here without that stupid dog going on. Open the door, Mike. I'm finished.

I'll race you up the stairs.

Hey, what's she still doing here? And what is she doing in our bed?

"It's okay, Cody. You know Jen."

Yeah, I know her. But why is she sleeping here?

"I think he's surprised to see me here. It doesn't fit what he's used to."

"You're probably right. Come on, Cody. Jen lives here now."

Lives here! You wouldn't let me live here. Don't expect me to sleep beside her. Move over, I don't want to fall off the bed.

Jennifer sat up in bed. "I thought this might happen. Come here, Cody."

I'm asleep.

"Look what I've got for you."

I'm still asleep.

"Do you want some cheese?"

Cheese? I'm awake. Here I come.

"That's a good boy. You're so cute. Here have some more."

This may not be so bad. But I'm staying in the middle, outside the covers, to keep you two separated. Now go to sleep. And she better not be going camping with us.

****

Uh oh, here comes Jennifer down the stairs.

Chapter Twelve

Michael looked up and smiled. "Hi, sweetheart. I hope our packing didn't wake you?"

"No, not at all. I can't find my running shoes. I'm sure I left them beside the bed. I've looked everywhere."

"I didn't see them when I got up. Are you positive you took them off there?"

"Yes. Do you think Cody took them? He didn't seem too happy that I was here last night."

Hey, don't go blaming me for your stupidity.

"He wouldn't do that."

Thanks, Mike.

"What am I going to wear to go running? They're the only pair I have."

"It's okay, sweetheart." Michael took her into his arms. "I'll help you look, and we'll stay home until we find them."

Just great. That backfired. Here.

"Cody, thank you. Where did you find them?"

Right under the sofa where you left them.

"We're all packed, Jennifer. We're going to take off. I'll see you on Saturday."

Yuck! Kissing right on the lips. Break it up! How can you breathe? I said break it up!

"Bye, guys. Have a good time." Jennifer waved from the front door. "Be careful, I love you."

Thanks. You're okay, but I wouldn't go that far.

Hey, Mike, your car's awfully full. What is all this stuff? It smells kind of musty. Hey, I smell hot dogs back there. Let me check it out.

"Cody, no! Stay up here with me."

Okay, okay, you don't have to yell. Where are we going?

"We have about a three-hour drive, so you might just as well relax."

Relax? No way. I'm going places I've never been. I'm not going to miss a thing.

Hey, Mike! Smell! What is that? Stop! Look!

"*Bark, bark, bark!*"

"What? That's just a cow. I'll pull over and let you see. I bet you have to go out anyway."

Now that you mention it. I'll go pee-pee first, but I have to see this thing. Look at the size of the legs on that! I bet he can run fast.

****

"Here we are. What do you think?"

Hey, there's no house here. Where are we going to sleep?

"Stay in the car until I get your porta-pen set up."

Hurry up. I need to explore.

"There you go."

Get me out of here! I didn't come this far to sit in this stupid little yard.

"*Bark, bark, bark.*"

"Cody, stop digging. What's wrong with you?"

What do you think? I want to walk around, and I'm not going to stop barking 'til you let me out.

"Okay, okay. Stop it! I'll let you out, but you can't run free. I'll put you on a long rope."

That's all I'm asking for. What are you hammering? Wow, an instant house. Let me in.

"This is a tent. We're going to sleep in here."

Kind of flimsy, don't you think? It better not fall on us.

Oh man! You scared me! Why are you blowing into that thing? What is it, a flat balloon?

"This is my air mattress. I even brought a little one for you. Now get off, or I'll never get this thing filled."

I'm going out to look around.

Mmm, this smells good. I think the hot dogs are in here. I wonder how this opens? I'll try to push the top off. Nope. Maybe I should lift. Ah, it moved. Maybe just a little harder.

"Cody!"

Busted.

"Get out of that. Here let me put the cooler and boxes up on the table, then we'll go for a walk. When we come back, we'll have lunch."

Okay, Mike. Isn't this nice. It's something like the park back home but bigger and better. Not so many people, and it's got lots of different smells. I bet Andy would like it here. Look! There are lots of soft houses—I mean tents.

Hey, squirrels. They're as bad as cats.

"*Bark, bark.*" Let me go, Mike.

"Cody, no. You can't chase the squirrels."

Uh oh. Put on the brakes—water. A lot of water.

"It's okay, Cody. You don't have to go in. Come on, let's sit over here and watch for a while."

I can't believe people would actually go in there to play. Looks like they're having fun. Then again, this is the species that likes showers. Maybe it's just me. As long as I don't have to go in, who cares.

"Cody, you stay here. I'll just put your lead around this tree. I'm going in to cool off. I'll be back in a minute."

Hey, if my options are to stay dry or go in the water with you, I'm happy to stay. Don't go far.

Mike, are you all right? Why are you swinging your arms and kicking your feet? I hope something in the water didn't grab him. It did, and it's dragging him out!

Oh no, it took him under! Mike!

There he is. He must have gotten away. Thank goodness, he's coming back. At least he won't try that again.

"Aw, that felt good."

You don't have to be brave with me. I totally understand. I know that water isn't safe.

"Come on, I'm starving."

Me too.

"Here, Cody. I brought you a chair. Hop up, and you can watch me cook."

Whoa, this seat's kind of saggy. It must go with the tent. I'd better sit down.

"Come on, Cody. I forgot to get some water, and I bet you're thirsty too."

I don't want that water you were in. There's something living in it.

"Here we are. Stand back."

Cool, a tap coming right out of the ground.

This is the best water I ever tasted. It doesn't even smell the same as the hotel's.

"Here you go. You can have a hot dog, but don't get too used to it."
Why not?

There goes another squirrel. Mike, look out! There's one sneaking up behind you. I'll get it.

Get out of here!

I guess I showed him.

"That's a good boy, Cody. You better not go too far, or you'll get choked. I'm going to do up the dishes, then I think I'll sit and read for a while."

This is living. Out in the woods. Just Mike and me. A few people walking by, but not close enough to bother us. I think I'll take a snooze. I wonder how Andy's mother is...

****

"Come on, Cody. Let's go for a walk before supper."

I could get used to this.

"Let's go the other way this time."

Suits me, away from the water. Hey, look, Mike. Some people have houses on wheels.

"Hi, how are you?" A man and a little girl approached from the opposite direction.

"Fine, thanks."

"Can I pat your dog?" the little girl asked.

"Sure. His name is Cody."

"Hi, Cody."

Hey, gently. I'm just little.

"My name is Allan. We're having a big bonfire about 8:00, down by the recreation field. Why don't you come join us?"

"Nice to meet you. I'm Michael. That sounds good."

"Great, see you later."

The little girl waved. "Bye, Cody."

Bye, kid.

****

"Damn!" exclaimed Michael. "Those darn squirrels got into the bread. It was my own fault. I should have put the food in the trunk."

Why should you have to hide your food? Let me loose. I'll solve the squirrel problem.

"At least the steak was safe. I'm really looking forward to it. Nothing better than cooking outdoors."

Steak! This is sounding better and better.

"Here's your supper, Cody."

Hey! This is my regular old food. Where's my steak?

"Sorry, Cody. That's all you're getting. Here, I'll put a little steak juice on it."

Better than nothing, I suppose.

****

Wow! Look at that big red dancing thing. I've got to check this out. Phew! It's hot. Put the chairs back here.

"Hi, I'm Cheryl. Your dog is so cute."

"What's your dog's name? He's so cute, sitting in that chair," said another woman.

"Hello, I'm Ann Marie. I just love your dog."

"Hi, I'm Roxanne. I've been watching your dog, and I think I'm in love. What's his name?"

"Cody."

"Hi, Cody dude," Roxanne smiled and patted my head.

Hi, I like you too.

"What kind of dog is he?"

"A Westie—a West Highland White Terrier."

"Why don't you two come over for lunch tomorrow? We're at site #112."

"Sorry, but I don't think we'll be here. I'm going to try to rent a canoe for the day."

"No problem. Have a good day. Bye, Cody dude."

Did you see that? She kissed me.

"Man, Cody. If I was free, I'd have some good pickings."

What do you mean, free? I don't see a chain around your neck or a fence keeping you in.

"You sure are a great way to pick up women."

Don't start that. You already picked up Jennifer and look where that got you. Don't you think your house is full enough?

****

I love bacon fat on my food. Thanks, Mike. Shove over. I'm coming up for leftovers.

"Sorry, Cody. Nothing left today. Down you get. I've got to get the dishes done and pack up our lunch."

Where are we going?

"Here, try this on."

What is it?

"How does that fit? Good, I think. Can you walk with it on?"

It's okay, but don't you think it's a little warm to be wearing a coat?

"Good morning, Michael." Roxanne walked up to our table with a cup of coffee in her hand. "Hi, Cody dude. You look awfully cute in your life jacket."

Life jacket? Now where did I hear....Rachel. Oh no you don't! You're not putting me in the water. End of story. No more discussion.

"When will you be back?"

"Before supper, I hope."

"Have a great time, I just dropped by to see Cody. Bye, Cody dude. Don't fall in the water."

Fall in? You don't need to worry about that. I won't be close enough to fall in.

"Come here, Cody. I'll take that off you and snap it to my pack."

****

"Cody, come. I'll put you in the canoe."

No thanks.

"Come on, you're not going in the water."

I know I'm not.

"It's safe. Look, it floats."

Yeah right, it's so safe I need a life jacket.

"Here, you sit right in front of me. Hold still while I push off."

Don't worry, I intend to.

****

"So you're finally awake. Boy, did I have you pegged wrong. I thought you would try to jump out."

Hellooo! I don't think so. That's water out there. Have another coffee and wake up.

"That looks like a nice place to stop for lunch over there. Let's check it out. I bet you need to pee, too."

Sure do.

"What a great spot—our own little private beach. I'm going to have a swim to cool off before lunch. Do you want to come?"

I don't think so, thanks.

"Come on, Cody."

I said no thank you.

"Come on, Cody."

No.

"Come on."

What part of no don't you understand?

"You must be hot, let's get your jacket off. Cody, you're boiling up. I have to put you in to cool you down."

Oh no you don't. Put me down.

"Cody, stop it. You don't even know what you're missing. You might like it. Ouch! I can't believe you scratched me."

Then put me down. No, not in the water! Something lives in here. It's going to drag me out, and I'll disappear.

"Stop it! We're not going far."

We're already too far.

"Here you go. You can swim."

Aahh! I don't like it. I'm going under. I can't move my feet any faster. Pick me up.

"Cody, no! Ow! Stop scratching! Turn around and head for shore. It's not far."

Maybe not for you. Mike, help! There's something under my feet! It's going to eat me!

Oh, it's land.

That really worked! I'm hotter now than when we started. Boy, I haven't had so much fun since Mr. Jennings yelled at me. Now do you believe me? I *don't* like the water.

"Okay, you win. I won't put you in again. I'm sorry. You sure don't swim very well. It must be because you're so solid and heavy for your size. Ooh, Cody, don't roll in the dirt."

I always roll around after my bath. I can't help it.

"Let's eat our ham sandwiches."

These are good. What else do you have?

"Sorry, Cody. I've only got a chocolate bar, and dogs can't have chocolate."

Of course not. Give me some water. I'm thirsty after all that exercise and food.

"What are you looking for? There's nothing else."

Water.

"Are you thirsty?"

That's what I said.

"I didn't bring any water. You'll have to drink out of the lake. Come on."

Not again.

"It's all right; you don't have to go in. Look."

You don't have to splash the water up with your hand. I know it's there. Why do you think I'm back here?

"Cody, this is ridiculous. Come here."

Put me down.

"Now drink."

All right! You didn't have to stick my nose under. I get the message. Get off my case.

"Good boy. That wasn't so bad, was it?"

I'm not answering one more stupid question.

"Let's head back to camp."

I think this is one experience I could have done without.

****

What's that noise? Mike, wake up!

"What is it, Cody? The rain? It's loud on the tent, isn't it? I love that sound."

I guess it's not too bad. At least I can't hear anything else out there. Wow! Mike, let me in, the sky is falling!

"Aw, Cody you can't fit in…I guess you can. What scared you?"

I don't know what it was, but it was loud. There it is again.

"That's just thunder, Cody. You can stay in my sleeping bag, but go to sleep."

I'll try.

****

"Cody, we have to get up sometime. I need to go to the bathroom."

Me too.

"I hate the rain."

Boy, you make me laugh. You swim in the lake and stand under the shower every morning, but you don't like the rain. Is there a difference?

"At least it's dry over the table so we can cook. Why don't we go for a drive after breakfast and check out the countryside?"

****

"Michael!" Jennifer ran and jumped in his arms. "I missed you so much. Hi, Cody. Did you like camping?"

Everything except Mike trying to drown me.

"How did he make out?"

"He was great."

"Wasn't he afraid in the canoe?"

"No, I couldn't believe it. He looked over the side a couple of times, then laid down and went to sleep. I think I wasted the money on a life jacket for him."

"I think it was smart just in case you tipped. Are you taking him back tonight?"

"No, I thought he could stay here, and I'll take him back Monday when I go to work."

"I have to work tomorrow afternoon. What about your slow pitch game?"

"He can go with me. I can tie him behind the fence or one of the guy's wives can look after him. After all of the women he attracted at the campground, that shouldn't be a problem."

"Oh yeah? Tell me about these women."

Tell her about Roxanne.

"Nothing to tell. I just couldn't believe all the people, mostly women, who came over to talk to him."

Jennifer crossed her arms, tilted her head, and wrinkled her brow.

"Are you sure it was Cody they were interested in?"

"Yes I am. Come here. I really missed you."

I didn't hear you mention her all week. Here we go, kissing again.

Michael pulled back and held Jennifer at arm's length.

"If you don't cut this out, I'll never get the car unpacked and the gear cleaned up."

Jennifer moved closer. "Would that be so bad?"

"Not usually, but everything is wet from the rain, and I don't want it to get mildewed. Now quit teasing, and let me get to work."

"You win, for now. Let's have an early supper. And then…"

"My thoughts exactly."

What are these guys talking about?

****

"Hi, Michael. Who's your little friend?" A.J. asked. "A new ball boy?"

"He probably could be. This is Cody. Hi, Chelsea."

"Michael, he's so cute. Is he yours?"

"No, he lives at the hotel where I work. I look after him. We just got back from camping yesterday, so I decided to keep him until tomorrow. I was wondering if he could stay with you during the game?"

"Sure thing. Hi, Cody."

Hi. Where are you going, Mike? Wait for me.

Chelsea knelt down and held onto me.

"It's okay, Cody. Look, we'll sit right here, and you can see Michael."

I don't want to see him. I want to be with him. Why isn't he playing catch with me? I can catch that stupid ball, and I'd bring it right back to him. He wouldn't have to reach all over the place to catch it.

Man! What are they yelling at? I think I will stay here after all.

"Let's go, guys," Chelsea yelled.

No sense yelling at them to go. They're not listening. Besides, we just got here.

"Look, Cody, Michael's playing shortstop. If anyone hits the ball near him, he'll try to throw it to the base before the batter gets there. Watch now! This guy's a big hitter."

Who is he a big hit with? I don't know him. I see, he's going to try to hit the ball with that metal stick.

Wow, look at the ball go.

"Go, A.J., go!" Chelsea jumped to her feet. "What a dive! Good catch—did you see that? A.J. caught him out. One down, two to go."

What's so fun about this? A guy hits the ball, you go chase it and catch it.

"The next guy, Gary, is good too."

Big deal, he didn't hit the ball as far as the last guy. He only hit it on the ground to Mike.

He's afraid of something, he's running away. No wonder, Mike's going to throw the ball at him. Get him, Mike. Rats, he would have hit him if that guy on the white square hadn't caught it.

I have to give Gary credit, he's coming back. That's right, go sit down.

Okay, Chelsea, what's this next guy going to do?

Good hit—the ball's rolling to the guy way out in the field. He's got it. Wait a minute. Why is he staying on the white square? Throw the ball at him. He's too stupid to run.

"Let's go, guys. Never mind him. Two out. Get the batter."

Mmm. So this guy is the batter? I wonder what he does different than a hitter? And what are the two out of?

Nothing, there goes the ball again. Catch it, A.J.!

"All right, way to go, A.J. Three out."

Everyone is coming in. Is the game over? Wasn't that fun!

"How's Cody doing?" Michael asked.

"Great. He's sitting here watching the game. If I didn't know better, I'd say he's trying to figure out what's going on."

"I wouldn't be surprised."

"Hey, Michael, you're up," A.J. called.

"Go get 'em, Michael, and don't worry about Cody."

Yeah! Go get them, Mike. Go get who? Okay, he's got the club now.

Good hit! Nobody can catch that. Look at them run for it. Why is Mike running? He's not afraid of anything. Mike, no! Don't go into the middle of them. Here comes the ball, they're going to hit you! They made him fall down. Let me go! Mike needs help! "*Bark, bark!*"

"Cody, no. It's all right. Michael's fine. He just slid into second. That was good. Way to go, Michael!"

This is one crazy game. How could sliding on that hard dirt be good?

"Come on, A.J. Hit Michael in."

Hit him in what? I think he's had a bad enough time already. "Yes! Home run! Good hit, A.J.!"

Run, Mike! A.J. missed you with the ball, but he's chasing you. Don't slow down, here he comes.

This is so stupid. First he tries to hit you, then he chases you, and then you turn around and slap hands with him.

This is too much. I'm going to sleep. I think this type of game is on TV. Maybe I'll watch it with Scottie and try to figure it out later.

Chapter Thirteen

Monday morning we walked to the hotel. Mitchell came out the door and smiled.

"Welcome back, you two. I think everybody will be glad to see you. The place seemed strange without Cody around. How did he make out camping?"

"He was great. I think he really liked it."

"Hi, Cody. Come here, I need a hug." Laura bent down and picked me up. "I really missed you."

Okay, okay. That's long enough. Let me go. I need some food.

"It got pretty exciting here. Dusty thinks he's found his daughter. I told him you'd be back today. He's going to come over later."

I'd better not go too far. I'll eat quickly, so I won't miss him.

Carter bent over to rub my back. "So the world traveler is back."

I think world is an exaggeration. Let me out, I just ate.

Hey, Andy's here. Wait—Andy, what's wrong? Why are you crying?

"Cody, where have you been? I waited every day, but you never came out. I went in your building yesterday, and Carter said you went away. When I started to cry, he said you'd be back today."

It's okay. I'm back. Boy, I didn't know I meant this much to him.

"Something awful happened."

Stop crying, and tell me.

"The last day I saw you, I went home and my mom was sicker and I couldn't wake her up and I didn't know what to do. I sat and held her hand all night. In the morning she opened her eyes and said, 'Andy, I love you. I'm sorry I haven't been a very good mother.' Then she closed her eyes and stopped breathing. I shook her and told her I loved her and that she *was* a good mother and she still wouldn't wake up. I went to get Harold, so he could give her some drugs to make her feel better."

Andy, this is so sad.

"When Harold came in, he looked at my mother and went right back out and then the police came and then the ambulance came and took her away. They wouldn't let me go with her. I started screaming at them."

I know the feeling. That's what happened to my mother.

"The police took me to the station. They wouldn't tell me where my mom was, and they wouldn't let me go look for her. I kicked one trying to get away."

That's not good, but I understand.

"Then a woman came and said I had to go with her. I asked if we were going to see my mom, but she said no."

It's all right, Andy. I mean it's all right to cry. I know what's coming.

"She…she said Mom was dead. I told her it was a lie and that I wanted to see her. She told me when I saw Mom not breathing that meant she was dead."

I can't stand this.

"I told her she was a liar and I wanted to see my mom and I kept yelling and yelling and calling her a big old liar. Finally she said I could see her the next day."

Oh, Andy, no.

"They took me to sleep in a house with a whole bunch of other kids. The next day, the woman took me to the hospital. My mother was in the basement and she had a sheet over her face like on TV. I knew then she was dead—they're always dead when they have that sheet on. She looked like she was just sleeping. I kissed her on the cheek and said, 'Bye, Mama. I love you.' They had to pull me away from her. I miss her so much." Andy dropped his head onto his knees and sobbed uncontrollably.

"Cody!"

Mike, come quick. Andy needs you.

138

"Andy, what's wrong? I'm Michael, remember?" Michael jumped over the fence.

"My…my mama died. I was just telling Cody about kissing her bye. She's in the basement at the hospital."

"Oh, Andy, I'm so sorry." Michael gathered him into his arms. "Do you have any other family?"

"No. Except for Cody."

"Would you like to go inside the fence to sit with him? I can lift you over."

Mike, you're so sweet.

"Ye…yes, please."

Michael lifted Andy over the fence and hopped over behind him. "There you go. Why don't you sit down? Cody can sit on your lap, and I'll sit beside you."

"Thanks, Michael."

"When did this happen, Andy?"

"The day after I met you."

"Where are you living now?" Michael slipped his arm over Andy's shoulder.

"They put me in a foster home. It's not too far from me and Mom's apartment. There's three other kids there. I don't like them and I don't like the house, but don't tell anyone, okay?"

"Why not?"

"They might move me further away, and then I couldn't visit Cody." Andy began to cry again.

Oh, Andy, here—have a kiss. I love you too.

"Andy, I don't think any foster home would be good right now. Your mother just died, and it's a very sad time. Maybe it will get better after a while."

"Maybe. Where did Cody go? I…I was looking for him every day."

"I'm sorry, Andy. Cody and I went camping for a week. If I had known you needed Cody, we would have come back."

"Re…really?"

"Of course. What are friends for?"

"Do you want to be my friend, too?"

"I would love to be your friend. After Cody, of course."

"Right, 'cause Cody is my best friend."

Thanks, Andy. Thanks, Mike.

"Is there anything I can do for you, Andy?"

"No, you already let me in with Cody."

"You don't have to meet him out here. He's in the lobby almost every day. You could come in there to ask for him. Just come around the building and in the big doors."

"I know where it is. I was there yesterday. I had to find out if Cody was gone away too. I thought I might have lost my mother *and* my best friend." Andy spoke softly as he wiped his eyes on his sleeve.

"Cody isn't going anywhere. You can count on it. You come visit anytime during the day until school starts again."

"Thanks, Michael."

"No problem."

"What time is it?"

"Almost noon."

"I have to go. My foster parent doesn't like me to be late for lunch. Thanks for putting me over the fence. Bye, Cody. I'm glad you're back."

Don't squeeze too tight. Oh, who cares.

Michael lifted him back over the fence. "Bye, Andy, come back anytime."

"Thanks, I will." Andy turned and ran off down the hill.

"Man, Cody. That was sad. What a tough situation for a little kid. I don't think I could handle it as well, even at my age."

Appearances can be deceiving. I should know, I can sense things you humans can't.

****

Dusty!

"Hi, Bud."

"Hi, Code."

"Hi, Cody. Did you have a good trip?"

Sure did.

"Hi, Laura. Is Michael around?"

"He's in with Mr. Ellis. He should be out anytime. Why don't you go have a seat over there? I'll get you some coffee while you're waiting."

"Thanks. Please join us if you can."

"I'll try."

"Code, tell me 'bout your trip."

"Bud, it was great! Mike took me camping. We lived outdoors all day in the woods and slept in a tent at night."

"What's a tent?"

"It's like a tiny, tiny room with soft walls. You zip it open, walk in, and sleep in it. It wasn't even big enough for Mike to stand up all the way."

"Sounds crowded."

"No, cozy. The best part was living outdoors all day. You would like that."

"I think I lived outdoors enough in my life."

"Sorry, Bud. I forgot."

"Hi, Dusty," Michael said as he walked toward us. "I hear you might have some good news?"

"I found my daughter! Or rather I know where she is. Well, not exactly where she is, but kind of where she is."

"Dusty, calm down and tell me what you know."

"Sorry. Laura's friend Morgan finally got confirmation that one J.E. Kronby we e-mailed is Jane Ellen Kronby, who just graduated from Georgetown with a masters in computer science. He tried to get an address from her for an alumni listing, but she wouldn't bite. She said she called the university, and they never heard of Morgan or such a listing being compiled. She hasn't answered since. Smart girl. All we know is she's in California. Her server won't give us any information."

"It sounds like you have one option: e-mail her and tell her the truth."

"I was hoping to just go out and look at her. You know, make sure she's all right."

"I thought we had decided she had a right to know about you."

"We did. But now that I've found her, I'm not so sure. I don't want to disappoint her. I don't know what she thinks happened to me or what she's been told. Maybe her story is better than the truth. Would you like to find out your father is a bum?"

"Dusty, you are not a bum. You're not the same person you were two months ago. You're even running a successful business again."

"What does that matter? It's what I did to her that matters, and that makes me a bum. I just want to see her and make sure she's okay. If her life is fine, then I will just slip away. I don't want to cause her any more pain."

"How could you tell by looking at her if her life is fine? You won't know what she's thinking or what she's feeling."

"She must be doing all right; she just graduated from Georgetown. I can't believe she's gone into computers. Isn't that ironic?"

"Maybe not. What if she got involved in computers because she knew her father was in computers and she wanted to hold on to her memories?"

"Do you think that's possible?"

"Sure it's possible, or maybe she just inherited your ability to work with computers. But none of that matters. What really counts is that you are her father and she deserves to know what happened to you."

Dusty slumped back into his chair and sighed. "Michael, I don't know what to do,"

"E-mail her. Let her know you are alive and would like to talk if she wants to. Give her your phone number and e-mail address, and then just wait."

"What if she doesn't answer or call back?"

Don't be so silly. Of course she will.

"I think that's just a chance you have to take. Besides, if she doesn't answer, you could still hire a private detective to locate her. Then you could still go out and see her. Or at least look at her."

"All right. I'll do it, but I always was more comfortable with computers then people. Would you help me with the e-mail?"

"Sure. Just say when."

"Whenever you can." Dusty unclenched his fists and his face relaxed.

"Why don't I come over to your place after work?"

Hey! What about me? I want to know what's going on.

"Okay, let's say around 7:00….And thank you, Michael."

"No problem. I'll see you then. Come on, Cody. We'd better go start looking for someone to stay with you tonight."

"Bud, you pay attention tonight. I want to know what they put in that e-mail."

"Sure, Code. See ya later."

I don't believe him. He couldn't even stay awake to hear Dusty's life story.

****

"Good evening, Mr. Knox," Krista said. "Here's Cody. He just came in, so he should be fine for the night. Call down to the front desk if you have any problems. He should sleep well tonight because he's just back from a week of camping."

"Call me John. Hi, Cody."

This guy's a little hyper. He seemed calmer this afternoon when I met him.

"This is a great suite you have here, Cody. Look at the size of it. A dining room, living room, two bathrooms, a huge bedroom, its own dining room."

Two dining rooms, huh? You said that already. What's wrong with you? Maybe we should play a little to calm you down. I want to go to bed soon.

"You want to play do you? Well, let's go."

Ow! Take it easy on the teeth. You're just supposed to try to take it—not rip it out of my mouth.

Hey, throw it across the room, not up the wall. That's it.

Ow! I told you about the teeth. Now you can play by yourself.

"Are you quitting? We just started. Come and have a little candy. That will pick you up."

Sounds good. I like jujubes. Nice and chewy. Hey, that's not candy. It looks like the artificial sugar Jennifer puts in her coffee.

"Want some? I need some more."

Now I *know* there's something wrong with you. Sniffing sugar through a straw up your nose. The mouth is for eating, and there are spoons in the dining room.

"I'm ready to go now."

Oh great! What about bed?

"I have to work on my presentation for tomorrow. I'm being interviewed for a position with the top advertising agency in the city. These guys like hype and excitement."

You don't need to worry about that. You just better hope they don't find out you eat through your nose.

"I haven't done real drugs before, but Donald said this would get me up. He's right—my portfolio sure looks good tonight."

Great, drugs! No wonder you put it up your nose. People do strange things on drugs. I heard Mike telling Jennifer about his friend who died from too much drug use, and Andy's mother probably died from them too. That's all I need, someone to die here. At least it would be quiet, and I could get some sleep. No, no, I didn't really mean that. It's just that I'm so tired.

Come on, John. Let's go to bed.

"Let go of my leg. I can't go to bed yet. I have to look at this some more."

Looking won't get you anywhere. You already said it was good, and they wouldn't be interviewing you if they hadn't already seen your work.

"I'm wired. I've got to go down to the training room and work out. Do you want to come?"

No. But I'm not letting you go alone. Let's make this fast.

****

Aren't you done yet? I can hardly stay awake.

"Boy, what a good work out. Holy snappin! It's 3:00. I've got to get some sleep."

My thoughts exactly.

Wait up. Didn't you forget someone?

"I've got to get a shower."

Yippee.

"Let me see, my interview is at 9:00. I should be there by 8:45. It should take about half an hour to get there, 8:15. Eat, shower. Alarm at 7:00. I think I'll have another small snort."

Oh no you don't. Hasn't anything sunk in?

"Hey, where are you going with that bag?"

I'm putting it exactly where it belongs.

"No! Not in the toilet. You ruined it. Now what am I going to do?"

You're going to go to sleep and rely on your own abilities tomorrow.

"I can't get through the interview without some help. I'll have to get up at 6:00 to find some more coke. I don't even know where to start looking."

If it's help you need, look inside yourself. I know a little girl in a wheelchair who is more self-reliant than you. Now go to sleep.

"If you think you're sleeping with me after what you did, you're sadly mistaken. Get off the bed."

All of a sudden we're not so jovial, huh? I don't want to sleep with you anyway. The sofa looks fine to me. I'm so tired, the floor even looks good. I'd better wait until he's asleep. I've got one more plan for him.

Carter comes to get me at 8:00, so if John hurries he can still make his interview. I hope I can do this. I'm not supposed to touch anything plugged into the wall.

Good, alarm clock unplugged. Can I finally get some sleep?

****

Knock, knock.

That must be Carter. Come on in, this guy's still out of it.

"Excuse me, sir. I've come to get Cody. I thought you must have left when you didn't answer the door. I'm sorry to wake you."

"What time is it?" John sat up, shaking his head.

"Eight o'clock, sir."

"Eight? Oh my God, I must have overslept. Hey, my alarm clock's been pulled out of the wall. You did that, didn't you, Cody?"

Yup!

"I don't think so, sir. He's been trained never to touch the electrical outlets."

"Yeah right! You don't know half of what this dog does. Just get out of here. I have an interview in fifty-five minutes. I want a taxi at the front door in fifteen minutes. If I blow my interview, this hotel is going to hear about it. I'll collect my stuff when I get back."

"Yes, sir."

"And take that mutt with you."

"Yes, sir. Come on, Cody."

You don't have to tell me twice.

"Boy, Cody. What did you do to him?"

Nothing.

"No one has ever complained before. They're usually saying how wonderful you are."

Sounds about right.

What's Dusty doing here so early?

"Hi, Carter. Mike in yet?"

"No. He usually gets in about 8:30. Why don't you get a coffee and wait for him?"

"Thanks."

"Bud, what's going on?"

"I dunno."

"What do you mean, you don't know? What did the e-mail say?"

"Dunno. I fell asleep."

"Bud, I asked you to pay attention."

"I know, but I was tired."

"Some things are more important than sleep."

"I'm sorry, Code. I just need more sleep than you."

"I can't believe you couldn't just do this one thing."

"I'm sorry. I blew it. And I owe you so much."

"No, that's all right. You don't owe me anything. You're my best dog friend. I'm sorry I snapped."

"Thanks, Code. You're my best friend, too."

"Morning, Dusty," Michael said. "What are you doing here so early?"

"Michael, you won't believe it. Janey e-mailed me back! That e-mail address was at her work, so she got it as soon as it was sent. She e-mailed back two hours later, when she got home."

"Well?"

"Here. You read it." Dusty handed him a piece of paper.

Michael unfolded it and read aloud,

Chapter Thirteen

James,

I was glad to hear from you. I started looking for you about a month ago. Mom is very sick and is expected to die within two weeks. She asked me to try to find you. She has questions she needs answered. I hope you can help. I've included my home number. If you can come out, please call and I'll make arrangements to pick you up at the airport.

Jane

"Dusty, I'm sorry. Are you going out?"

"I have a flight this afternoon. I called Janey to let her know. She was very abrupt, like her e-mail. Not that I can blame her. At least she wrote. Then again, I guess she did that for her mother. It will be a rough trip."

"Maybe Jane is cold because she doesn't know what to expect. She probably doesn't want to be hurt again. Plus her mother is dying, so I wouldn't expect too much."

"Don't get me wrong—I was thrilled that she wrote me, no matter what the reason."

"I think your best bet is to just be honest and answer all their questions, no matter how difficult."

"Don't worry. I don't plan to make any excuses. I'll answer everything I can."

"Good luck, Dusty. We'll all be thinking about you. What are you doing with Bud?"

Yeah, what are you doing with Bud? Let him stay with me.

"Kiki, the manager of the animal shelter, is going to look after him. She'll take him home at night and let him hang around the office during the day. He's familiar with the office, and he likes her. I hope he doesn't think I'm leaving him."

"What do you think Bud?"

"'Bout what?"

"Staying with Kiki."

"Why? Where's Dusty goin'?"

"Bud. Don't you listen to anything? Dusty is going to see his daughter. He'll probably be gone a few weeks. You are going to stay with Kiki."

"Guess that's all right. I like her. Dusty comin' back?"

"Yes, of course."

"We'd better get going. Thanks, Michael. I'll call you in a week or so."

"How are you getting to the airport?"

"The subway, I guess."

"Why don't you let Cody and Jeffrey take you? They were going for a drive this afternoon anyway."

"Thanks. That would be great. Do you think they could pick me up at my place at 1:30?"

"They'll be there. Good luck." Michael stood and shook Dusty's hand.

"Bye, Bud. Enjoy your stay with Kiki."

"Sure."

****

"Hi Cody, did you have a good trip to the airport?" Mitchell asked.

I think I'd only call it a drive. Uh oh, there's John. I hope he's not looking for me.

"Cody! I've been looking for you."

Rats.

"This might seem strange, but I wanted to thank you for last night. I don't know what got into me."

I know the answer to that.

"I got the job, and I was clean."

Hmm. I didn't think you'd have time for a shower this morning.

"If I had been high, I would have thought the drugs got me the job. Who knows where that would have led? I hated the way they made me feel. It was like someone else had taken over my body. Thanks to you, I don't have to go through that every day. Thank you. I'm sorry I yelled at you."

No problem.

"Mr. Knox, I'm Michael Goodwin, the concierge. I understand you had some trouble with Cody last night."

"No. Actually he might have saved my life in the long run. It's a long story, but I'm sure glad I spent the night with him. I don't know if you realize how smart this little fellow is."

"Oh, I think we do," Michael said with a grin.

Chapter Fourteen

Michael came over and woke me up.

"Cody, come on over and meet Mr. and Mrs. Higgins. This is their fiftieth anniversary. How 'bout we make it special? What do you think, can they spend the night in your suite?"

Let me check them out. Yes, they'll be perfect. A nice older couple. I bet they'll be in bed early too—exactly what I need.

"Mr. and Mrs. Higgins, we'd like to offer you the complimentary use of a suite tonight, if you don't mind sharing it with this little guy."

"My goodness! Wouldn't that be wonderful. Please, call us Bert and Betty. You know, we spent our honeymoon in this city. My husband has developed Alzheimer's, and I thought a trip back here would spark some memories. Unfortunately, the hotel we honeymooned in has been torn down and replaced by an office tower. Thank you very much."

All right, this should be good.

****

Betty looked around. "Cody, this is a beautiful suite. What a marvelous way to spend our anniversary. I hope Bert doesn't disturb you too much tonight."

Oh great! What does that mean?

"He sometimes wanders around because he doesn't know where he is."

So? Tell him; it's no secret. Or is he blind like Emmy's mistress?

"He forgets nearly everything because of this hideous disease. It's very difficult to spend a lifetime with someone you love and not have them remember all the good times we've had."

Wow, that would be hard. I bet it's hard on Bert too.

"Who is the dog?" asked Bert.

"This is Cody. Remember I told you this is his suite?"

Do you want to play grr-toy, Bert? "*Grr, grr.*" That's it, now throw it.

"Fetch, Sammy."

Sammy?

"No, Bert, that's Cody. Sammy was our poodle."

"Where's Sammy?"

"She died ten years ago."

"I'm so stupid. I'm sorry, Betty. I forgot."

"No, Bert, you're not stupid. It's the stupid disease."

Wow. This must be more difficult than I thought. I would feel terrible if I forgot my mother or Dusty or anything else from my past.

"What's his name again?"

"Cody."

"Fetch, Cody," commanded Bert as he threw the toy across the room.

Aaah, Bert. Take it. Did you forget you were playing with me?

"Hi, Sammy."

Hi, Bert.

"Come on, Bert, let's get ready for bed."

I knew this was a good choice. It's still early. I should be able to get a good sleep tonight.

"Are you going to sleep with us, Cody?" asked Betty. "That would be nice. Sammy used to sleep on our bed. I miss her sometimes."

"Good night, Betty. Night, Sammy."

Night, Bert.

****

Hey, Bert! Where are you going? What are you looking for? You shouldn't go out in your pajamas. No! Get back here. I'd better get Betty.

"*Bark, bark, bark!*"

"Cody, what is it?" Betty sat up, shaking herself awake. "Do you have to go out?"

No, Bert's gone.

"Oh my! Where is Bert?"

"*Bark, bark!*"

"Bert, where are you?" Betty got up and put on her robe.

Come on, follow me.

"Cody, are you trying to tell me he's gone out the door? Goodness! Let's go."

Come on. This way. There he is down by the elevator.

"Bert, you scared me! What are you doing out here?"

"I was looking for the bathroom." Bert began to cry. "Look—I wet myself."

"It's all right, sweetheart. Come on in, and we'll get you cleaned up."

This is tough.

"I don't believe it. I forgot the key. We're locked out. What are we going to do?"

Come on, we'll get another key from Krista.

"We can't go downstairs. What will people think of two old people wandering around in their night clothes? It's 2:00 A.M.," exclaimed Betty.

Don't worry about it. This is a hotel. Lots of strange things go on here.

"I guess we don't have any choice. Come on, Bert. We have to go downstairs to get a key."

"Where is our key?"

"I forgot it."

"Welcome to the club." Bert started laughing.

"I'm glad to see you haven't lost your sense of humor," said Betty, chuckling along with Bert.

"Here we are." Betty peeked around, as the doors opened into the lobby. "Thank goodness no one is waiting for the elevator.... I don't think I can do this."

Stay here. I'll go get Krista.

"Cody, how did you get down here in the middle of the night?"

"*Bark, bark, bark!*"

"Okay, I'm coming."

Follow me.

"Mr. and Mrs. Higgins, good evening. Can I help you?"

"Yes, dear, we're locked out of the suite. We need another key."

"No problem. You just stay there, and I'll be right back."

See, I told you she'd help.

"There you go." Krista returned with the key.

"Dear, you certainly are good at your job. You must be wondering how we got into this mess."

Krista gave them an encouraging smile. "I'm sure you have a good explanation that is really none of my business. Here come some other guests. Maybe you'd like to get going."

"Thank you, dear," Betty said as the elevator door was shutting. "Come on, Bert. Let's get you cleaned up and back into bed. Thank you, Cody."

No problem.

"Cody! We're ready to go back to bed. Where are you? Are you going to sleep by the door? What a sweetie you are. I think you actually know what's going on. Thank you, Cody."

Sure thing. Now let's get to sleep.

****

Here he comes again!

"*Bark, bark, bark!*"

"I'm here. Bert, come back to bed. Thanks again, Cody."

Yup.

****

"Are you leaving, Mrs. Higgins?" Michael asked. "I thought you were staying for a couple of nights?"

"I guess I didn't really think everything through. Bert wanders through the night. He left the suite last night. If it hadn't been for Cody, I don't know where he would have ended up. I guess it was too much to ask of him, to put him in strange surroundings. At home all our outside doors require a key to open, so he is relatively safe. I hoped when he saw the city, it might spark a few memories. I forgot about him possibly wandering out of the room. I'm sorry we won't get to see more of the city, though."

"Why don't you let Cody's chauffeur give you a tour before you leave? He'll take you anywhere you want to go. What time is your flight?"

"That would be wonderful, but you have done so much for us already. We don't want to be a bother."

"Please. I wouldn't offer if it was a bother."

"Thank you. You're such a sweet boy. Our flight's at three, so we certainly have time and would appreciate it. We can be ready in about an hour. Come here, Cody. Let me give you a hug."

All right, but not too tight.

"Thank you, Cody. I don't know what I would have done without you last night. Bert might have gotten hurt or so confused I might never have settled him down. I would have had to stay up all night just to keep an eye on him."

Right! Better me than you.

"I was thinking perhaps we should get another dog. Maybe it could help me look out for Bert. If it was half as smart as you, I'd be happy."

If he was half as smart as me, he'd be a genius.

"Thanks again. Maybe we'll see you before we leave."

I'll be the round white ball sleeping in the chair.

"Well, Cody, it looks like you helped another guest," Michael said. "I'd love to know what goes on up in that suite."

I bet you would.

"It seems like half the people who stay with you end up wanting a dog."

Of course. Now let me get some sleep.

****

"Cody, I'm sorry to wake you. Bert wants to say goodbye. Thank you for the suite and the use of your chauffeur. I can't get over a dog with his own suite and limo. Wait until I tell our friends about this. Say goodbye, Bert."

"Bye, Sammy."

Bye, Bert.

"What was that all about?" Michael asked as the Higgins walked out the front door.

It's a long story.

I can't believe I've gone through another sleepless night. I'm staying in the lobby tonight.

****

"Hi, Cody. Sorry I couldn't come yesterday. It was raining bad."

"Hi, Andy," Michael said. "I'm glad you've come to visit Cody."

"It's pretty fancy in here."

"Yes it is. I'm afraid you won't be able to play in here. If you want to play chase or ball, you'll have to go out in Cody's yard."

"That's all right. I just want to sit and talk to Cody. We can go sit in a corner."

"That won't be necessary. Come with me. Here's a nice sofa you two can sit on. Can I get you some milk and cookies?"

"No thanks."

"Are you sure? It's all right."

"No, I don't want you to have to spend any money on me."

"Why would...Oh no, I can get all the food I want free. It's a service that all Cody's guests can have. Since you're here to visit Cody, you're his guest. Are you sure you wouldn't like something?"

"Okay. I mean, yes, please."

"I'll be right back. Make yourself comfy."

"Hi, I'm Laura. Who are you?"

"I'm Cody's friend."

"Hello, Cody's friend. Do you have a name?"

"Yeah. It's Andy."

Michael returned with a plate of cookies and a glass of milk. "I see you've met Andy. He and Cody have been friends for months."

"But how—"

"Enjoy your visit, Andy. Laura, can I talk to you for a minute?"

"He's nice, isn't he, Cody?" said Andy. "I felt a little bit better yesterday after I told you and Michael about my mother. I had a good sleep. I never once dreamed about her being dead."

I'm glad.

"Is there a clock in here?" Andy looked around. "I can only stay one hour. I can tell time, you know. I'll be six next week."

Oh good! We can have a party for him, like we did for Dusty. How can I tell Mike? I'll have to think on this.

"I don't feel like talking much today. Is it all right if we just sit?" Andy picked up a cookie and settled back onto the sofa.

Chapter Fifteen

"Andy sure has been visiting Cody a lot," Carter commented on his way past Michael's desk.

"Three days in a row. There haven't been any problems, have there?"

"No. They just sit on the sofa, and Andy talks. Sometimes he doesn't say anything. He just sits, and Cody lies with his head on his lap. He seems so sad. How can a boy that age sit for so long at a time?"

"His mother died two weeks ago. They took him to the morgue to see her. I don't know why they would do that to a child that young. It seems awfully cruel to me."

You didn't hear the whole story. He wouldn't believe she was dead until he saw her. At least he got a chance to say goodbye.

"Who is he living with now?"

"A foster family somewhere close to here. I really don't know too much."

Why don't you call them? Maybe they'll tell you his birthday is in a few days. I don't know what else to do. Man, I wish I could talk.

I think I'll go into the lounge until it's time to go up to the suite. Maybe there will be a ball game on. I just hope the game on TV is the same as Mike's. The only difference I can see so far is the size of the ball and the way the pitcher throws it at the batter. See—I've learned some terms already.

"Hi, Cody. Did you come to watch some TV?"

What else?

Look at those two over there. I hate people kissing. Not little kisses, but those big long sloppy kisses. Hey, he's giving her a present! I wonder if she needs my help to open it. Wait for me! I'm a good present opener.

"Get out of here, dog," the man snarled and kicked out at me.

"Don't yell at him, Ron. He's not hurting anything," said the young woman.

"Bartender, get this dog out of here."

Hey, you don't have to tell me twice. I'm out of here. What a grouch! I hope she doesn't get stuck with him for life. Hey lady, don't let him pick you up. You'll end up living with him. Trust me, I've seen it before.

"Oh, Ron, it's beautiful!"

"Here, move the paper out of the way, and I'll show you how to set it."

See, I had him pegged. Just shove the paper on the floor. Let someone else pick it up.

"This is the nicest birthday present I've ever had."

Birthday present? That's it! I need that paper.

Got it!

"Cody, give me that." Scottie came around the bar.

No way, Jose. See ya. Now what am I going to do? If I carry it around, someone will take it from me. I know. I'll put it in the corner behind the plant. There, that should do.

"What have you got there, Cody?" Krista asked.

Busted.

"Get back here!"

I don't think so. I can't lose this paper. Think. That's it. I'll put it under the cushion on our sofa until tomorrow. That vacuum cleaner better not eat it!

****

"Hi, Andy." Michael smiled and ruffled Andy's hair.

"Hi, Michael. Would it be all right if Cody and I went outside today?"

Nooo! You have to sit on the sofa.

"Sure. Come this way." Michael headed for the back door.

Not me.

"Michael! Cody's not coming. Doesn't he want to play with me?"

"I'm sure he does, Andy. Cody, come."

Mike, please don't make me. I have to show you something.

"Cody! Come!"

Rats. What am I going to do? I'm coming.

"Look, Cody! I have a new ball we can play with. Can he play fetch, Michael?"

"Sure he can. But don't run him too much. It's quite hot out today. I wouldn't want him to get heat stroke."

"Oh no, I'd never hurt him."

"You come back in whenever you want, and I'll get you a cold drink of lemonade."

"Thanks, Michael. You're nice."

"Hey, what are friends for?"

Come on. Let's get out, so we can get back in.

****

"Did you have a good time, Andy?" Michael asked.

"Yeah! Cody's a good player. He can catch the ball right in the air, and then he brings it back to me. We played, and then we rested. I didn't tire him out."

"That's good, Andy. Why don't you go sit on your sofa, and I'll get your lemonade."

"I can't. I have to go."

No!

"Cody! Don't grab Andy's leg!"

"I think he wants something. Look, he's trying to pull me somewhere."

Finally. Follow me.

"Nope, he's just going to the sofa. I think he wants me to stay. Sorry, Cody, I have to go."

No! Look! I guess I'll just have to pull it out.

Michael took a step forward. "What do you have there, Cody?"

Andy took the paper and looked at it. "It's an old piece of wrapping paper."

Not just wrapping paper, it's birthday paper. Mike, ask Andy when his birthday is.

"Where did you get that, Cody?"

It doesn't matter. You're missing the point. Look: Andy…paper…Andy…birthday paper. Do you get it?

"What does the paper say, Andy? Can you read it?"

"Yes. It says, 'Just For You.'"

What? Doesn't it say "Happy Birthday"? Great. Just great.

It's still present paper. Come on, work with me here. Think about it. Follow the dog. Mike to Andy. Give a present.

"He's trying to tell us something, Andy."

"Maybe he knows who put the garbage in the sofa, and he's trying to tell on them."

"Could be, but I can't make any sense of it. Give me the paper, and I'll put it in the garbage."

"I have to go. I might see you tomorrow. Bye, Michael. Bye, Cody."

Aaahh! I wonder which day is Andy's birthday? He said next week, so it's probably today or tomorrow. I know he'll tell me. I can hear him now—"Hi, Cody. Today is my birthday."—but by then it will be too late to have a party for him. And what if no one is around to hear him? I can't believe this.

****

An angry-looking woman entered the hotel and looked around. She strode to Michael's desk. "I'm looking for Cody."

Hey, that's me.

"I'm not sure he's around right now."

Of course I am. I'm right here.

"Can I help you?"

"Are you telling me that there is such a person who lives in this hotel?"

"Kind of."

The woman leaned across the desk and raised her voice. "What do you mean, 'kind of'? There either is or there isn't, and I demand to know."

"Ma'am, please. If you could tell me what this is all about, I'll try to help you."

"I'll tell you what this is all about! My son has been meeting some pervert by the name of Cody who lives in this hotel. I demand to know how this could happen with so many people around."

Hey, who are you calling a pervert? Whatever that is.

"What are you grinning at?" demanded the woman.

Michael bent over and picked me up. "I'm sorry. Ma'am, I'd like to introduce you to Cody."

"A dog!"

"Yes, ma'am, and I presume you're talking about Andy."

"Yes, I am. I'm Keltie MacNeil, Andy's foster mother."

I thought she smelled familiar.

Mrs. MacNeil stepped back and sighed. "Andy disappears for a couple hours every day. When I ask him where he's been, he just says out. He hardly ever talks at home, so we don't know what he's doing or thinking. Yesterday I demanded to know where he goes. I threatened to keep him in the house if he didn't tell me. Finally he admitted he visited a friend. You know how it is these days; you can't be too careful. I asked who his friend was and where he lived. He eventually said his friend's name was Cody and that he lived in this hotel. My heart sank. You can imagine what I thought." She shook her head, but she smelled less angry now.

"I'm sorry, Mrs. MacNeil. My name is Michael; I'm the concierge and I am Cody's main care-provider. Andy started coming around in the spring. He and Cody would sit side by side on either side of a wire fence and talk. I don't know how long he was coming before I found out. After Andy's mother died, I invited him inside to see Cody. They usually just sit over on that sofa and talk. That is, Andy talks and Cody listens."

"Andy talks?"

"Yes, ma'am. With Cody, he's a real little chatterbox. They've just started going out in Cody's yard to play."

"I'll be darned! Andy hardly speaks at home, and he never plays. I have three other foster kids, and they're always playing and roughhousing. I've been very worried about Andy. I think he might need professional help—or at least I did. Maybe now we can talk about Cody. It would be a great start. Tomorrow is his birthday, and he doesn't seem at all interested—not that we can do much, but we try to do something special on the kids' birthdays."

Yes! Did you hear that, Mike?

"Did you say Andy's birthday is tomorrow?"

"Yes, he'll be six."

"Amazing. Cody, that's what you were trying to tell me yesterday."

Finally!

"What do you mean, Cody was trying to tell you?"

"Andy must have told him that his birthday was coming up. So he found an old piece of wrapping paper and was running back and forth with it between Andy and myself. He must have been trying to get one of us to say something. I'm sure he wanted to buy Andy a present."

No—have a party, and everyone buy him presents.

"I just realized he hid the paper in the sofa waiting for Andy. Cody, you never cease to amaze me!"

"He did all that?"

"Yes, he did."

Yes, I did. I am the Codyman!

"Does he really live in the hotel?"

"Yes. His owner died and left him in the care of myself and the hotel. She provided for his maintenance."

"That's kind of sad. No wonder Andy and he are friends; neither one has a real family. They've just been dumped into the system."

Hey, I've got it better than Andy. I've got lots of people who love me. I like my life.

"Mrs. MacNeil, maybe we can make Andy's birthday special by letting him spend the day with Cody. I'm off tomorrow, so I could take them to the park or whatever Andy wants. I could pick him up in the morning, and we could all spend the day together."

Mike, you're so nice.

"I guess that would be all right. But I want him home for supper. I'm planning a special meal, and I have a cake for him."

"Yes, of course. Would it be all right if we took him shopping?"

"I guess so, but don't go overboard."

"Thank you, Mrs. MacNeil."

"Thank *you*. It's about time that poor little boy had something good happen in his life. What time do you want him tomorrow?"

"Any time that is convenient for you."

"Would 9:00 be too early?"

"No, that's perfect. Thank you for dropping by. It was nice to meet you. If I had known you were worried, I would have called you. Why don't you leave your number in case I ever need to contact you? And you can always call me here at the hotel. Let me give you one of my cards."

"Thanks. I'll just jot my number down. I'm sure Andy will be here later, so you can make your plans with him."

"Goodbye, Mrs. MacNeil."

"Please, call me Keltie. Thank you, Michael. Goodbye, Cody."

I can't wait for Andy to hear this!

****

Andy! Andy! Did you hear?

Andy dropped onto his knees and wrapped his arms around my neck. "Cody, I'm so sorry. I had to tell my foster mother about you. She might try to stop me from coming here. If I argue with her, she might send me away."

No, Andy, she's been here. Everything is fine. She seems like a nice lady.

"I'll run away and hide in the hotel. I bet you know lots of hiding places."

Sure, but not for something as big as you.

"Hi, Andy," Michael said. "Are you all right?"

"I'm okay."

"Mrs. MacNeil was in earlier this morning."

"I know. I'm in trouble, right? I'm not allowed to come anymore, am I?"

"Of course you are. She's very nice. She was just worried, that's all. You didn't tell her Cody was a dog, so she just wanted to find out what was going on. She's happy you have a friend you can talk to."

"Really?"

"Really. Remember Cody was trying to tell us something yesterday?"

"Yes."

"Mystery solved. He was trying to tell me that your birthday was coming up. Did you tell him when your birthday was?"

"Yeah. But that was last week. Why would he wait until yesterday to tell you?"

"I guess he didn't know how. Maybe when he found that paper, he thought he'd try that. We didn't even figure that out. I don't know what he would have done if Mrs. MacNeil hadn't dropped in."

"It must be hard not to be able to talk, huh, Michael?"

It is, trust me.

"I spoke to Mrs. MacNeil, and she said you could spend the whole day with Cody and me if you wanted."

"Really!"

"Yes, as long as you're home by suppertime. She's planning a special meal for you."

"How early can I come?"

"Why don't you meet us here at 9:00?"

"Wow, it really will be the whole day!"

"Where would you like to go?"

"I don't know. I've never been anywhere hardly."

"The circus is in town. Would you like to go?"

"Can Cody go there?"

"No."

"Then I don't want to go. I just want to go places Cody can."

"That's very nice of you, Andy. I'm sure Cody appreciates that."

I do.

"Okay, let me think about it," Michael said. "I'll make plans and surprise you in the morning. Now, what about a present? What would you like for your birthday?"

"Just spending the day with Cody is enough!"

"I don't think Cody would be happy about that. I think he was showing us that paper yesterday because he wanted to buy you a present."

"He can't buy anything. He's a dog."

"You're right, but I do his shopping for him. He has lots of money that can be used for things like this."

"How much money does he have?"

"A whole lot."

"Really?"

"Really. Now what would you like? A new bike?"

"Can he afford a bike?"

"He can afford a hundred bikes."

"Boy, he is rich!"

"Yes, he is. Do you want a bike?"

"No, 'cause it would get stolen, and I'd be sad."

"Okay. What sounds better?"

"I don't know. I can't think of anything. Wait. We need a new toaster. The one at my house broke. I like toast, and we haven't had any for a week. That would be nice."

"But, Andy, this is your birthday. You should get something for yourself."

"I don't need anything." Andy lowered his head.

"Andy, look at me. What's the real reason you don't want anything?"

"I...I don't want the other kids in the house to feel bad."

Michael had to turn his head away for a second. When he looked back at Andy, he had a smile on his face.

"Why don't we buy something for everyone?"

"Really?" Andy's face broke into a big smile.

"Sure, we can do that. Tell me about the other kids."

"There's three of them. All boys. Mark, he is the oldest, he's 12. He likes sports. Jason's 10. He likes fighting. He's always in trouble at school. The other one is Tommy, he's 9. He has a bad leg. I think his father broke it. He doesn't go out very much. He watches a lot of TV. I like him the best 'cause he doesn't pick on me. Mark and Jason don't like me. They push me around when Mrs. MacNeil isn't looking and say awful things to me."

"Is there a Mr. MacNeil?"

"No, he died a long time ago."

"When I talked to Mrs. MacNeil this morning, she seemed nice and she was very concerned for you."

"She's nice, but it's not like having a real mother."

Michael put his arm around Andy's shoulder. "I know. So, what do you want to buy for these guys?"

"I don't know. What do you think?"

"Wow, I don't know either. I haven't bought much for kids. I don't even know kids that age. Maybe when you go home you could ask them what they want."

"Oh no, I want it to be a surprise."

"Maybe you could say something like, 'If you could have anything you wanted, what would it be?'"

"No. They'd either say a real home or something stupid like 'get rid of you.'"

"What about, 'If you had a hundred dollars, what would you buy?' That should do it."

"That's a good idea. Will Cody be allowed in the stores?"

"No, but if we're busy all morning, he'll be ready for a nap."

Especially after the past few nights.

Andy grinned the biggest grin I'd seen in two weeks. "Okay, then let's do that."

"Good. I have to get back to work. We'll see you in the morning—9:00, right?"

"Okay. Thanks, Michael."

"Don't thank me, thank Cody. He brought the paper over, and he's got the money."

"Yes, but you're going to take us out."

"All right then, you're welcome." Michael walked away smiling.

"Cody, I'm so excited. I can't wait. I wonder where we're going?"

So do I.

Chapter Sixteen

Michael pulled into a parking spot by the harbor. "Here we are. I just have to get something from the trunk."

"Where are we going?" Andy hopped out and followed.

Oh no you don't. This is supposed to be a fun day.

"What's that, Michael?"

"It's Cody's life jacket. A friend of mine has a boat, and he's going to take us out for the morning."

"I've never been on a boat!"

"There's an aircraft carrier in port we might be able to take a look at. And then later there's an island out further where we can moor and have lunch. We could even go for a swim."

"I don't know how to swim."

"Don't worry. With your life jacket on, you'll float like a duck. Here, you take Cody and his jacket, I'll take the picnic basket. Hold on tight to his lead."

Give me a break.

"Michael, I'm so excited."

"Good. Here's A.J.'s boat. Permission to come aboard, Captain."

"Hi, guys. Come aboard."

"A.J., I'd like you to meet Andy."

"Hi, Andy." A.J. extended his hand. "Happy birthday."

"Thank you. And thanks for taking me out in your boat. It's my first time."

"My pleasure. Hi, Cody, welcome aboard."

Yeah right.

"Michael, you can put Cody's life jacket on, and I'll get one for Andy. I'll get one for you too. What do you need, a small?" A.J. laughed and slapped Michael on the back.

"No, you can use that one. Better get me an extra extra large."

"In your dreams."

This has got to be bad if everyone needs a life jacket.

"There we go, all set. Michael, cast off, and we'll be on our way."

"Can your boat go really fast?" Andy asked.

"Pretty fast, but you're not allowed to go fast in the harbor. When we go out further, I'll open her up. How's that?"

"Okay."

"Andy, do you want to sit up front on the deck? We'll be able to see everything better," Michael asked.

"How do we get there?"

"Just walk up the side."

Andy took a step back and hesitated. "It isn't very wide."

"It will be all right. Watch, I'll go first. See, hold on to the bar and walk sideways."

"What about Cody?"

No way am I walking along that skinny path. Dog overboard! Dog underwater! Dog gone.

"Cody, come."

Dog overboard!

"He's scared, Michael. Don't make him."

Thanks, Andy.

"I don't think I could make him. He hates the water. I'll come back and carry him."

"How will you get back?"

"I can make it with one hand. Come on, Cody."

Hold on tight.

"Cody, be still or you'll end up in the water."

Look. Statue dog.

"Good boy. Come on, Andy. Thatta boy. Good job."

"I did it! That wasn't hard."

"Okay, let's sit here. Cody can sit between us."

"This is fun, isn't it, Cody?"

Yeah it is. The wind blowing in your face and so many good smells.

Michael stood up and turned around. "Hey, A.J., can we take a look at the aircraft carrier?"

"Yeah, but we can't get too close. They've got a buoy line to keep other boats away."

"How many planes are on the carrier?" asked Andy.

"I don't know. Maybe we could look that up sometime. Here it comes."

"It's so big! How can it float? Does it have a life jacket too?"

"It's just the way it's built."

"What's that little fat boat do?"

"That's a tug boat. Two of those probably brought that big carrier into the harbor and pushed her to her mooring."

"But they're so little!"

"That's right, but they are very strong. They're a good example of why we shouldn't judge people by their appearance. You never know what's inside someone."

Yeah, just like Dusty.

"Michael, are you trying to teach me about more than boats?"

"Yes, I guess I am. Sorry."

"No, I like to learn. I read everything I can find. My social worker told Mrs. MacNeil that I read at a fourth-grade level."

"No way."

Andy turned toward Michael with a big grin on his face. "Yes way."

"Andy, that's wonderful. You must find school pretty easy."

"Yup, I like it."

"That's good because school is very important. Do you know what you want to be when you grow up?"

"A doctor. I'm going to work cheap, so everybody can afford to see me. If there was a doctor like that around, maybe he could have helped my mother."

"Andy, you are a very special boy."

"Okay, you guys, hold on. I'm going to open her up," A.J. yelled.

****

"Here's the cove we're going to moor in for lunch. Let's go back and help A.J."

"Michael, before you come back, will you release the anchor?"

"Sure."

"How did you like that, Andy?" A.J. asked.

"It was awesome."

"And what about Cody?"

"He liked it too. I could tell because he had his head up sniffing everything."

It was all right, but I'm not happy about all the water around.

"Michael, do you want a swim before lunch?" inquired A.J.

"I'd love one. Can't you see how hot I am from working so hard?"

"Yeah right. How about you, Andy?"

"I can't swim, and these are the only clothes I have with me."

"No problem. I've got some extra swimsuits for my nephews below. Come with me. What about you, Michael? Did you bring a suit?"

"Yup."

You guys are all crazy.

Andy stood beside Michael and looked over the side. "Are you sure this jacket will keep me up?"

"Sure, watch." Michael jumped into the water.

Mike, no!

A.J. put his arm around Andy's shoulder. "See, Michael has his hands in the air and he's not sinking. Michael, come here. I'll lower you down to him. Andy, Michael will hold on to you until you're ready to be let go. I'll stay right here on board. If you don't like it, I'll bring you right back up. Okay?"

"All right."

"Here he comes, Michael. Ready?"

"I've got him."

"Are you going in, Cody?" A.J. asked.

No, and don't come near me.

"Andy's fine, A.J. Come on in."

They're all nuts.

****

A.J. stood up and stretched. "We better get going if you want to be back by two. Have you had enough to eat, Andy?"

"Yes, thank you."

"Good. Michael, grab the anchor and we'll head back to port. Andy, do you want to steer for a while?"

"You bet!"

****

When the boat was secure, Michael turned to Andy. "I left my swimsuit on board. Can you go back and get it?"

"Okay." Andy scampered up the ramp.

"Thanks, A.J. I owe you one."

"You don't owe me anything. I had a good time, and he's a great kid."

Andy returned with a big smile on his face. "Here, Michael. Thanks, A.J., for everything. I'm going to remember this forever. This is the best birthday I ever had."

"You're welcome, Andy. Here's a little something for your birthday."

"Wow! Five dollars. I can buy a whole bunch of stuff! Thanks!"

"Thanks again, A.J. I'll see you at the game tomorrow. Come on, Andy, we've got some shopping to do. We'll run Cody back to the hotel so he can have a nap."

I am awfully tired.

****

They're back. I wonder what they got? Bring it over here.

"Cody, get out of the bags," Andy demanded.

"He won't hurt anything. He's always sticking his nose in bags. I think that's where the term nosy comes from."

Yeah, yeah. Empty the bags.

"Can I show him what we got for everyone?"

"I think you better. After all, it's his money we spent."

"I'm sorry, Cody. I forgot."

Don't worry about it.

Andy ran over and hopped up on the sofa. "You come sit beside me, and I'll show you everything."

Sounds good.

"First of all, I got you a new chew bone with the money A.J. gave me. Thanks for telling about my birthday, buying me all this stuff, and being my friend."

Andy, you're so sweet. You shouldn't have. But I'm glad you did.

"We got the toaster for Mrs. MacNeil. Look, it holds four slices. We got a portable CD player for Mark and four CDs. For Jason, we got Rollerblades. He's really going to like them! And for Tommy, we got a Sony Playstation 2. Now he can do something besides watch TV. Michael says we can pick up a used TV on the way home, so Mrs. MacNeil won't miss her soaps. We also got everyone a new backpack for school. Isn't that great?"

Wonderful, whatever all those things are. What did you get?

"I got all kinds of things. School starts soon, so I got a backpack full of stuff for that. New running shoes, too. Look—aren't they awesome? I got two pairs of pants, five T-shirts, and a new jacket. Look, Cody, they're all so cool."

Yeah, great. Didn't you get anything fun?

"And look, I got a Game Boy from Michael."

What's in it?

"See, it's got four games and rechargeable batteries. Now for the best thing. Ta da! A watch! It's from you. Look—it's so great. It's waterproof, so I never have to take it off. Thanks, Cody."

Yes, once again, I am the Codyman! I guess you'd better start calling me a watch dog. Ha ha!

"Andy, we'd better get going. You have to be home by 5:00, and we still have to pick up that TV for Tommy."

"Okay. Here, Cody, I need to hug you. Thank you for giving me such a wonderful birthday. I love you. Bye."

Bye, Andy. I love you too.

****

The next time Andy visited, he sat down and started rubbing my back. "You know, Cody, after my birthday I started thinking about how nice it would be to have a father. I sure had fun with Michael and A.J. You know, just doing guy things. No, not guy things—I know women can do all that—but I mean with guys."

I know what you're saying, Andy.

"I wish I could have a real family. I asked Mrs. MacNeil about it. She says it's called adoption. People that can't have their own kids adopt children who have no parents. That's a good idea, isn't it?"

A really good idea.

"She said she would speak to my social worker about it."

****

Andy, what's wrong? You feel so sad.

"Hi, Cody. I don't want to play today. I just want to sit on the sofa."

Sure, Andy.

"My social worker came over yesterday. She said I probably won't get adopted. She said I'm too old. Most people want newborn babies."

That's stupid. With a baby you never know what you're getting. With an older child you can see what the kid is going to be like. It's like buying something—wouldn't you like to see what's in the box before you buy it?

"Mark told me I'd never get adopted. I'm too big. He's been waiting for eight years. I told him I would get adopted, and he laughed at me and shoved me down on the floor."

Oh, Andy, I'm so sorry.

"I guess I'll be in a foster home all my life. I hope I can stay with Mrs. MacNeil; at least I'll be near you."

Thanks, Andy.

"School starts tomorrow. I can't wait to wear all my new clothes. I hope I get Miss LeClair for a teacher. She's nice."

****

"Hi, Andy," Michael said. "How were your first four days of school?"

"Weird."

"Weird? What do you mean?"

"The first day I was in Miss LeClair's first grade."

Good. That's what you wanted.

"Today I got put into Mrs. Arthur's second grade."

"Wow, Andy, they moved you ahead. That's great."

"No it's not. I wanted Miss LeClair for a teacher."

"Don't you like Mrs. Arthur?"

"I don't know. I just met her. She seems all right."

"Give it a chance. You must be very smart for them to move you into second grade. Why don't you wait and see how it goes?"

"Yeah, I guess." Andy sighed and sat back.

"Is there anything else bothering you?"

Tell him, Andy.

"No."

"Why don't I believe you? Come on, Andy. You know you can tell me anything, don't you?"

"Yeah."

"Well then, what else is wrong?"

"I was hoping to get a real family. You know, a mother and father? But I'm too old."

"Who told you that?"

"My social worker, Mrs. MacNeil, and Mark."

"Did they actually say, 'Andy, you can't be adopted because you're too old'?"

"Kind of."

"What does 'kind of' mean?"

"They said most people want babies and that it's really hard to find someone who wants a bigger kid."

"Most people might prefer babies, but not all people. Andy, I'm telling you, if a couple ever met you, there is no way they wouldn't want you. You're smart, cute, clean, polite, and thoughtful. With all the bad luck you've had in your life, I don't know how you turned out so good. You're the best kid I know."

"You already told me you didn't know any kids."

Michael chuckled. "You know what I mean. You're a nicer person than most adults I know."

"Really?"

"Really. Now get those bad thoughts out of your head. Sometimes good things do happen to good people."

"They already have." Andy grinned. "I met Cody and you."

"Thanks, Andy."

Yeah, thanks, Andy.

Chapter Seventeen

"Michael, have you heard from Dusty?" Laura asked. "He's been gone a month."

"As a matter of fact, he called two nights ago."

Hey! Why didn't you tell me? Is he home? Did he make up with his daughter? Come on—spill it!

"His ex-wife died four days ago. He had just gotten back from the funeral when he called. His daughter wants some time alone, so she told him to go home and she'd be in touch later. That's all I know. Jeffrey is picking him up at five and bringing him here. Can you have supper in the restaurant with us after work? Jen's coming."

"Sure. I want to hear everything that went on."

"Good. Meet us at six."

Hold on just one minute. I'm not allowed in the restaurant, and I want to hear everything. Maybe I can sneak in like I did to talk to Emmy. But what if I get caught? I'll have to think about this.

****

Mike! Here's Dusty!

Hi, Dusty. I'm so glad to see you!

"Hi, Cody. That's the warmest welcome I've had in a while."

Michael gave him a quick hug. "Welcome back. Man, you look tired."

"I'm beat. It's been a long month. Thanks for sending Jeffrey to pick me up."

"No problem. Laura and Jennifer are through work in fifteen minutes. Would you like to have a drink in the lounge?"

Wait for me. At least I can go in there.

"What will you have, Dusty?"

"A club soda will be fine, thanks."

"Scottie, will you bring a club soda and a beer?"

And some cheezies.

Scottie came over and put the drinks on the table. "Here you go."

"Thanks. Put it on my account."

Hey! You forgot my cheezies!

"How was your flight, Dusty?"

"Long. I hate that cross-country flight. At least coming this way my body still thinks it's early."

"You better not tell me too much. The girls will want to hear everything. I went to check on Bud a couple times. He was sleeping in the office of the animal shelter. He looked good and seemed content."

Hey, you never told me that. Why didn't you take me with you?

"Thanks, Michael. That was very thoughtful of you. I called a couple of times. I think Bud is just happy to be inside and have regular meals. I doubt I'll get as warm a welcome from him as I did from Cody."

Don't make judgments. Just wait and see.

"Hello, Dusty," Jennifer said, giving him a hug. "I'm so glad to see you."

Laura also hugged him. "I'm glad you're back."

"I'm certainly a lucky man to have friends like you three."

I think that should be four.

"Do you ladies want a drink before we go to dinner?"

"No, we'll get something with our meal. Is that all right, Laura?"

"Sounds good."

Michael stood up and pushed his chair back. "Let's go then. I have a table reserved. I asked for the one in the far corner, away from the other diners."

Just great! I'll never get all the way across the room without being seen. Now what? Maybe if I just walk in like I belong.

Michael stopped and blocked my path. "Cody! You can't come in here."

I can't hear you.

"Cody, no! What's wrong with you? You know better."

I'm not missing Dusty's story.

"I don't know what's wrong with him. He knows he's not allowed in here. Even if he didn't, he always obeys such a strong command."

Dusty came back to join us. "You're going to think I'm nuts, but I think he wants to hear about my trip. I know that sounds far-fetched, but after these past six months, we know he's no ordinary dog."

"So what? He's still not allowed in here."

"What harm will it do?" Laura asked.

"First of all, it's against health regulations. Second, I don't want to confuse him by allowing him in sometimes but not others."

"Look, why don't we take the table by the door," suggested Dusty. "Dogs have incredible hearing, so if he lies outside the door, he should be able to hear everything we say."

"All right. Let's give it a try. Ladies, have a seat. I'm just going to take...well, I'll be. Look, Cody's already gone out and lain by the door. Sometimes he scares me."

I don't know why. Do you think I couldn't hear Dusty's suggestion? This is the only way I can tell you that I agree with it.

"Good evening," said Craig, one of the waiters. "I thought you had that other table reserved?"

Michael shook his head. "We did, but Cody wants to listen to our conversation, so we'll sit here."

Craig started to laugh. "Michael, I think you're working too hard."

"It's a long story. Craig, this is our friend Dusty Kronby."

"How do you do, Dusty? Do you want something to drink before you order dinner?"

"Why don't we just order now and have wine with dinner?" suggested Laura. "Then we won't have too many interruptions."

"There you are, Cody," Carter said. "I've been looking all over for you. Your supper's down."

No way. I'm staying here.

"What's wrong with you? I've never seen you miss a meal unless Michael was away. Now come on."

No.

"All right, Lazybones. I'll carry you."

Put me down. Mike, could you help me out here?

"Stop fighting me. It's hard enough lugging you all this way. Here you go. Doesn't that look…hey, get back here."

Catch me if you can.

"Cody, I can't fight with you. I was supposed to be off twenty minutes ago. Now come with me. I'm not playing games here."

Mike! Get out here!

"*Bark, bark.*"

"Hi, Michael. I'm trying to get Cody to eat his supper, but he won't come. I already took him down once, and he ran right back here."

"Sorry, Carter, just leave him. I'll look after him later."

Thanks, Mike.

"Okay. See you tomorrow."

Carter left, and Michael stood looking down at me. "So you do know what's going on. You're a nosy little thing."

I don't see you going home and missing anything.

"You won't believe what Cody just did." Michael returned to the table. "Carter just took him to get his food, and he ran right back here."

"There you have it," said Dusty. "I don't know why we're surprised anymore by anything he does."

"You're right, but it's hard to believe a dog can be so smart or human-like. It's kind of freaky."

"Maybe we should stop trying to understand," Jennifer said, "and just accept him for what he is."

Finally, a voice of reason.

Michael picked up his glass and took a drink. "Okay, Dusty, fill us in on your trip."

"First, Janey picked me up at the airport. I wish you could see her; she's beautiful. I'm not just saying that because she's my daughter. I'm telling you, she could be a model or something.

"We didn't talk too much in the car. I think we could both feel the tension. She told me about her new job at a big computer company. She does everything, from programming to troubleshooting. Sounds like she's the best they have. Everything is so easy for her."

"I guess she takes after you," Michael said.

"Only in her computer skills. She's compassionate, kind, articulate, and totally loyal to her mother. All the traits I was missing when I was married. Maybe if I had had some of those, I wouldn't have made such a mess of my life.

"By the time we got to her house, it was already late. We sat up for a while, and she told me about Sara." Dusty paused. "They arrived in California the middle of May and bought a lovely house about twenty minutes from Janey's work. Sara was still living off the trust money I had left her. She put all her effort and time into Janey.

"On the first of June she went to the doctor because she wasn't feeling well. Two days later she was diagnosed with cancer, which had already spread throughout her body. She died exactly three months later."

Laura reached across the table and touched his hand. "I'm so sorry, Dusty."

"By the time I got there, she was already in the hospital and not expected to last more than two weeks. When we arrived at the hospital the next morning, I was scared to death. It took every ounce of courage I had to enter Sara's room. When I went in, I was shocked. She was so pale and thin. She had lost all her hair from chemotherapy. Janey asked me to wait outside for a minute while she woke her up and got her ready.

"When I went back in, she was raised up in the bed and had a scarf on her head. She was smiling. I could only stand there with tears running down my face. I didn't see anything but my beautiful Sara. She was so gracious; she said, 'Don't just stand there crying. Get over here and give me a hug.'"

Dusty sighed. "Can you imagine it, after all these years with no communication and she asked for a hug? I broke down and sobbed. Here she is, dying of cancer, and she's comforting me. Finally I sat up, took her hands, and apologized for the way everything had turned out. She told me not to feel bad; I was there now and that was all she wanted.

"She told Janey to go to work. She wanted to talk to me alone. That is how we spent the next two weeks. Janey would drop me off at the hospital at eight. I'd fix Sara up, feed her the tiny bit she would eat, and we would talk for a couple of hours—as long as she could stay awake.

She'd wake up again for another couple of hours, then go back to sleep until Janey arrived. Janey would feed her supper and tell her about her day at work. I learned a lot just listening. I didn't say much during the evening, so they could have some time to themselves. I tried to leave the first day, but Sara wanted me to stay.

"It was difficult but wonderful. I told Sara everything. She wanted me to thank you all for your kindness, and she sent you all her love. She especially wished she could meet Cody."

I'd like to meet her too.

Jennifer wiped her eyes. "Dusty, this is so sad. She sounds like a wonderful person."

"She is—was. She loved me all these years. She never once considered remarrying. She blamed herself for our divorce—felt she walked away too quickly. When she found out that I ended up on the streets, she felt worse. I think I had her convinced that nothing was her fault. I tried to explain how the old James thought and acted. I put most of the blame on my lack of communication. She finally agreed that it had been difficult to talk to me, and that the new me was a totally different person. She even started calling me Dusty."

So what? That is your name.

"That's so sweet," Jennifer said.

"That's a good word for her...sweet. What a mess I've made of things." Dusty rubbed his temples.

Michael sighed. "You can't dwell on the past."

"I know. But it's difficult not to. While my days with Sara were going well, my nights with Janey were strained. We talked a little the first week, and I let her direct the conversation. By the second week, I thought it was time to tell her everything. She listened without interruption but didn't have a lot of questions. Finally she told me about her life."

Dusty had a sip of coffee and slowly continued. I could barely hear him. "She was very hurt when I left and her mother took her to Chicago. She couldn't understand why I didn't come to get her. She knew I didn't love her or I would have tried to find her.

"I tried to explain how none of this had anything to do with my love for her. It was my own selfishness for money and power that drove me away from the things that should have been important.

"When they moved, she went into a shell for a while, spent most of her time alone in her room with her computer. This lasted about six months until her mother took the computer away. Sara didn't want Janey following in my footsteps—a whiz on the computer but a social misfit. Her mother enrolled her in a community acting company and made her volunteer at the children's hospital. I guess she blossomed during this time. She became more outgoing, and after seeing some of the children at the hospital, she realized her life was pretty good.

"She got her computer back, finished first in her high school class, was president of student government and homecoming queen, and started a computer club. Janey was given a full scholarship to Georgetown and finished first in her class there."

"Boy, Dusty," Michael said, "she must be brilliant."

"She is that. She was offered the job she has now at the end of her freshman year. Thank goodness she didn't need the money. I think even after all her success, she still hurts from being abandoned. Now that her mother is gone, it's like being abandoned twice."

Dusty brushed back tears. "After the first two weeks, Sara started to fail. She was only awake an hour at a time, and I could tell she was in extreme pain although she never complained. Janey took the time off work, and we sat at Sara's bedside all day. We took turns reading her favorite books to her. Sometimes she would smile. I like to think it was from pleasure and not pain.

"The final week she dropped into a semi-coma. We stayed with her day and night. The hospital put a cot in the room, and we took turns sleeping. Then one day she partly sat up and said, 'Janey, you've been a wonderful daughter. Give your father a chance; he's a good man. I love you both. Please look after each other.' Then she laid down, closed her eyes, and died."

"Oh, Dusty. What a wonderful thing for her to do," said Jennifer as everyone at the table wiped their eyes.

"It was. It was also the first time Janey and I hugged. We cried together for a couple minutes, then Janey pulled away and went to get the doctor.

"We buried Sara two days later in a beautiful plot under a big oak tree. A few of Janey's co-workers were there, but that's about all. They hadn't been in California long enough to make any friends. Sara would have liked the simplicity of the service. Janey and I both spoke. It was difficult, but it was cleansing. I am so glad we started our search when we did. I'll cherish my time with Sara for the rest of my life."

Michael leaned forward. "What about Janey? How did you leave it with her?"

"I'm not sure. She wanted to be alone for a while. But she said she'd call, and she hugged me goodbye at the airport."

"It must have been a very difficult month for her," suggested Laura. "She finds a father and loses a mother. Either one of these would be emotionally draining, but both at the same time must be pulling her apart. Do you think she's all right?"

"I think so. She seems so strong, but…I'll give her some time. If I don't hear from her in a couple of weeks, I'll call her."

What a story. I'm glad I didn't miss that.

Dusty pushed back his chair and stood up. "I'd better get going. It's already 8:00, and I want to pick up Bud. Thank you all again for all your help."

"Good night, Dusty," said each of the three as they gave him a hug.

"I'll give you a call if I hear anything. Bye, Cody. I hope you didn't miss anything."

Don't worry. I didn't.

Chapter Eighteen

Michael woke me up. "Hey, Cody. Why don't you come spend the weekend with Jen and me?"

Is she still living with you? Why can't we spend the weekend alone? You and I are buddies. We don't need anybody else.

"We have some good news to tell you."

She's moving out! No, that wouldn't be good news to Jennifer. She's got it made living with you all the time. I guess I'll just have to come and find out.

Just great. A couple of days of trying to put that Doberman in his place.

****

"Hi, Cody." Jennifer bent down to pat my head. "I'm glad you came. We're going to have a good time. Michael's team is in the championship game on Sunday; we can both go to cheer him on."

Good. I've been watching the game on TV. I'll know what's going on this time.

"Do you have to go pee-pee?"

Yes, I do, but I don't want to go out. I'll wait.

"The Doberman is gone, so you don't have to worry about him. There's a nice German Shepherd there now."

In that case, I will go out.

"Hi, I'm Cody."

"Hi, I'm Sarge. What kind of dog are you?"

"I'm a West Highland White Terrier."

"I hear you terriers are tough little guys."

"I can be if I have to, but I'm a lover not a fighter."

"Good. Me too."

"What happened to the Doberman who lived here?"

"Ah, they put him down."

"Down where?"

"No. To sleep."

"When is he going to wake up?"

"No, putting him down means they killed him."

"What? Why?"

"He was too mean, I guess."

"But his owners made him that way to keep people away from the house."

"I know, but I guess they went too far. I heard them talking about not making me like that. They just want me to bark when someone comes to the door. If they say, 'It's okay, Sarge,' then I stop."

"It's sad, isn't it? These people made him mean, and then they killed him because he was. Somehow it doesn't seem right."

"I agree. Where did you come from? I haven't seen you here before."

"I live in a hotel. Michael looks after me there. Sometimes he brings me home with him. "

"I've got to go, Cody. See ya later."

"Sure. Nice to meet you."

"Cody, come here. Jen and I want to tell you something."

Here it comes.

"This feels weird talking to a dog." Jennifer laughed.

Hey! Who are you calling a dog? Oops, that would be me.

"I know, but you saw how he insisted on staying with us to hear Dusty. What harm can it do? If he does understand, I want him hearing this from us first."

"All right. Fair enough."

Come on, spill the beans.

"Cody, Jen and I are getting married."

Uh oh. Is this good or bad? What's married?

"That means we will become husband and wife." Jennifer had a stupid grin on her face, so I knew this was only about them. "He looks confused," she said.

"Okay, listen. Next February, Jen and I will get all dressed up and go in front of a minister to tell him we love each other and want to live together forever."

I guess she's not leaving.

"This man will say okay and pronounce us husband and wife. Nothing will change in how we live. It will just be official, and Jen will change her last name to Goodwin."

You still haven't mentioned me.

"Cody, nothing will change for you. We'll even take our camping trip every summer."

It's kind of strange to go through all this just so Jennifer can change her name. Bud changed his name from Jake without getting married. But I guess it sounds all right. She's not going to move anyway, so I don't care what her name is.

Jennifer leaned over and kissed Michael on the cheek. "I was talking to my mother today, and she's getting so excited about the wedding too. She asked me to thank you for letting them stay in Cody's suite. They're all hoping Shelley isn't too pregnant to travel. I'd be so disappointed if my sister couldn't stand for me."

"I'm sure everything will be all right. Do you think our invitation list is complete? They need to be sent out this week."

"I guess so. Last count was one hundred and ten. It's a good thing we both come from small families."

Wow, this sounds important. What about me?

"Sweetheart, are you sure you only want your sister Shelley to stand for you? I thought all women wanted a big wedding."

"I never did. The only thing I'll miss is a little ring bearer. I always thought they were adorable."

"Don't any of our friends have kids that age?" Michael asked.

"Not that I would want to have. I don't think the two I know would be well enough behaved. Too bad, Cody—wait a minute. Michael, why don't we have Cody carry the rings? Just listen a minute. He's really important in your life. Everyone knows him, and a lot of the people coming work at the hotel. And he's so cute."

That's all true. But what would I have to do?

"Do you think he could do it?"

"Of course. Listen. We can put the rings on a ribbon around his neck. He can come out with you and sit by your side. Michael, it will be so cute."

"I guess he can do that. If we have a couple of practices, he should be fine. I think it would be kind of neat."

All right. This doesn't sound so bad. I'm going to walk with Michael and sit beside him. What's there to practice?

"Let's get to bed," Michael suggested. "It's supposed to be a the perfect Indian summer day tomorrow. Do you want to take a picnic to the park?"

"Why don't we get out of the city? Let's go to that picnic area by the lake we found last summer."

By the lake? No thanks.

"Good idea. Should be fun."

Doesn't anybody ever think of me?

****

Mitchell opened the door to let us in. "Hi, Michael. How was your game yesterday?"

"A squeaker. We won, three-two."

Yeah, Mike was the hero. He got a home run at the end to win. I'm so proud of him.

"Mr. Ellis asked to see you as soon as you came in. Just a warning—he seemed a little ticked."

"Great. I hope there's no problem with you-know-what."

What?

"If there is, you better grab Jennifer and Laura before they do anything."

"Right. I'd better go find out."

Wait for me.

"Cody, no. You stay here. Go get your breakfast."

What's going on? You're hiding something from me.

****

"Laura, change of plans. We can't use the meeting room today. Mr. Ellis doesn't think it's appropriate," said Michael, sighing.

"Great. Now what are we going to do? Everyone was looking forward to it."

"Come here for a minute. Cody, stay."

Hey! Get back here, I want to hear. What's going on? It must be bad if they are keeping it from me. Something has happened to someone or they are taking me someplace I don't want to go. The vet's, I bet.

I think I'll eat quick, then stay out of sight. Maybe they'll forget about me.

****

That seemed to work pretty good. No one's bothered me all day. Maybe they can't see me behind the plant, or they forgot about my appointment or whatever. It must be getting close to supper. I'll check with Scottie's TV.

"Hi, Cody. I haven't seen you all day."

That was the plan.

"I bet you're checking to see if the news is on. You've still got another half-hour."

Okay, I'll just lie under the table until then.

"Hi, Michael. Are you looking for our little friend?"

"Yeah. He was sleeping out behind the plant most of the day. Now he's disappeared."

"Look under there."

Thanks a lot, Scottie. Hi, Mike.

"Good evening, and welcome to the six o'clock evening news."

Good, supper. Did you come to take me to eat? Hey, what's with the lead? I know my way to the kitchen.

"Come here, Cody. We're going up to the suite."

Not before I eat we're not. Besides, I haven't met any guests today, so I shouldn't even be going to the suite. Did you forget? No guest, night in lobby. Now get out of my way. Hey! Get that lead off me. I want to eat.

"Come on, Cody. You can eat after."

After what? What are you going to do to me? I don't think I like this. You know I'm a dog of routine, and right now it's time to eat. See ya.

"Look, Cody, you're coming with me. So you can either walk or I'll carry you."

You'd better carry me then.

"What a funny little guy you are. One little change and you get all worried. Don't you know by now I would never do anything to hurt or scare you?"

Uh, hello! Vet's, Cathy's, drowning—need I say more?

"Here we are. Do you think you could walk in the door?"

I guess. That way I can get behind you if something isn't right.

"Surprise!" The room was full of people. "Happy birthday, Cody."

"Happy birthday," Michael said.

Wow—a birthday party for me! I love you, Mike. Hi, Jennifer, Laura. Hi, Carter. You too, Mitchell.

"Happy birthday, Cody." Andy dropped on to his knees and patted my back. "Mrs. MacNeil is letting me stay out late. Michael's going to take me home later."

Andy, I'm glad to see you. I was hiding all day, I was hoping you hadn't come in.

Wow. Hi, Dusty.

"Bud, you're here too!"

"Yup. Happy birthday, Code. I think Dusty and I are spendin' the night."

"Great. That's a wonderful present. How did you and Dusty get in? I didn't see or smell you."

"In the back door again."

"That was kind of sneaky."

"Had to be a surprise."

"It sure was. I didn't pick up any clues. I'll see you later. I have to visit everyone."

Dusty, thanks for coming.

"So, Cody, I get to come to your party. Maybe now I can pay you back just a little of what I owe you."

You don't owe me anything. I just hope you hear from your daughter. Hi, Laura and Jennifer. What do you have?

"Happy birthday, Cody," Jennifer said. "Do you want a piece of ham sandwich?"

No, I want the whole thing, but I'll take what I can get.

"Here, Cody," said Laura. "Have a piece of my salmon one."

This could be good. I'll just keep wandering to everyone, then start again.

Hi, Adam. I didn't expect you! How many lawyers does it take to...oh, never mind. I don't really mean it anyway. I hate it when people lump others into groups and then dislike the whole bunch. Remember that Jennings guy that came in and hated me just because I was a dog? He didn't even get to know me.

What are you eating anyway, Adam?

"Do you want a cheese sandwich?"

Of course.

"Hi, everyone. Did I miss anything?" Scottie asked as he entered the suite.

"No. We've just been eating," Carter replied.

"So, Cody, were you surprised?" Scottie picked up a couple of sandwiches.

Why do people keep asking me questions that require a verbal answer?

"He seemed to be," Michael said. "He knew something was going on. I had to carry him up here, but when I opened the door and everyone yelled surprise, he came running into the room."

"I thought he might hear us this morning when we had to change places," Laura commented.

Adam sat back and shook his head. "Doesn't it seem kind of weird that you had to sneak around and whisper to keep a dog from finding out about a party? He wouldn't have known what was going on."

"I'm sorry to contradict you, Adam," Dusty replied, "but you must not have spent much time with this dog. Some of us believe Cody understands everything. Maybe even more than words. You'd have to hear some of the things he's done to fully appreciate what a special dog he is."

Thanks, Dusty.

"He's very smart, Mr. Park," Andy added.

"Sometimes I think he's just a little person inside a dog's suit."
Carter laughed at his own stupid joke.

"Time for presents?" Laura asked.

Yes! I love presents.

"Let's go to the living room," Jennifer suggested.

"How old are you, Code?"

"Three. How old are you?"

"Dunno. 'Bout five, I s'pose."

Laura sat down on the floor and looked around the room. "Why
don't we each give out our own presents? That way, Cody will know
who they are from."

You could just tell me. Remember—little person, dog's body. Ha
ha!

"I'll go first," Adam said. "Cody, I hope you'll like this. Here, I'll
help you open it."

I don't think so.

"Wait," interrupted Michael, "just give it to him. Sorry, but he
enjoys opening presents."

Thanks, Mike. Okay. What is it?

A new ball. It's perfect. It just fits my mouth. Want to play?

Michael took the ball and put his hand in front of me. "No, Cody.
We'll play later. Go see Laura."

Okay. What do you have for me, Laura?

"Will you look at that?" exclaimed Adam. "He went right to her."

Duh! Whatcha got, Laura?

"Winter's coming, so I thought this would be nice when you and
Michael go for your walks."

A coat. Good, but I like toys better. What's next?

Jennifer picked up the coat to have a look. "Laura, this is cute. It
will be really nice after his Christmas grooming."

Grooming? Let's not spoil the party.

"Me next," Jennifer said. "Here, Cody."

I know what this is. I can smell it.

"Look, Bud, two rawhide bones."

"Gimme one."

"You just have to ask."

"Sorry, Code. Can I have one?"

"Sure. Here."

"I'll be," exclaimed Adam. "He gave Bud one of his bones. I don't think many dogs would do that. And look, he's not even going to chew one himself."

It will keep. I see more presents.

"My turn," Scottie picked up the present beside his foot.

Mmm. A faint smell of food. What is it?

"I'll open this box for you. These are mini dog treats. I thought I'd keep them in the lounge, so you can have a treat when you come to see me."

Good idea. Mmm, these taste good. Give me another one.

"That's enough, Cody. Go see Dusty," Michael butted in.

What's in this, Dusty? Perfect! A new stuffed banana. That was my favorite thing to play grr-toy with before I ripped it. Thanks, Dusty. Do you want to play?

Who's at the door?

Jennifer ran out to get the door. "Hi, Cathy. I'm glad you could make it."

"Thanks for inviting me. I've never been to a birthday party for a client before."

Hey! What's she doing here? I'm gone.

"Cody! Get back here," demanded Michael.

Why do I have to get groomed in the middle of my birthday party?

Cathy sat down on the floor. "Come here, sweetheart. I'm not going to bathe you."

You're not?

"I brought you a present."

Sure. What is it, a new brush?

"Here, open it."

You open it. I don't want any new grooming supplies.

"Look. Beef jerky for dogs." She took one out and handed it to me.

Wow! These are great.

"Hey, Bud, come try this."

Where is he? Sleeping again? He's starting to get a little boring. Thanks, Cathy. Move over and feed me another.

"Can I go next, please?" Andy asked.

"Sure, Andy," replied Michael.

"Cody, I bought this with my own money. I hope you like it."

I'll like it because it's from you, Andy. A toy boat! At least it's not in water. Cool. Listen to that squeaker. It's great. Thanks.

"I have something else for him, but I have to whisper something to him first. I know it's not polite to whisper, but I have to."

Michael smiled. "It's okay, Andy. Go ahead."

"Cody, this is for you in case I ever get adopted. You'll be able to remember me."

"Can you open it for him, Michael, please? I don't want it to get ripped."

"Sure, Andy."

"It's my school picture. I wanted him to have it. You know, just in case."

"I know, Andy."

"I guess you're next, Carter," Laura said, trying to keep things moving.

"If it's all right, I'd like to go last."

"Okay. Do you want to go next, Michael?"

"Sure. Here, Cody."

Wow, this is big. What is it? You better help me get it out of the box.

A chair? There are lots of chairs in the hotel. Why do I need another one?

"This is for our camping trip next summer. You remember the saggy chair you had? This one has a nice solid seat and a cushion. Here, try it out."

Thanks Mike. This is perfect.

"That's great, Michael." Mitchell pushed another present forward. "Here, Cody. Open my present to you."

Another big one. I hope it's not a chair too.

Nah, this is soft. What is it? It's like a pillow. Don't you know I sleep under the covers? I don't need a pillow.

"It's for the lobby. I hope Mr. Ellis doesn't mind. Cody is always lying by the window in the sun. This should be more comfortable for him. We can put one of those plants in front of it, and no one should ever see it."

This is great. And so comfy.

"What a good idea, Mitchell," said Michael. "Don't worry about Mr. Ellis; we'll work around him. Okay, Carter, looks like you're the last one."

"All right. I have to go into the bedroom for a minute. I'll be right back."

Wait for me. It's my present.

"No, Cody. Stay."

All right. You don't have to yell.

"Is everyone ready?" Carter returned with something in his hand.

"Carter, you didn't!" exclaimed Michael.

Didn't what? What is that in your hand?

"I couldn't help it. I saw it and just couldn't pass it up. I love remote controls. Ready?"

I sure...Rat alert! Rat alert! I'll save you.

"*Grr...grr...grr...grr...*"

"Cody, no!" yelled Michael. "Give."

"*Grr...grr...grr...*"

"Give!"

Okay, okay. But I think I killed it. It stopped moving. What's everyone laughing about?

"Carter! Are you nuts? Don't you know Westies were bred to hunt rodents?" Michael asked.

"I know. But I couldn't help it. I wanted to see what he'd do. I don't care if he breaks it. I thought he probably would."

Break is a strange word. I killed it.

"Put it down, and let it go again. I'll try to keep it away from him."

Carter, it's dead. It's not going anywhere.

"Okay. It's your money."

He bought this? Why would you buy a rat? The streets are full of them. You just had to go catch one. That's it! He couldn't catch one. He should have taken me with him. I would have caught a bunch. Mind you, they'd all be dead.

Besides, I thought these guys were pretty nice people. Why would they get a kick out of watching me kill a rat?

"Put it over by the door again, and I'll try to run it under the sofa."

How do you run a dead rat?

"Okay. Come here, Cody. Sit by me. Ready."

It's still alive! It won't be when I get through with it this time. Get out from under that sofa.

"*Bark, bark, bark!*"

Yes! I've got you now.

Look out, Michael! Here it comes.

Got it!

"*Grr...grr...grr...*" Die!

"Cody, give."

What is so funny? You guys are sick. Why aren't you all scared? I thought people hated rats.

"Cody, look. It's not real."

What do you mean not real? Did you ever see anything that is not real running around?

"Carter, turn it on. Look, Cody. See the wheels moving? Look, I'm going to put it down."

I've got it.

"*Grr...grr...*"

Die! Rat! Die!

"Cody. No, give. I don't think we'll convince him of this one. Cody, look! It's a toy."

A toy? This is totally stupid. You guys are sick.

I'll see you all later. I'm going to bed. Shut the door when you leave.

"Uh oh," Jennifer said, "I think he's mad."

"Why would he be mad?" Adam asked. "You've taken other toys from him tonight."

"I think he's mad because we tried to trick him," Dusty replied, "and I think he's very sensitive. I don't think he likes being laughed at."

"All right. I believe you," conceded Adam. "Cody is no ordinary dog."

Carter came to the bedroom door. "Come back, Cody, please. I'm sorry. I didn't get the rat to tease you. I guess I didn't think about the consequences. Come here, I'll get you a cheese sandwich."

Oh, all right.

"I wonder where Donald is?" Jennifer asked. "He should have been here...Good, that must be him now. You guys get ready."

My own birthday cake! I'm going to sit up on my new chair for this. I'm ready. Start singing.

****

"Michael, that was a great party last night," Dusty said on his way out. "Thanks for inviting us."

"Hey, you're as close to Cody as most of the staff. It wouldn't be a party without you."

"I didn't want to bring this up last night, but I need a favor."

"Anything, Dusty. You know that."

"I heard from Janey yesterday. She's coming here next week for a seminar and workshop. I was wondering if she could stay with Cody that week?"

"You bet. We'd love to have her."

She'd better. I want to meet her.

"She just called to let me know she was coming. She suggested we might get together. I was thrilled. I'll call her later and offer her the suite with Cody. I hope she says yes. I'd really like all of you to meet her."

"And we'd love to meet her. Let me know exactly when she's coming, and I'll book her in."

This will be great. I can't wait.

"Hi, Cody," Andy came skipping across the lobby. "That was a cool party, wasn't it?"

It sure was.

"I'm sorry they teased you with that toy rat. I was going to tell them to stop, but how can a kid tell a bunch of adults what to do?"

If it's right, it's right, no matter how old you are.

"It made me sad. I almost started crying."

It's all right, Andy. I made Carter apologize; he'll think twice before he teases me again.

"That was the first birthday party I've ever been invited to. I'm glad it was for you. You sure do have a lot of friends."

Yeah, I do.

Chapter Nineteen

Mike, look at that beautiful woman. She looks lost.

"Good afternoon. I'm looking for Michael Goodwin."

"Good afternoon. I'm Michael, what can I do for you?"

"I'm Jane Kronby. I know I'm not suppose to be here until tonight, but I took an earlier flight. I hope that's not an inconvenience."

"Not at all. I'm pleased to meet you. This is Cody."

"Hi, Cody. Thank you for sharing your suite."

I think I'm in love.

"I'll find Carter to get your luggage and take you to the suite. Please feel free to order anything from room service and when you want to go out, call down to the front desk and Cody's limo will be at your disposal."

"Thank you, but I don't think I can use the limo. It might be a little pretentious for a seminar. My meetings are just down the street, so I'll probably walk."

"Whatever you decide. If you change your mind, just let me know. Excuse me. I'll be right back."

"So, you're the famous Cody. My mother sure enjoyed stories about you."

I didn't know I was famous.

Michael returned with Carter. "Miss Kronby, this is Carter. He'll take you to the suite."

"Please call me Jane. Hello, Carter."

"Hello, Miss—ah, Jane. Is this all your luggage?"

"No. I have two more pieces over by the door. Thank you, Michael, for suggesting I stay here. I'm sure I'll see you around."

Hey, it was Dusty's idea.

"You're welcome. Perhaps we can have dinner some evening?"

"Sure, that would be fine."

Carter returned with the luggage on a cart. "If you'll follow me, I'll take you upstairs."

Wait for me.

"Cody, where are you going? You don't go upstairs this early."

I do today. I'm staying with Jane.

"It's all right with me if he comes up now. If we're going to be roomies for a week, we should get to know each other."

She's perfect.

"Doesn't he need a lead or anything?"

"Not in the hotel," replied Carter. "He pretty well comes and goes as he pleases. He has his own little routine."

"What about going out to do his business?"

"He eats down by the kitchen. Close to that area there's a door that opens into a fenced-in yard. I put him out after his meals and first thing in the morning. If he has to go out at other times he just sits by the door. There are always waiters and waitresses going by. They open the door and let him out. We've arranged that whoever puts him out brings him in. That way he won't get left outside. It hasn't happened yet, so I guess it works."

I never thought I could be forgotten outside.

"Here we are." Carter opened the door and stepped aside.

"Oh my goodness. This is a real suite. It's beautiful."

What did you expect, a fake suite?

"If you need anything else, you just call the front desk, and if you ever need help in a hurry, just push this panic button. We'll be here before you know it."

"Thank you," Jane said, handing him some money.

"Thanks, but no. You might as well forget about tipping. No one will take money from Dusty's daughter. We're all just glad you're staying with us."

"It seems like you folks think a lot of James."

"We sure do. You enjoy your evening, and I'll see you later."

"Thank you, Carter." Jane turned around with a smile on her face. "Well now, Cody, I guess it's just you and me. James suggested I talk to you as if you were human, so I'll do that."

Why are you calling your father James? If you can't call him Dad, you could at least call him Dusty.

"I have to unpack. Do you want to help?"

Sure. Here's a sweater.

"No! I didn't mean that literally. You can watch me unpack."

Sorry. I'll just lie on the bed and watch.

"I guess you are smart. I'd better watch how I phrase things. Sit up....Go sit on the chair....Get down....Come here...."

You're not going to be bossy, are you?

"Good dog, Cody. You're a little bit scary. Dogs aren't supposed to understand so easily."

Hey, that was easy stuff. You ain't seen nothin' yet.

"I think I'm going to enjoy staying with you, and look at that face. You're so cute."

I know.

****

Knock, knock.

Jane walked over to open the door. "Hi, Carter."

"I'm sorry to bother you, but Cody needs his supper. He usually eats at 6:00."

"What time is it?"

"6:15," replied Carter.

"I'm sorry. I've been preparing for a workshop I'm giving in the morning, and I must have lost track of time."

"What's Cody been doing?"

"Just lying at my feet. He's been great."

"Good. Come on, Cody."

No.

"It's time to eat."

I don't care. Jane has to eat sometime. I'll wait for her.

"You see how he's looking the other way? That means no. I don't know what's gotten into him. He never misses a meal. Food is his life."

"Maybe he's not feeling well," Jane suggested. "Could he be sick?"

Yeah, lovesick.

"His nose feels all right. Has he been acting sick?"

"I don't think so, but I don't know him well enough. Look, I'm going down to the dining room. Maybe he'll come down with me."

My suggestion exactly.

****

"Carter, why is Cody lying outside the dining room?" Krista asked.

"Dusty's daughter, Jane, checked in today, and I think Cody has really taken to her. He wouldn't come down to eat until she did. Then he gobbled his food, ran outside quickly, and has been lying by the dining room door waiting for her."

"Wow. He doesn't usually take to someone that quickly."

I haven't met anyone like Jane. Here she comes!

"Hi, Cody. Are you waiting for me?"

Sure am.

"Hi, I'm Krista. I work the front desk during the evening and some nights. I see you've stolen this little fellow's heart."

No she hasn't. It's right where it belongs, except it's beating faster.

"It looks like it. I'm not sure why. I haven't done anything special."

You didn't have to. I just feel you're special, plus you are Dusty's daughter.

"Are you going back upstairs?"

"Yes, I have work to get ready for tomorrow, and I want to get to bed early."

"Cody usually goes out at 9:00. I'll send Gord up to get him if that's all right."

"I don't mind bringing him down. I'll need a break about that time. Where do I take him?"

"Just go through those doors over there to the end of the corridor. You'll see a door beside his water dish."

I'll show her where to go.

"If you need anything else, just call me at the front desk. Have a good night. You be good, Cody."

204

Aren't I always?

****

"I'm going to shower. You don't want to come with me in there, do you?"

Mmm…for once that's almost tempting, but I'm not *that* crazy over her.

I wonder why I like her so much. It's not because she's beautiful. After all, Bud is my best dog friend and he's no looker. I just feel good things about her. She has a nice warm feeling about her. I like her in a different way than Michael and Andy.

"What are you thinking so hard about?" Jane came out of the bathroom wearing a robe.

You.

"Are you ready for bed?"

Don't you want to talk? Most people tell me about themselves or their problems. Do you want to play grr-toy?

"You want to play?"

That's the idea. Take it, if you can, and throw it.

"*Grr…grr.*"

"Aren't you the vicious little fellow?"

Not really. It's just a game. I don't hold on long.

"Good boy. Go get it."

Okay, five times is enough. Shove over. I'm coming up. Scratch my ears, and tell me why you call your father James.

"Are you ready for bed now?"

I could be, but don't you want to talk?

"I get it. Your head turned away means no. You obviously don't want to play anymore, so what do you want?"

I'll snuggle in, and you talk.

"It's not like we can sit and have a conversation. It would be kind of one-sided."

So what? Come on, give it a try.

"I suppose you want to know how I feel about James?"

You got it.

"Aha! That made you look at me again, so I must be on track. To be honest, though, I'm not really sure how I feel. I was pleased when he called but hesitant at the same time. My mother wanted to see him. She was dying, so I didn't protest. I hope him being there made her final weeks easier. And it made it a bit easier for me, too. She wasn't alone all day while I worked. I couldn't just take time off—I've only been with my company for three and a half months.

"He helped me understand why my parents' marriage fell apart, but that doesn't change how abandoned I felt as a kid. I suppose in some way he had no choice. The thirst for power and money can be as all-consuming as the thirst for a drink is for an alcoholic."

I never thought of that, but he's not like that anymore.

"I hope he's changed, but I'm afraid. I don't want to get close to him and have my heart broken again. He started another computer business, and if it keeps growing this way, we'll lose touch again."

That will never happen.

"I know I'm a big girl and don't need a father anymore, but it would still be painful....I spoke to him on the phone earlier tonight."

When?

"He wants to know when we can get together. I put him off because I'm scared."

Don't be scared, Janey. Here.

"Thanks, Cody. I needed that kiss. Now can we go to bed?"

Sure.

****

Michael got up from his desk and came over to meet us. "Good morning, Jane. Did Cody keep you up talking last night?"

"That's an interesting question. Why do you ask?"

"Well, I'm not sure how he does it, but a lot of Cody's guests come down the next morning and say it was so nice to talk to him. He doesn't actually talk back, does he?"

Jane laughed. "No, but I have to admit I wanted to go to bed earlier than I actually did. And yes, I did stay up a bit later to talk. I sat on the easy chair, and Cody jumped up into my lap. I started patting him, and it just seemed natural to start talking out loud. Maybe that's what it is—

a feeling of relaxation and also knowing no one will be judgmental about what you say. Come to think of it, it was good to talk to him."

"There you go. It wasn't a totally wacky question. And I think you've answered a few of the questions I've had about people talking to him. Thanks. Would you like to have dinner tonight, or do you have other plans?"

"My father wants him and me to get together. Would you mind having dinner with the two of us?"

"No, of course not. I think that would be great. Do you want to eat in the suite or in the dining room? Or would you like to go out to a restaurant?"

Don't even think it. Mike, remember me!

"Cody. Don't pull on my pants. What do you want?"

Eat here.

"All right, let go. I get it. Jane, maybe we could stay in the hotel—at least for the first meeting. I think Cody wants to be there." Michael smiled.

"Don't you think you give him just a little too much credit?"

She'll learn.

"I don't think so. I'll tell you some stories later, then you can judge for yourself."

"All right. Let's eat in the dining room, say 7:00. I've got to get going. Do you think you could arrange it with James?"

"Sure. Have a good day. I'll see you later." Michael watched Jane walk away. He didn't notice me.

"Whoa, Cody. Where do you think you're going?" Mitchell stepped in front of me. "I thought you'd given up trying to get out the front door."

It's okay; I'm with her.

"I guess he's following me. I'm Jane Kronby. I'm sharing Cody's suite this week. He hasn't left my side since I arrived yesterday afternoon."

"Good morning. I'm Mitchell. I take it you're Dusty's daughter?"

"That's right. Does everyone here know my father?"

"A lot of us. We're all really proud of how he pulled himself up and turned his life around. He's an inspiration."

"Thanks." Jane bent down and took my face between her two hands. "Cody, I have to go to a meeting all day, and you cannot come."

Come on, Janey. I'll just lie at your feet.

"I'll see you when I get back. Go on."

Why doesn't anyone just give me a chance?

I'm going to lie right here and wait for you. Bye.

****

"Michael, what's wrong with Cody?" Laura asked. "He's been lying at the front door all day. He didn't even move when Andy came in."

"I think he's waiting for Jane to return. Remember he went up early to the suite yesterday? Well, he wouldn't come down for supper until Jane came down to the dining room. I think he's taken with her."

"Isn't that sweet?"

"I'm not so sure about that. I don't want him so attached that he starts pining when she leaves."

"Good point. What should we do about it?"

"I don't know. At least her conference isn't here, so he can't be with her all day. I'll try to make his days a little bit busier. It's time for our walk anyway. Maybe if we do a few different things, it will help keep his mind off her."

"Good luck! We all know what he's like when he puts his mind to something."

"Please don't remind me," said Michael as he went to get a lead.

I thought you told Laura we were going for a walk. Why are we in the limo? We better not be going to Cathy's or the vet's....Okay, so it's the park. A guy can't be too careful. What's on your mind? You haven't spoken since we left the hotel.

"Thanks, Jeffrey. We'll be about an hour....Cody, sit. Look at me," demanded Michael.

All right, what are you mad at?

"We're going to start working you off lead."

Yippee! Finally. Thank you, Mike. I love you.

"Now listen."

I'm listening, I'm listening.

Chapter Nineteen

"We're going to start on a long, light lead, so if you take off, you're in for a violent jerk when you get to the end. All your commands are identical to what you do on the regular lead. Just stay beside me and you'll be fine. All right, here we go."

"Heel." Michael walked about fifteen steps, then halted.

I know, stop and sit beside you.

"Good job, Cody. Let's work on stay and come. When you come back, sit in front of me. Ready."

"Stay."

Don't go too far.

"Cody, come."

"Good boy. Something new. After you sit in front of me, I'll say, 'Beside.' Then you return to a sitting position beside me. Ready. Stay."

"Come."

"Beside." Michael grabbed me and placed me beside him.

"Good boy. Stay."

"Come."

"Beside." Michael pushed me into the same position.

Hey. I got it the first time. Stop pushing.

"One more time. Stay."

"Come."

"Beside."

"Good boy, Cody. You're so smart. I bet no other dog ever learned it faster."

Yeah, yeah, I could have done it the first time. I'm glad he doesn't know I've seen this on TV. I'll take the credit.

"All right, enough formal training for today. Let's just go for a run."

Sounds good, but you said we were going to be training off lead. I thought that meant without a lead, not some other human double-talk.

****

"Cody, let's go to your yard. I want to train some more."

Why? What didn't you get at the park?

"Out you go. Go pee-pee."

"Cody, come."

"Beside."

"Heel."

"Good boy."

Why are you so happy? We just did all this in the park. Don't you think this is enough?

"Good job. You may be ready to go without the lead tomorrow."

Hey, I didn't have a lead on. I forgot. I can't wait until tomorrow!

****

"Hi, Dusty. How are you doing?" Michael asked

"I'm a little nervous. What do you think of Janey?"

"I have to tell you, Dusty, she's very beautiful. Are you sure she's your daughter?" Michael chuckled.

"No wisecracks tonight. Besides, I was a looker in my day. Then again, she looks a lot like her mother."

"Seriously, Dusty, she seems very nice—which she must be because Cody is smitten with her. He's acting like a lovesick puppy."

So what? I'd be with her now if you had told me she was back from her meetings. Yippee, there she is! Hi, Janey.

"Hi, Cody. Did you have a nice day? I missed you up in the room."

I missed you too. Guess what? I'm going off the lead tomorrow. It's so exciting.

Dusty came over to join us. "Hello, Janey. Did I exaggerate when I told you he was a special dog?"

"No, you sure didn't. Hi, Michael."

"Hi, Jane. How was your seminar today?"

"It went very well. I had two job offers. I can't believe the money I was being offered."

"Are you interested in any of them?" Dusty asked.

"I don't know. I haven't thought about it. I haven't even been at my present job for half a year, and they were so good about giving me time off when Mom was sick. I'd hate to walk out on them."

"Why don't you just go to them, tell them about the offers, and ask for them to match your best offer?" suggested Dusty.

"These new jobs have greater responsibility and more challenging work. I don't think it would be fair."

"So ask for a more challenging job."

"Doesn't that seem a little presumptuous for a new employee?"

"Jane, if there's one thing I've learned in life, it's that you have to enjoy your job to fully enjoy the rest of your life," Michael interjected.

"I suppose you're right, but I owe my company so much."

"Janey, do you think your company was good to you because they are compassionate and caring?" asked Dusty. "No. They knew you were valuable, and they didn't want to lose you."

"Maybe, but I'm not going to think about it until I get through this week. Let's go in and eat. I'm starving."

A girl after my own heart.

Michael pulled a chair out for Jane. "We have to sit at this first table so Cody can hear our conversation."

"What if we sat on the far side?"

"He'd bark and carry on. He'd probably even try to sneak in; we've gone through this once."

"I'll take your word for it. Where is your dog, James?"

"I left him home. He's quite content to curl up on a soft sofa and sleep."

Sounds like Bud.

"Janey, I understand you can't call me Dad, but I'd like you to call me Dusty. James is a person I'd like to forget. I hope I've left him behind and become a better person. The new me is nothing like the old James."

Jane dropped her head. "I'll try, Dusty."

Yes! The first step.

Jane raised her head and looked at Michael. "Are you allowed to tell me anything about how Cody ended up living in the hotel? Or at least why the hotel would agree to let a dog stay here? James—Dusty—didn't seem to know too much."

"I can tell you a little. His mistress and he lived in the suite until she died suddenly. In her will, she asked that Cody be allowed to stay here. I get a certain amount for being his primary caregiver. When anyone retires, they get a certain amount for each year they work while Cody is here. When he dies, the hotel gets a very large sum—plus of course he pays for his suite every day."

"Wow! That's cool. She sounds like she had everyone pegged. I bet everyone who's employed here works hard so they don't lose their jobs."

"I must admit, the hotel has worked very efficiently the last seven months."

"Do you think Cody is happy?"

"I think so. He has lots of people fawning over him. I take him home occasionally, and last summer the two of us went camping."

"You like him a lot, don't you?"

"Yeah, I do."

I like you too, Mike, and I am happy here. At least I'm never bored.

Jane turned to her father. "Tell me about your business, Dusty."

"I'm about as busy as I want to be. Mostly training people on new software, sometimes on new computers. I've been in computers so long, it's hard for me to believe some people are just buying them for the first time."

"You've been out of computers for a long time too. How do you know how to use the new programs?"

"I just play with it for about an hour. Glance at the manual, and I've got it."

"Jane, how did you get into computers?" Michael inquired.

"It's a long story, but the short version is that I inherited Dusty's computer genes. I just always found them easy. I almost feel guilty taking money for working on them because it's usually more like playing. I get such a kick out of solving a problem."

"I envy you both. I'm computer illiterate. I haven't really had a need for one, and I can't see spending that kind of money to play games."

Jane shook her head and smiled. "But Michael, you have a perfect job for a computer. You could have all the attractions of the city on the computer. You could print out maps with routes from here to any place anyone wanted to go. You could keep all your clients in the computer so when they check in, you punch up their name and all the things you've found out about them are highlighted. You know, like, 'Good afternoon, Mr. Smith. How is your daughter doing at USC?' You could also keep their requests on file, so you don't forget. Geez, I could talk for another ten minutes on ways a concierge could use a computer."

"Wow, I didn't realize. See—I am computer illiterate. I was considering maybe getting one for home so I could go on the Internet and have e-mail."

"That's a start," said Dusty. "Once you get it, I'll show you a few more things you could use it for."

"All right. I'll think about it. At least I know two computer geniuses who could help me. Right?"

"Absolutely," said Jane. "Wherever I am, we could still e-mail."

"Well then, maybe I will get one. So, Jane, tell us about growing up a computer nerd. Did the kids at school give you a hard time?"

No way, who'd give her a hard time?

"Not too much. I didn't flaunt my abilities, and I don't think I look like the stereotypical computer nerd."

"No, you certainly don't."

Easy, Mike. I've seen that look before. Your house isn't that big.

Jane's face turned red as she turned to her father. "Dusty, what are you going to do with your business? Are you going to branch into other lines of computer technology or stay with the same kind of work?"

"Actually, I've been working on something new. I'm not quite ready to discuss it though."

"Are you afraid I might steal it?" Jane sat back and crossed her arms.

"No, of course not. I'm hoping to have everything ready by the end of the week before you go. If it's okay, I'd rather wait until then to show you the finished product."

Jane relaxed a little. "Oh sure. I didn't mean to imply anything. You know, I wouldn't mind starting some kind of computer business of my own. I think it would be neat to do whatever you wanted, whenever you wanted."

"I wish it were that simple. Most of the time you're doing things you don't want to do. What you need is a company with a very good managing director. That would free you up to do what you want. You could use your trust fund to start your own company—that would give you money for a good business partner."

Janey stumbled over her words a bit before answering. "Actually the money is all gone. We used some for the down payment on the house, and then Mom's hospital stay used up the rest. I can't believe how expensive it all was."

"Do you still owe the hospital, Janey?"

"A little."

"How much is a little?"

"Not too much. After all, I have no other debts, and I'm making plenty."

"How much, Janey?" demanded Dusty.

"I'm not sure that's any of your business. After all, you did leave us enough money to live comfortably all those years, and your money enabled me to buy my first house. So I'll handle this."

"Janey, I know this is difficult, but I still feel an obligation to your mother and you. I feel bad enough that I wasn't around all that time. I don't want you to be in debt for years on top of everything else. Now please, tell me how much you still owe the hospital."

Jane leaned forward and glared at her father. "I told you it's none of your business."

"Please, Janey."

"Butt out. I can handle it."

"Please. I'd like to help, if I can. I don't want you to be paying a hospital bill for years. Now, how much do you owe?"

"$150,000. There, are you satisfied?"

Michael whistled so softly, I'm not sure anyone could hear it but me.

"Janey, I'm so sorry. I have a few thousand saved up. You can have that, and I'll give you some every month to help."

"I can handle it. I've worked out monthly payments with the hospital. It will just take a while that's all."

"Janey, why should you be burdened for years to come? Let me help, and you can go on with your life."

"Will you give it a rest if I promise to think about it?" Jane stood up and dropped her napkin on the table. "If you two will excuse me, I have work to do for tomorrow. Thank you for the lovely dinner, Michael. Good night, Dusty. I'll put Cody out on my way."

"Good night, Jane."

"Good night, Janey."

Chapter Twenty

"Cody, I don't know why I get so upset with Dusty. After all, lots of marriages end in divorce, and most husbands aren't as generous as he was. But I never heard from him for all those years. Every birthday and Christmas I'd watch the mail so closely in case he sent anything. After a few years I just gave up. I resent all those years of heartbreak."

I can't blame you, Janey. But that person no longer exists. Dusty is a different person. Give him a chance to prove it.

Ring, ring.

"Hello?...I guess we could. I'll come back here to shower, and then we'll come over around 6:30."

We? Does that mean me, too?

"Don't you think a limo is a little much?"

Must be.

"Okay. We'll see you then." Jane hung up the phone. "That was Dusty. He wants you and me to have dinner with him and Bud. He already checked with Michael."

Yippee! I've never been to Dusty's.

****

Jeffrey opened the limo door to let us in. "Good afternoon, Michael, Cody. Where are we off to today?"

"Take us to the ball field on Oak Street."

I thought your ballgames were all over.

Hey, there's nobody here. Are we going to play catch?

"Jeffrey, you can just wait if that's okay. We'll only be about twenty minutes, then I want to go down to the park."

"Cody, heel."

Aaah. He's testing me. Look, ma, no lead.

"Stay."

Wow, he's far enough away. What's he doing? Hey—he's eating. Save some for me. Here I come.

"Bad dog. You were told to stay."

Bad Mike. You tricked me.

"Get back here. Sit. Stay."

Go where you want. Do what you want. You won't trick me again.

"Cody, come."

Here, I come on the run. Sit, look up.

"Good dog. Beside. Heel."

Aren't I great?

"Good boy. I bet everyone would like to have a dog who learns as quickly as you."

I bet they would.

"Okay, let's go to the park and try this where there are more distractions."

****

When we returned to the hotel, Andy came running to meet us.

"Cody, where have you been? I've been waiting forever."

Hi, Andy. I've been in the park off the lead.

"Sorry, Andy," Michael said. "We've been down at the park doing some training. You look awfully bubbly."

"I am. My social worker thinks she has a couple that might want me because they're looking for an older child. I'm so happy. I wanted to tell Cody because I won't be able to come over for a few days but I'll come back to see you before I go live with them because even though I'll be happy to get a new home, it's going to be sad to leave Cody. I'd stay here, but I really want a mother and father."

"Don't feel bad, Andy. This will be wonderful. You can write Cody, and I'll write you back for him. We'll keep in touch."

"Promise?"

"I promise."

"Maybe I could get a dog of my own."

"Maybe you could."

Here we go, another dog named Cody.

"I'd never call it Cody, you know, because there could never be another Cody. I might call him Tugboat to remind of my first real birthday with Cody and you."

"That would be cool, Andy."

"I have to go, I'm late."

"Bye, Andy, good luck."

"I don't need good luck. You said anybody would want me. I'm a shoe-in. Bye."

"I hope that boy isn't in for more heartbreak."

Why? You did say that. Didn't you mean it?

****

This is so exciting; Janey and I are going out together in the limo. I wonder what's for dinner. I hope Dusty made Bud and me some real food.

"Hi Janey. Welcome to my humble abode. Hi, Cody."

Hi, Dusty. I'm really glad to be here.

"Hi, Bud. Have you met Dusty's daughter, Jane, yet?"

"Nope."

"You're in for a treat."

"Janey, this is Bud. He's not much to look at, but he's been a great companion when I really needed one."

"Hello, Bud." Janey bent down to pat his head.

"I like her, Code."

"I told you."

"Tell me about how you two met."

"It's an interesting story. I'll tell you exactly what happened, and you can draw your own conclusions. Let me put the dogs out first; Bud hasn't been out for a while."

No way! Not me. I'm not going to miss a thing.

"Why didn't you go before we came, Bud?"

"Sleepin'."
Surprise.
"Cody, you go out too."
No thanks.
"You're not going to miss anything. You of all people know how I found Bud. Now go on out. I bet you have to go too."
All right, but don't forget about us. I don't want to miss anything else.

****

Hey. This is long enough, open the door.
"Code, what's the rush?"
"I need to get in there."
"Why?"
"Dusty and Janey are still not very close. I don't want to miss anything that I might be able to help them with. Don't you want to go in?"
"Yeah. I guess I'm gettin' sleepy."
"Bud, why don't you wake up and smell the coffee?"
"What does that mean?"
"I don't know. I just thought it might fit. How do you get Dusty to open the door?"
"Easy. Scratch the door and bark. Sometimes he gets on his computer and forgets. I always hafta remind him."
"Well, do it."
Scratch, scratch. *"Bark. Bark."*
"Sorry, guys," Dusty said, opening the door. "I got carried away with my story. Don't worry, Cody, I just finished."
You better have.
"So you guys honestly believe Cody knew what he was doing?" Jane asked.
"I know it's hard to believe, but I truly think so. Are you ready to eat? I'm not much of a cook, but I've learned a little over the past several months. I made beef stew with dumplings. I hope that's all right."
"That will be fine."

Sounds good to me. I wonder what stew is? The beef part sounds perfect.

"What about the dogs?" Jane asked.

Yeah, what about us?

"I'll treat them to a little beef and gravy over their regular dry food."

Yahoo!

"Here, guys. No fighting."

Why would we fight? We each have our own bowls.

"Shove over, Code. I'm done with mine."

"What? I barely started!"

"You snooze, you lose."

"What does that mean?"

"I don't know. I just thought it might fit."

"Good one. Now get out of my bowl."

"Sorry."

"Hey, you ate it all."

"If you don't eat fast, someone else will take it. I learned that on the streets."

"But, Bud, you don't have to eat like that anymore. Does Dusty forget to feed you?"

"No, but it's a hard habit to break. Besides, it got me extra food tonight."

"Sure, but it was my food. I thought we were friends."

"Yup. So you shouldn't mind sharin'."

"Yeah but...you're right, Bud, I don't. Be quiet, I want to hear what these two are talking about."

"So you have what, five job offers? Are you considering any of them?"

"At first I didn't, but a couple of today's offers sound good. They're both here on the East Coast, but I don't know if I want to make that long move again."

"Would it bother you to sell your house?"

"No. Mom and I bought it together. I've been finding it hard to go home and not have her there. I was thinking of handing it over to a rental company to rent out as an investment."

"Good idea."

"Both companies offered to pay my moving expenses, so I wouldn't even need money for that."

"They must be offering you a whack of money to get you to consider such a move."

"An extravagant amount, but it's also the job challenge."

"Would you like to take a coffee into the other room?"

"Sure. The stew was great, by the way."

"Thank you."

Yeah it was. The little bit I had. Hey, Dusty, what's your wallet doing on the floor? He'll get it later. No, I'd better take it into the other room.

Janey, put this on the table.

"What's that, Cody?"

Dusty's wallet.

"Here we go." Dusty came into the room with the coffee. "How did my wallet get here?"

"Cody just brought it in."

"I must have knocked it off the counter. Thanks, Cody."

No problem for a dog who can walk off the lead.

"Do you want it?" Jane asked, leaning over to pick it up.

"No, it's okay. I'll get it later. What do you want in your coffee?"

"Just milk, please."

"Hi, Bud. I thought you were sleeping?"

"Woke up to smell the coffee. Ha ha."

"Funny."

"Nah, I'm just gettin' more comfy."

"How can you sleep through this?"

"Code, you should know by now that all dogs aren't like you."

"I could explain things to you."

"No thanks. Night."

"Good night, Bud."

"How many computers do you have here, Dusty?"

"I don't know. Eight, I think. I've only bought one. Some are from people who were throwing them out, others I took in lieu of payment. I had about twelve, but I've stripped them down and rebuilt them. I have some of them networked. I've learned a lot just playing around with them."

"That's one thing I haven't done a lot of—actually stripping a computer down. I've put in new memory chips, you know, easy stuff like that, but I've never stripped one down completely."

"Do you have any interest in doing that?"

"I don't think so; there's way more money in coding. Are you going to hire more people to help you in your company? After all, you're limited by the number of hours you can work in a day."

"I don't think I want to get into handling employees again. I wasn't very good with people. That was one of my biggest problems."

"What about the new Dusty?"

"You got me there. I think I would be a lot better the second time around, but I don't want to get that busy again. I don't want the money and power I had before. I just need enough money to pay the rent and help you out if you'll let me. But I still enjoy working on the computer and developing new software."

"Are you ready to tell me about what you've been working on?"

"Almost. Janey, do you think we could meet Friday evening? I should have everything by then."

"I'm supposed to fly out late Friday afternoon."

"Oh." Dusty sighed and sank back into his chair.

Come on, Janey. Stay an extra night. What harm can it do? Aren't you curious?

"I guess I could change my flight to Saturday and ask Michael if I can extend my hotel stay. Where do you want to meet?"

"I'll come over to your suite about 7:00. You have a laptop, right? I'll bring one of these old things over too."

Jane looked down into her coffee cup and took a deep breath. "Dusty? All those years you were gone, did you ever think about me?"

Uh oh!

"Nearly every day, Janey."

"Then why didn't you ever call or write?"

"Like I said—at first, I didn't want you to see me as a drunken egoist, and then when I hit the streets, I was too ashamed. I know that was no excuse, but that was how I felt. Please believe me when I tell you, you were never out of my thoughts."

"I wish I could."

Oh great. How do you prove a thought? Wait...

"Cody! Where are you going with my wallet? Give."

No way. I'm on a mission.

"Cody, come," demanded Jane.

Sorry, Janey. This is for you. I'd better get under the sofa before they grab me.

I've got to get this wallet open.

Rats, here comes a hand.

"Give!"

I'm off. Catch me if you can.

Phew! Back under the sofa. Come on, wallet, open.

Yes! Where is it? Come on. Come on. Yes again! Watch out, Dusty, 'cause here I come.

"Cody, I can't believe you remembered that." Dusty took the picture and handed it to Jane.

Jane's mouth dropped open as she took the picture. "That's my fifth-grade picture."

"That's the last picture I ever had of you. I looked at it nearly every day."

Jane's eyes filled with tears. "You did remember me."

"Of course I did. I'd stare at your picture and wonder what you were doing and how you had turned out. I felt so bad for the mess I'd made."

"Why didn't you start looking for us earlier?"

"I was afraid. I didn't think you would forgive me. I'm so sorry, Janey. I made such a mess of everything." Dusty wiped a tear from his eye.

"It's okay, Dad."

Wow! I think I'm going to cry, just like them.

"Can I have a hug?" Jane asked.

"It would be my greatest pleasure." Dusty stood to hold his daughter.

Mission accomplished. I am the Codyman!

"How did Cody know about the picture?" asked Jane when she returned to her chair.

"The first night I spent in his suite it fell out of my wallet. I don't know why, but I told him about you and all about my life. I had never talked like that before. It made me realize all the terrible decisions I'd made in the past. That was the beginning of my thoughts that maybe it would be good to look for you and your mother. I'm so glad I did, or I wouldn't have had those final weeks with Sara. They mean a lot to me."

"They meant a lot to her, too."

"I think if I hadn't been there, you would have resented me more, and I would have even more regrets."

"I'm sorry, Dad, but I have to get going. I still have work to do. Thanks. I'll see you Friday at seven." Jane gave her father a quick hug. "Come on, Cody, we're late. You know, Dad, I think Cody went and found Bud for you because you were both alone. After what he did tonight, I'll believe anything about him."

"Good night, Janey. I love you. Bye, Cody, and thanks."

No problem. I love her too. Bye.

"Good night, Dad."

Chapter Twenty-One

Jane and I snuggled into one of the overstuffed chairs.

"Cody, thank you so much—thank you, thank you, thank you—for bringing my dad and me closer together. I don't know what will come of it, but I feel so much better."

No problem.

"It's been wonderful staying with you and a comfort talking to you. No wonder Michael says all your guests leave singing your praises."

I don't think I know that song, but I love the title. Could be a hit.

"Are you feeling all right? Your nose is warm."

Now that you mention it, I don't feel good. I think my supper made me sick. Sleeping usually helps, but I don't want to miss Dusty's visit. You guys might still need me.

Knock, knock.

"That must be Dad. You stay here, and I'll let him in."

Okay.

"Hi, Dad. Hold on, I'll hold the door so you can get the cart in. Good idea to bring the computer up on it."

"I'm getting too old to be lugging an old computer around."

Jane had to laugh. "Yeah, right. You're nearly ready for the nursing home."

"Where's Cody?"

In here.

"He's in the living room. I don't think he's feeling well. His nose is warm, and his ears are hot."

Dusty came over and put his hand on my nose.

"Hi, little guy. Are you all right?"

No. I'm sick.

"Dad, do you think we should call downstairs and let them know?"

No way, I'm not leaving.

"Nah. He'll be all right. Most dogs will just sleep it off. We'll keep an eye on him, and if he gets worse, we'll let them know."

Thanks, Dusty.

"Okay. It's your turn, Dad. What have you been working on?"

Dusty hesitated. "Please have a seat. I have a gift for you. Read this while I set up the computer."

Have you got one for me too?

"What is it?" Jane asked as she started to open an envelope.

"It's your future."

"I don't understand."

What does this all mean?

"Please, Janey, just read the information while I get ready. Then I'll show you."

Jane settled back in her chair and began to read while Dusty started putting the computer together.

"My God, Dad, do you realize what you have here?"

"I think so."

"This could be worth a fortune."

"I know. Here look at this." Dusty handed her another envelope.

"Why does this have my name on it?"

"I applied for the patent in your name."

"No way, you can't do that. I can't take credit for your work."

"It doesn't say you did it. It says you own the patent, or at least will own it when it is finalized."

"I can't accept this."

"We'll discuss that part later."

Dusty turned on his computer. "Come here, and I'll show it to you in action."

Computers? Is this all they're going to talk about? Mike and I hate computers. I'm going to bed. I'm not feeling well.

****

I wonder how long I've slept. I hope I haven't missed anything important.

"I don't think I can make a decision tonight, Dad."

Nope.

"Take your time. There's no need to decide tonight; you only heard about it two hours ago. What time do you leave tomorrow?"

"Eleven. I can't believe you've developed this concept when you've only been back into computers for such a short period of time."

"I guess I have a knack for it."

"Or you're more of a genius than you appear to be."

"Yeah, right. I'm so smart I lost my family."

"Dad, let's not talk about that any more."

"Whatever you say, sweetheart." Dusty sighed. "So, what are you going to do?"

"If I wanted to create my own business, how would I go about it? The job seems overwhelming! I don't even have money to get started."

"Janey, I don't think you have to worry. I have an old buddy, Bob MacKay, who's a venture capitalist. I've already passed this by him, and he thinks money will be no problem. I wouldn't be surprised if he didn't want to be your first client."

"I don't want a big profit. I can't stand companies who rip off consumers, especially when they have a monopoly."

"Honey, listen! If you only made $1.00 per unit, you'd be a multimillionaire. Your problem isn't making money, it's getting everything up and running and distributed before anyone else copies the idea."

Jane sat down and buried her face in her hands. "I don't think I can do this."

"Then don't. Sell your patent to someone else and start your own company doing something else."

"But they would just rip everybody off."

"Honey, that's what business is all about. Most companies have shareholders they have to make money for."

"Do you think it's possible to do everything fairly quickly?"

"I have a few ideas. You have to decide what you want to do first."

"I think it could be exciting. But, Dad, I can't do it alone. Will you help me?"

Dusty put his hand on her shoulder. "Of course, honey. Where do you want to work from? I'll move to California if you want me to."

"I think maybe we should work right here. It's close to the manufacturer and a large workforce. Plus, it might be good to be in the Eastern time zone. I'll go back tomorrow. I have to talk to my boss and put my house up for sale. I'll get back as soon as possible. I'll aim for next Thursday. Can you can make an appointment to meet with Bob on Friday?"

"Sure. We could be a while yet, Janey. Why don't I take Cody out while you order coffee and something from room service? Come here, Cody. How are you feeling? You've been sleeping for hours."

A little better, but not much.

"Do you know where to take him?"

"Not exactly, but I'm sure Cody will show me."

****

I can't believe it's morning. I must have been really out of it. I didn't hear Dusty leave, or Janey come to bed. Look at her. Isn't she beautiful? I hate to wake her, but I have to go out. How can I do this gently? I know—I'll kiss her on the cheek. I hope it takes a few times.

"Mmm." Jane stretched. "Good morning, Cody. What time is it?"

Hey, you're the human. What are you asking me for?

"Half past eight? I'm sorry. You must have to go out. I'll call down to the desk and get someone to come and get you. I need a shower. How are you feeling?"

Better.

Jane reached up and felt my nose. "Good. It's cool and moist again."

Check my ears.

"Good morning, this is Jane Kronby with Cody. I was wondering if someone could come up to take him out. I just woke up, and I don't think he can wait."

"No, not today. I'll be down in an hour."

What was that all about? "No, not today?" Regardless, I think whoever is coming had better hurry. I hope the elevators aren't busy.

Knock, knock.

It's about time.

"Good morning, I've come for…"

No time, let's go.

"I guess he's in a hurry. Hey, Cody, wait for me."

Get a move on. Hold that elevator!

****

Hey, this is Janey's luggage. Rats, I forgot she was leaving this morning.

I should have gone back up to the suite to help her pack and spend some time with her. All week I've been going back up to the suite while she got ready for her meetings, and now on her last day I'm stuck down here. I wonder why they—that's it. That's what the phone call was about. "Not today." She didn't want me to help her pack, just like she didn't want my help when she was unpacking. I'll show her. I'm not going to say goodbye.

What's Dusty doing back this morning? I'd better get under the chair and at least listen to what's going on.

"Good morning, Dad." Jane greeted her father with a hug. "Did you have trouble getting up?"

"No, I was anxious to see you. Having you back in my life is still so new."

Ho hum.

"How about you? It was three when I left. Did you wake up all right?"

"Yes, I woke up to Cody kissing me on the cheek. It was sweet."

Oh sure. It was so sweet you didn't want me to come help you pack or say goodbye.

"Where is he now?"

"I don't know. Someone came to take him out, and I haven't seen him since."

You could have.

"I don't want to leave without saying goodbye to him. He's so sweet, and he's done so much for us. We owe him a lot."

Now *you* can feel the pain.

"We can't wait much longer, honey, the limo's outside. You don't want to be late for your plane. I'll take your luggage out while you look for him."

"Okay. I'll check at the desk."

You might not want to find me. You could feel worse if I ignore you.

"Excuse me. Have you seen Cody anywhere? I have to leave, and I wanted to say goodbye."

"He was around a little while go," Shannon replied. "He has to be here in the lobby or down by the kitchen. I'll check it out for you."

You won't find me. I'm too well-hidden.

"I'm sorry, Miss Kronby," Shannon said, returning to the front desk, "he's not down there. We can look around some more. Maybe he's in the lounge. He lies in there occasionally, but not usually this early in the day. Why don't we just call him? He usually comes when he's called."

"All right, but I don't have much longer. I have a plane to catch."

"Cody."

I can't hear you.

"Cody!"

La...La...La...

"I'm sorry, I can't wait any longer. I know this is going to sound strange, but could you please give him a message? Tell him goodbye, and I hope to see him in a week or so. Tell him he is the sweetest thing I know and that I owe him my future. Tell him...tell him I love him. Thank you." Jane sighed and her eyes glistened as she turned away and headed for the front door.

Goodbye, Jane. Darn, I can't do this. Wait!

"*Bark, bark.*"

"Cody!" Jane bent down to pick me up. "I was so afraid I wouldn't see you before I left. Thank you for sharing your suite, and thank you for being my friend. I love you so much. I have to go now, but I should be back next week. Maybe I could stay with you until I find my own place."

I'd like that.

Wow! She kissed me right on the mouth.

"Bye, honey-bunny."

Bye, Janey. You'll always be my favorite guest

"Sorry, Cody. You can't come any further. You sit by the window, and I'll wave goodbye to you."

I think I feel exactly how people do when they cry. I wish I could cry. Bye, Janey. Can you see me standing up at the window?

Sigh.

I think I'll just stay here for a while. I'm too sad to move. I'm not choosing a guest tonight. I just can't go up to the suite with anyone else. At least not tonight.

****

Shannon came over and woke me up. "Cody, are you all right?"

No, I'm not. Janey's gone.

"You've been lying by this window all day. I don't think you've been out."

Just this morning.

"Come on, I'll put you out."

No thanks.

"Cody, it's almost 2:00. You must have to go out."

Will you leave me alone! If I have to go out, I'll go to the door. Have you ever seen me mess in the hotel? I don't think so. Get lost. I want to lie here and think about Janey. I miss her already. We didn't even spend our last hours together. I didn't even have a good evening with her. I should have sat beside her while she talked to Dusty. But, oh no, I had to pull a Bud and go to bed. Look at all those wasted hours.

Sigh.

****

"Cody it's 5:00. Aren't you going to choose a guest for tonight?" Shannon asked.

No.

"You must have to go out by now."

Sigh.

Hey, get that lead off me.

"There is no sense fighting me. You've been lying in the sun all day. You need a drink, and you're going out."

You need a drink, and *you're* going out!

"Heel."

All right, all right.

"Drink some water."

I don't think so.

"You stubborn little thing."

Getting a little nasty, aren't you?

"Look, Cody. I'm just trying to take care of you. I don't want you getting sick. If anything happened to you, I'd lose my job."

So now the truth comes out. It's not me you're worried about. It's your job.

"Come on, Cody. I need this weekend job. My husband ran off and left me with two little kids. We live with my mother, and I'm the only one with a job. I don't want my kids raised on welfare. Besides, your trust fund will pay for their college education. This is the only chance my little babies will have."

Don't start crying on me. Look! I'll drink. I must admit I am thirsty. You're right; I was just being stubborn. Put me out, and go back to work.

"Good boy. Out you go. I'll be back to get you in a while."

Yeah, yeah.

Hi, Andy. What are you doing out here so late? What's wrong? Why are you crying?

"Cody, where have you been? I've been waiting for you forever. I couldn't come in. I didn't want anyone to see me crying."

Calm down and tell me what's wrong.

"They…they didn't…want me."

What? Who wouldn't want you? I agree with Michael; you're a great kid.

"I went to meet them yesterday. I was all dressed up and smelled good. I liked them and I was very polite and on my best behavior and I thought I did good. I just knew they wanted me. I could tell."

Andy, please don't sob like that. There has to be a mistake.

"I went home yesterday so stoked. I even started packing. Then this morning my social worker called to say they changed their minds.

Nobody will ever want me. I bet they think I hurt my mother and they're scared of me."

Andy, no. Stop it. You have to talk to someone. I wish Michael was working. Please, Andy, don't cry.

"Cody, I think you're the only person who will ever love me. You know how bad I am, and you're still my friend."

You're not bad. Look out, someone is coming!

"*Bark!*"

"Hi, Mark."

"Hi, Andy. I heard what happened. I'm sorry. It will get a little easier each time."

"There won't be another time. I'm never doing that again."

"Yes, you will."

"Oh no I won't. I'm just going to stay with you and Mrs. MacNeil and stay friends with Cody."

"Is this Cody?"

"Yeah. Cody, this is Mark."

"Hi, Cody. Thanks for my CD player."

You're welcome, but if I ever hear about you shoving Andy again, you'll answer to me. I'm little, but I've got big teeth.

"It feels weird thanking a dog for a present. He's kind of cute, isn't he?"

"He's more than cute. He's smart, friendly, and he listens to me."

"We have to go, Andy. Mrs. MacNeil sent me to look for you. She's worried. She was ready to call the police."

"I'm coming. Bye, Cody. Thanks for listening."

Bye, Andy. Why wouldn't those people want Andy? They couldn't make their own child that good. There has to be a mistake.

I feel so bad for him. I don't know what I can do to help him. I've helped so many people but he's the hardest yet.

Shannon opened the door. "Cody, it's 6:00. Are you going to eat?"

Sure, why not? I may be sad that Janey left, but my problems are nothing compared to Andy's. Come to think of it, I have no problems. I've had guests coming and going for months, lots of them I really liked, and I survived when they left. Besides, she'll be back next week, and she's moving here permanently, so this is even better than usual.

Chapter Twenty-Two

Bruce and Kim Grant entered my suite and looked around. "Cody, this is beautiful!" Kim exclaimed. "Thank you for sharing it with us."

Yeah, no problem. I needed some guests to take my mind off Andy and Janey.

"Maybe things might finally be turning around for us," Bruce commented. "We've spent enough money in this city. It's nice to finally get something free."

Not only is the room free, but you get a bonus prize—me.

"Bruce, we can't regret spending that money. We both agreed we had to try."

"Don't get me wrong; I think I wanted to try more than you did sometimes. It's just that after three failed in vitro fertilizations, it's hard not to think about all that money wasted."

What are you guys talking about?

"But, honey, if one of them had taken, then the price would have been cheap."

Hellooo. I'm still lost.

"I know. I guess I'm still disappointed that I'll never have my own child." Bruce sank into the sofa and put his head back.

"You're not having second thoughts about tomorrow, are you? I thought we had thoroughly discussed this, and you agreed we should adopt a baby. If you're not one hundred percent sure, we shouldn't go ahead. It wouldn't be fair to the child or to our marriage."

"No, I just always imagined having my own child."

Oh my gosh, I don't believe it! They're here to adopt a kid. Things don't happen like this. I have to make the most of it.

"Once we hold that new baby, it will be just like our own. Trust me."

"But waiting six months, or even a year….It seems like an eternity."

Hey, I can get you a terrific boy tomorrow.

"Maybe if we make a good impression tomorrow, we could be moved up on the list."

"Do you think that's possible?"

"Why not? We would make terrific parents. You're a school principal used to dealing with kids, and I'm a pediatric nurse. Who would know more about children? We have lots of hobbies and interests to stimulate a child's development. What could be better?"

"I suppose you're right. I'm just nervous." Bruce sighed.

"Don't worry about it. Just be yourself and everything will be fine."

"All right. We'd better get to bed early, so we'll be at our best."

"Good idea," Kim agreed. "I wish we didn't have to wait until Tuesday for a decision."

"I know. The wait is going to be agony. What time will we be finished tomorrow?" Bruce asked.

"I think we should be back here around 3:30."

Yes! Andy should be here. I hope. Please, Andy, be here tomorrow.

****

Andy! Andy! Come sit on the sofa.

"Hi, Cody."

I know you're still sad, but I might have found some parents for you.

"Andy, are you all right?" Michael asked.

"I'm okay."

"Did you have your interview Saturday?"

"Yeah."

"Did something happen?"

"No." Andy's jaw started to quiver. He bit on his lower lip and lowered his head.

"Andy, I'm so sorry." Michael sat down and put his arm around him.

Andy pulled away from Michael's arm. "It doesn't matter if they didn't want me. I don't want to be adopted. I'm happy where I am. And besides, I don't want to leave Cody."

"But, Andy, I don't understand what happened."

"They didn't want me, all right?" Andy snapped back. "I wasn't good enough. That shows you how much you know. Leave me alone. I want to talk to Cody. He's the only friend I have."

Michael got up with a hurt look on his face. "I'm sorry, Andy. I'll be right back. Please don't leave."

Mike, don't leave. You can't give up. You have to help Andy.

"Cody, I got in trouble in school today."

What happened?

"Sometimes I help other kids with their work. Today Jonathan asked me to help him with his math. I told him to get lost, and I shoved him down, and he banged his head on the desk and started crying. I got sent to the principal's office. It was the first time I'd ever been there. It was scary. He made me sit on this big chair in front of his desk and—"

"Andy, listen to me." Michael sat down on the sofa. "I was just talking to your social worker. You didn't get the full story about your interview. There was a terrible mistake made. That couple you met really wanted a girl. They already have two boys, and they only want one more child. They had their hearts set on a girl, but somehow there was a mix-up, and they brought you in. They loved you. They even agreed to take you, but when they got home that night, they talked about it some more. They only have a three-bedroom house. The two boys are in one room, and they had gotten the other room ready for a girl. They felt so bad for you, but they called the next morning and said they would only take a girl. The social worker apologized for the mix-up. I told her it was a very cruel thing to do to a little boy, and she agrees. So you see, Andy, it wasn't you they didn't want. It was just that you were a boy."

"Really? You mean they wanted a girl, and they almost took me anyway?"

"That's right. They thought you were the best child they've ever met. They felt bad about not being able to take you, and they hope you find a home real soon."

"Thanks, Michael. I guess I feel better. I'm sorry I yelled at you."

"It's okay, Andy. I don't blame you. I have to get back to work. See you later."

"Cody, did you hear that? They did want me! They just couldn't take me. Where are you going?"

Wait here.

"Wait for me." Andy scrambled up from the sofa.

Kim, wait.

"Hi, Cody. Were you waiting for us?"

I sure was. I want you to meet my friend Andy.

Bruce came over to join us. "Come on, Kim. Let's get up to the room."

No. Wait!

"Cody, let go of my dress," Kim demanded. "Where do you want me to go?"

Stay here. Andy, come here.

"Hey, Cody. Stop pushing." Andy laughed.

"It seems like he wants us to meet," Kim said.

Good. A smart one.

"Hi, we're Mr. and Mrs. Grant."

"Hello, my name is Andy. I'm Cody's friend."

"I guess that's it," said Bruce. "We're staying in Cody's suite with him. I guess he wanted us to meet his friend."

"Are you a guest at the hotel, Andy?"

"No. I live down over the hill. Cody and I have been friends for a long time. I visit him on my way home from school."

"How old are you, Andy?" Bruce asked.

"I was six in August."

"Ah, first grade, right?"

"I'm supposed to be, but I got moved into second grade after the first day of school."

"You must be very smart."

"I guess. I just find the work easy, and I'm a very good reader."

"Your parents must be very proud of you."

"Yes, they are. I have to go now. Goodbye." Andy turned and headed for the front door.

Andy, you lied! How can I help you if you lie?

"Bruce, isn't he cute?"

"Yes, and smart too. I hope our child turns out that well-mannered."

He already has. You can have him; just go get him.

****

Uh oh, the Grants are back early, and they look upset. I'd better follow them upstairs and find out what's going on.

"Cody, how did you get up here?" Bruce asked.

"He must have followed us up from the lobby. You'd better let him in. I'll call downstairs to let them know he's here."

"Hello, Michael? This is Kim Grant. I just wanted to let you know Cody followed us upstairs....No, he's fine....Sure, I'll get Bruce to take him down....Okay, bye."

"Should I take him down now?"

I'm not going.

"No, at about three. He usually goes out then, and his friend Andy will be there. I wonder why that little boy comes to visit Cody everyday and isn't playing with other kids."

Go ask Michael. He'll tell you everything.

"Maybe he doesn't have any friends. It's hard, sometimes, for a child to be moved ahead. He starts to lose his peers. Maybe I'll ask him when I take Cody down."

Good idea. This is going to work out fine.

"Bruce, I can't believe that agency thinks we're too old to adopt a baby. I'm only thirty-eight, and you're only forty."

"I know it's ridiculous, but they didn't say we *couldn't* adopt a newborn, Kim. They said it would be more difficult, and that maybe we should look at adopting an older child."

Forget the baby stuff; they're more bother than they're worth. All they do is cry and sleep. They can't even play with you.

"More difficult!" Kim said sarcastically. "That means never. We've just been permanently placed at the bottom of the list."

"I don't think so."

"For Pete's sake, Bruce, face the truth. We'll never get a baby."

"Honey, please. Maybe we should look at getting an older child."

That's right. Older kids are good.

"Maybe we should just get a dog and forget the whole thing."

"Is that what you really want?" Bruce asked.

"No."

"Then let's look at this rationally. Let's look at all the pros and cons of adopting an older child, and then we'll decide what to do."

This is sounding more hopeful.

"All right, let's look at the pros first," Kim suggested. "I can't think of any."

"Yes, there are—the very first being that it is a child. We've tried for twelve years to have a baby, and a child of any age would fill that hole. By getting an older child, we also don't have to go through the sleepless nights a newborn would demand. Three, by getting an older child, we'd already know their basic personality and intelligence level. Four, with an older child, we could start right away to share all the things we enjoy, like camping, fishing, and skiing."

"It sounds like you've given this a lot of thought."

"Not really. That's off the top of my head, but they're all true, aren't they?"

"Yes, they are, but you forgot one other thing: We have so much love to give that a child of any age would thrive in our home."

"I love you, Kim." Bruce kissed his wife and smiled.

"I love you too. Let's go back tomorrow and look at videos of available children."

No. Don't do that. Take Andy. He's the best.

"Why don't we try to decide what sex we want? That will halve the number of videos we'll have to see. I think it will be hard enough seeing all those children. Knowing us, we'll want them all."

"Isn't that the truth. What do you want?"

"It doesn't matter to me. All my friends who wanted boys and got girls said it was the best thing that ever happened to them. Honestly, Kim, I don't care."

"I don't either. I really don't."

"Why don't we flip a coin?"

"What a callous thing to say."

"No it's not. Listen. If we had our own baby, we wouldn't get to choose. If we were allowed to adopt a newborn, we'd take the first one available. Here we have a choice and we don't care. So let's pretend we're going for an ultrasound to find out what the sex is. It's all by chance anyway, so let's flip and leave this to chance."

"That makes a strange bit of sense. I'm going to go into the bedroom and get my lucky charm."

"You've got a lucky charm? I didn't know that. What is it?"

"I found it when I was twenty. I wished I could meet a nice boy. The next day I met you."

"Then I guess it's my lucky charm too." Bruce winked as he met her at the bedroom door.

"Okay. It's got an eagle on one side and a river on the other. Which will be the boy and which the girl?"

"Let's try to use some logic so we never second-guess ourselves."

"I've got it," declared Kim. "The river is the girl, for long flowing hair. The eagle, a bird for a boy."

Great, we want the bird. Thank goodness I know what that is.

"Is that a 'b' for boy or bird for something else?" Bruce chuckled.

"Bruce, you're so bad."

I don't get it.

"I know. Go ahead, flip the coin."

"All right, here goes nothing."

I've got to get there before they do.

Rats. No bird. I'll fix that. There.

"Cody, no!" Bruce yelled.

"Did he touch it?"

No! Maybe.

"I don't think so. But even if he did, wouldn't that still just be luck?"

"I guess so. Bruce, I'm scared to look."

Phew! I got away with it.

Bruce took her hands in his. "Come on, we'll look together."

"A boy!" they both exclaimed.

"Bruce, I'm so glad."

"I thought you didn't care?"

"I didn't, but you're the one who's off most of the summer. A boy is more apt to want to go fishing and backpacking with you."

Andy would love that!

"I still don't care, but at least we can plan for our son."

"Bruce, we forgot to list the cons of taking an older child."

"Does it matter?"

No.

"I guess not, but we need to discuss things we should look for in the videos. We want to be as sure as possible before we meet the child. Can you imagine how cruel it would be to meet a child and then reject him? That poor child will have enough problems without adding more."

"I'm sorry, Kim. You're absolutely right. What do you think we should be looking for?"

"It depends a lot on what the video shows. But I know we should look for hyperactivity, aggressiveness, passivity, eye contact, and things like that. Once we've chosen one or two, we need as much family and medical background as we can get."

"That makes sense. Let's discuss it as we go."

"I'm getting kind of anxious."

"Me too."

Ring.

"Hello?…I'm sorry. We lost track of time. We'll bring him right down. Bye-bye."

"I guess they're looking for Cody," Bruce said. "I'll run him down. I won't be long."

"It's so nice out, why don't we go for a walk?"

"Good idea. I'll grab our sweaters."

Now comes the hard part.

"Hello, Andy. Sorry we kept Cody late," Bruce said.

"That's all right. You're his guests, he's supposed to be with you."

"Not really. As we understand it, he's just supposed to come up in the evening and spend the night. He followed us up this afternoon on his own."

"He must like you. Why are you staying at the hotel?"

Here it comes.

"We're in town on business. We'll probably be here another couple of days. We're going for a walk. Would you like to join us? We don't know the city very well."

Yes!

"No thank you. I'm going to play with Cody here, but there is a nice park down by the harbor. Ask Mitchell, he'll tell you how to get there."

"Thank you, Andy, we'll check it out. Have a good time with Cody." Kim touched him on the shoulder and smiled.

"Thank you. I will."

I can't believe it! They're going to look at other boys tomorrow, and here is a perfect one right under their nose.

"Come on, Cody. Let's go out back and play ball."

Sure, why not.

****

"I'm so excited, I don't know if I'll be able to sleep tonight," Kim declared.

"Me either."

Me either, and not because I'm excited. I'm so depressed. How can I help everybody? Especially when they lie. I need Michael.

Ah, Andy's picture! I think it's in the bottom drawer in the dining room.

Rats, I can't get it opened.

"*Bark, bark, bark.*"

Bruce came into the room in a hurry. "What do you want, Cody? I've never heard you bark before."

Open this drawer.

"Is there something in there you want?"

Yes, open it!

"Aha, Andy's picture."

Give me that.

"I don't think you should——"

"Bruce, look. Cody brought me Andy's picture."

"He had me get it for him out of the buffet."

"I wonder what it was doing there?"

"I wonder why he wanted it and why he took it to you?"

Ask Michael.

"Do you think he's trying to tell us something?"

Now you've got it. Think about it.

"Nah, he's probably just proud of his friend. Remember he introduced us in the lobby."

"Maybe he just wanted his picture out so he could look at it."

"I don't know. What dog looks at pictures? Cody's an interesting pet. Do you think our son will want a dog? How would you feel about that?"

"I don't think I'd mind," Kim replied. "It might help him to adjust. Let's worry about that later."

"Okay. Let's go to bed. I think we're going to have a very difficult day tomorrow."

Aaahh!!

Chapter Twenty-Three

"Hi, Cody." Bruce patted my head.

You're back early again. I don't want to hear it. I'll be too sad.

"Bruce, let's have a late lunch before we go up to the suite."

"Good idea. It might take awhile to decide between these three boys."

Oh no! They've already chosen three. I don't have much longer. Please sit close to the door.

Thank goodness. Nothing else has gone my way.

"Which one are you leaning toward?" Kim asked.

"I don't know. Pass me Bernie's file."

"Honey, could we call them by numbers until we decide? It will make the two rejected ones less personal."

"We can, but I don't think it will help. I already feel bad choosing these three over all the others we saw today. Please pass me number one."

"Darn, I'm sorry. How clumsy of me."

Yes! They dropped them. This is my chance.

"Cody, get back here with that! Pick up the rest, Kim. I'll get Cody."

In your dreams. Mike! Mike! Here look at this!

"What have you got there, Cody?"

"That's mine, please hand it over," Bruce demanded.

"Of course. Here you go."

"I'm sorry I snapped. My wife and I are in the middle of a big decision."

Here it comes.

"I guess I'm just a little edgy."

"No problem. Is Cody a bother?"

"No. We were in the dining room having a late lunch, and he was just lying by the door. When I dropped this paper, he grabbed it and ran. I guess he wanted to play."

"I'll keep him with me. Sorry for the inconvenience."

"No problem. Thanks."

"Cody, what's going on? You were trying to tell me something weren't you?"

Yes, Mike. Please you have to help.

"I didn't get a chance to look at the paper, and I can't just go ask them what's going on."

Why not? You're the concierge, you're supposed to know everything.

****

Andy came over and sat on the floor beside me. "Hi, Cody. What's wrong? You look sad today."

I am. Mr. and Mrs. Grant are going to pick a son tomorrow, and it should be you.

"Do you want to go out and play? No? Let's go sit on the sofa then. I wish you could talk. I'm always talking about my problems, and now you have a problem and you can't talk about it."

Andy, I don't know what to do.

"Come on, Cody. Let's go see Michael."

"Hi, Andy."

"Michael, why is Cody sad? What happened to him today?"

"I don't know. Something is going on with his guests, I think."

"Mr. and Mrs. Grant, right?"

"That's right. You know them?"

"Yes."

"Have they said anything to you about Cody or anything else?"

"No, but I don't like seeing Cody sad."

"Me either, but I'm sure he'll get over it. Besides, I don't think it's his problem; I think it's a problem with the Grants. Cody tends to become involved with his guests. They'll be gone in a couple of days anyway."

That's the problem.

"Come on, Cody. Let's go out."

No.

"Shh…come on," Andy whispered as he motioned me to follow him.

What's he up to?

"Come on, Cody, get in the elevator. I'm going right up there and ask the Grants why they made you sad."

Yahoo!

Knock, knock.

"Andy, hello. What are you doing here?"

"I've come to talk to you and your wife about Cody."

"I'm sorry, Andy, but we're kind of busy."

"Who is it, honey?" Kim came to the door. "Hello, Andy. Come on in."

"Sweetheart, we only have an hour before we have to get that form in."

"This won't take long, I promise," Andy pleaded.

"All right, son, come on in." Bruce stepped back from the door.

"Have a seat, Andy." Kim patted the seat beside her.

"No, thank you, I'll stand. I won't be long. Something has made Cody very sad. You know dogs can't talk, so I'm trying to find out what happened so I can fix it."

"That's very sweet of you," Kim said. "How can we help?"

"He was fine when I left yesterday, and he's mostly been with you people, so I thought you might know something."

"I'm afraid not. We were out all morning," said Bruce.

"Wait, he was running around here last night with your picture, and today he grabbed one of our papers and took it to Michael. Does that mean anything?"

"When he takes things to people, he's trying to tell them something."

"What was he trying to tell us about you, Andy?" Bruce asked.

"I don't know. What did he take to Michael?"

"Just a piece of our business papers?"

Come on, you guys. Tell the truth. Open up.

"I guess we can't help each other, Andy," Bruce concluded.

"I guess not. I'm sorry I bothered you."

No wait! You guys are looking for each other.

Ah! Another piece of paper. What should I do? I have to try something. Here goes.

"Cody, give me that paper back." Bruce reached to grab me.

Nope. See ya. I've got to think.

"Cody, come out from under that bed."

Nope. I'm safe here.

Kim came into the room, followed by Andy. "I'll call Michael. We need that paper."

"Never mind. I'll get it." Andy got down on the floor. "I can fit under there."

Please read it. Here! Look at it. Good boy!

"Here's your paper, Mr. Grant." Andy choked on his words.

"Thank you, Andy. Are you all right?"

"Yes. I have to go now. I'm sorry I bothered you." Andy headed for the door.

Andy, no. Say something.

As Andy opened the door, he turned around slowly. "Make sure you really want that kid before you interview him." Then he walked out and shut the door behind him.

I don't believe it!

"What was that all about?" Bruce asked.

"It sounds like he's been there before. Oh my God, Bruce, you don't think…Quick—get your coat, we have to catch up with him. I bet Michael knows what's going on."

Hey, you forgot about me! I can't stay in this suite by myself!

****

"Cody! We owe you a big apology." Kim dropped to her knees. "We're so sorry. We understand everything you were trying to tell us.

If we were as smart as you, this wouldn't have taken so long. Sorry and thank you."

No problem. After all, I am the Codyman.

"We didn't catch up with Andy, but we spoke to Michael and went right down to Social Services. We just made it before they closed. They've agreed to let us talk to Andy tomorrow. He'd taken his video out of the file after he was rejected last week. We feel so badly for him. I'm sorry we left you in the suite."

It's okay. It was worth it.

****

"Hello, Andy, may we join you?" Kim asked.

"If you want to."

Bruce sat down beside his wife. "How was school today?"

"Okay."

"We sure had a busy day."

"Did you take the boy you interviewed?"

"No, we didn't."

Andy put his head back on the sofa and closed his eyes.

"We didn't apply for an interview, so the boy never knew."

"Good."

"We didn't want an interview because we found another little boy. We think this new boy is the best in the whole world. We are so lucky nobody else has seen him, or he would have been snatched up quicker than you could say jack-sprat."

"He must be a good one."

"He is. I already love him, and I've only met him a few times," Kim added.

"If you already met him, why were you looking at other boys?"

"We didn't know this boy was available, and we don't know if he wants us."

"Why wouldn't he? You seem nice."

"I'm a school principal. Do you think a boy would like to have a principal for a father?"

"Sure. If you're a good dad, who cares?"

"Mrs. Grant here is a children's nurse. That should be good, shouldn't it?"

"I think that's a good job for a mother. Mrs. Grant, why are you crying?"

"I am so afraid he won't want us, and I do love him. Do you think it's possible to love someone so quickly?"

"Sure, I loved Cody the first day I met him."

"What do you think we should say to him, Andy?" Bruce asked.

"Tell him the truth."

Yeah, go ahead.

"Good advice. The truth is, Mrs. Grant and I have wanted a child for a long time. We thought we wanted a new baby, but the more we thought about it, the more we realized we wanted an older child. Then we met the perfect boy, we fell in love, and now we'd like that boy to become our son. That boy is you, Andy."

There you go, Andy. They want you.

"Andy, are you all right?"

"I'm afraid."

"Afraid of what?" Bruce asked.

"I'm afraid you'll change your mind."

"Oh, honey," Kim cried, "never. Can I hug you?"

Andy got up from the sofa and ran into her arms. Then he stood in front of Bruce and put out his hand. Bruce picked him up in his arms and gave him a big hug. Everyone was crying, and if I could cry, I would too.

Michael appeared, wiping tears from his eyes. "I see everything has worked out."

Bruce put Andy down and smiled. "Yes, thank you for your help yesterday."

"Are you really going to be my new parents?"

"We sure are, son."

"I don't even know where you live."

"In a small town about 100 miles west of here. We can't leave until Friday. We told Social Services we'd call as soon as we knew if you wanted us. They'll start the paperwork today and get everything finalized tomorrow. The final adoption won't be complete for about six months, but by tomorrow afternoon we'll be legally a family."

"Wow, that fast?"

"Yup, would you like to spend tomorrow night in the suite with us?"

"Yeah! What about all my stuff?"

"As soon as the papers are signed, we can get your stuff from Mrs. MacNeil's. Why don't you go to school in the morning and say goodbye to everyone. In the afternoon, as soon as we get the papers, we'll pick you up at your house. We'll go to the school, get your records, and then come here. How does all that sound?"

"It sounds quick."

"Do you want more time?" Kim asked.

"No, no. But I'd like to spend as much time as possible with Cody. I'm really going to miss him." Andy wiped his eyes with his sleeve.

I'm going to miss you too.

****

Andy crawled up on the sofa beside me. "We leave in fifteen minutes. Here, sit on my lap. I need to put my arms around you."

I need your arms around me too.

"Cody, I promise I will never forget you. You cared about me when nobody else did and you gave me my first real birthday and you found me my parents. I'm happy to be leaving, but I'm sad to leave you."

Please don't cry, Andy.

"I don't think I'll ever get a dog. I could never love one like I do you. I don't know what I'll do without you. You're my very very best friend. I'll miss our visits and talks. Thanks, Cody, I really really love you."

"Andy, honey, it's time to go," Kim leaned over and whispered.

"Cody, I'll write. Michael said he'd write back and tell me everything you've been doing. Please don't forget me," Andy cried.

I won't. *Bark, bark.*

"Come on, honey." Kim picked a sobbing Andy up into her arms.

I got down and followed them.

"Bye, Cody. Thank you for looking after our Andy." Kim turned quickly and walked out the door.

There he goes. Bye, Andy. I'm really going to miss him. I'll never be happy again.

"Hi, Cody."

Janey! When did you get back?

****

"Hi, Cody," Krista said. "Isn't Jane back yet? It's 10 P.M."

Tell me about it. I'm exhausted and need some sleep. I was awake half the night talking to Andy.

"Hi, Cody." Jane waved as she flew across the lobby. "Sorry I'm so late. Does he need to go out or anything?"

"No, he's all ready."

"Thanks. Let's go, Cody. I'm exhausted."

My feelings exactly.

"I have to be out early in the morning. Dad has five buildings lined up for us to look at."

How early is early?

"Move over, sweetie, and I'll tell you about my day."

Can't it wait 'til tomorrow?

"Dad designed a great business plan already, and Bob was very impressed. He gave us a huge line of credit from his own account until the venture capital comes through, so everything on that end is set. Dad was right about Bob wanting to be our first client, too. We're going in on Sunday to do that. The rest of the day we'll spend at Dad's organizing our plans. Tomorrow we're going to look at office and work space. It's exciting but scary at the same time. I'm afraid I'm going to be late most nights. I can move to another room if that would be hard on you."

I can handle it.

"I can't talk any more tonight."

Ah, good night.

****

"Cody, good news! Dad and I found the perfect building, and somehow it's still available. It's a two story with lots of work space on the lower level and good storage space for all our units. The best thing, it's not too far out of the city."

That is good news.

"The second level is a three-bedroom apartment, so Dad and I are going to move right in."

That's bad news.

"We ordered furniture for delivery on Monday, so I guess tomorrow night will be my last with you. I'm so sorry, but this is probably best for you anyway. I'm going to be late every night, and I know how you like your sleep. I am going to miss you though. You've been a great comfort to me, and I'll never be able to repay you for helping my father and for bringing us closer together. You'll always have a special place in my heart."

Thanks, Janey. You already had a special place in my heart.

Chapter Twenty-Four

I can't believe it. Two weeks, no problems, and sound sleeps. I could get used to this.

"You look pleased with yourself," Michael grinned. "You must have had another satisfied guest."

Of course.

"I have a letter from Andy for you. Come on over, and I'll read it to you."

Yippee!

Dear Cody,

I can't believe I've only been here three weeks. It seems like forever. I am so happy. I have a beautiful room all to myself. Dad is teaching me all about the stars—it's astronomy—so I have lots of neat star maps all over my room. I even have my own telescope. Every clear night we go out and look at the sky. I can name a whole bunch of constellations. Dad says I'm pretty good at it. I like my new school. My teacher Miss Bishop is really nice. When I finish my work, she lets me read.

Mrs. Grant is very nice. She tucks me in bed every night and reads to me. We're reading The Hardy Boys. *Don't tell but sometimes I can't wait to find out what happens so when she leaves I take my flashlight under the covers and read some more. Sometimes it's hard to be surprised when I know what's coming. The best part is she kisses me good night. I really like that.*

They asked me if I wanted a dog, but I said no. I don't think I could ever find a dog like you so I'm just going to wait. I started taking swimming lessons at the pool last week. I'm doing pretty good. The Grants do lots of canoeing and camping in the summer, so they want me to be able to swim. I can't wait to go camping.

This is the best house. Thanks, Cody. I have to go. I'll write you later.

Bye, Andy

I'm so happy for him.

"There's another note in here from the Grants."

Dear Michael and Cody,

Thank you both so much. Andy is wonderful. We wonder why we ever hesitated getting an older child. He marvels at everything and wants to learn so much. We love him dearly. Thank you.

Kim and Bruce

"Isn't that nice, Cody? I'll write Andy back in a couple of days. Anything you want to tell him? Oh, sorry." Michael laughed as he slapped himself on the forehead. "Now I'm beginning to think you're human."

Why is that funny?

****

"Hi, Cody," A strange woman in a beige raincoat came over and sat down. "How are you today?"

Fine. How do you know my name?

"You're so cute. Paul didn't say you'd be so adorable. Come sit beside me. I'll scratch your ears."

Sounds good. Ah, feels good. What's wrong with you? You seem frightened.

"Would you like to go for a walk? It's a beautiful day out. Here, have a doggie biscuit."

I don't know, something doesn't seem right here.

"Come on, honey, Michael said it's all right. I've got your lead right here. Let's go down to the harbor and get a hot dog."

Okay. Michael must have told her that is one of my favorite things to do. Let's go. Hey! That's not my lead. Hmm. It must be a new one.

"Excuse me, ma'am. Where are you taking the dog?" Mitchell asked.

"It's okay, Michael said I could take Cody for a walk."

"All right then. I'll get the door for you."

"Thank you." The woman smiled and started forward. "Come on, Cody."

"Excuse me. I just remembered we have a procedure to follow before he goes out. If I don't follow it, I could lose my job. I'll take Cody, and we'll be back in a minute. Would you like to come with us?"

"No, thank you." The woman hesitated. "I'll wait right here."

"Yes, ma'am."

Michael looked up from his paper work. "Hi, Mitchell. What are you doing with Cody on a lead?"

"The lady over there—hey, she's gone!"

"What about the lady?"

"She was going to take Cody out for a walk. She said that you said she could. She knew your name and Cody's name, but something just didn't feel right. I didn't recognize her, and she seemed skittish. I told her we had a set procedure to follow before Cody could go out, so I took him to see you first. She said she'd wait over there by the door. Now she's gone."

"Good job. Mitchell. You did exactly right. Look, this isn't even Cody's lead."

I knew that. What's going on?

"Do you think she was going to steal him?"

"Or kidnap him," Michael suggested. "After all, a lot of people know he's got loads of money. Let's go look at the surveillance tapes and see if we can find anything. Come on, Cody. You stay with me until we find out what's going on."

Sounds good.

"Rollie, will you roll back the tapes for the front door?" Michael asked as we entered the security office.

"Sure, how far?"

"Five minutes should do it."

"Okay."

"There she is, just leaving." Mitchell pointed at the screen.

"Go back a little," Michael suggested.

"There, stop! That's when I started to open the door and decided I'd better check this out. See, I take Cody, she watches for a second and then rushes out."

"Stop the tape!" Michael yelled. "Look, a car pulled in to pick her up. What kind of car is that? Does anybody know?"

"It's a 2002 Pontiac Grand Am," Rollie replied.

"Are you positive?"

"Sure, cars are my hobby."

"I guess we know for sure she was trying to kidnap Cody." Michael sighed and sat down.

"Wow!" Rollie exclaimed.

"Rollie, let's check the lobby tapes and see if we can find anything else."

"There she is. Keep going back until we first pick her up."

"Here it is." Rollie put his finger on the screen. "She comes into view and starts talking to Cody."

Look, I'm on TV!

"There, she sits with him on the sofa, talks for a minute, gives him something to eat, and puts the lead on him. Now they disappear. I think that's where we pick them up on the other camera at the front door."

"Roll that again," Michael said. "Stop. Right there. Can you zoom in? Good. See if you can clear that up and print me a copy. We'll give a copy of her face to everyone who works here and see if anyone recognizes her. We'll also keep one handy in case she comes back. I want a picture of that car too. And make me a copy of both tapes. I don't want them erased."

"Why don't we go back on that first tape and see if we can find her entering the hotel?" Mitchell suggested.

"Good idea," Michael replied. "You better get back to the front door. I'll let you know what we find."

****

Michael ran his hands through his hair. "I can't see anything. We've gone back two hours. I don't think she'd hang around that long.

"Why don't I check the elevator tapes coming up from the parking area?" Rollie suggested.

"Good idea. While you're at it, check the garage tapes and see if we can see that car again."

"Helloo, pretty lady."

"What time is that?"

"Two minutes before we see her talking to Cody."

Show me that part again.

"Print me that picture. It's clearer than the other one."

"Don't you think it's time we called the police?"

"Soon. Let's check the garage tape first. Take it back five minutes before we see her on the elevator."

"There's our car," declared Rollie.

"Are you sure?"

"Positive."

"Look. Two people in it. The driver looks to be a male, but he's got the visor down. Can you make out his face?"

"Nope."

"All right, continue. There's our woman getting out, and the car is pulling away."

"It's a rental, and the plate number is good and clear."

"Now I can talk to the police." Michael smiled.

"You know, Michael, I've been thinking. They might not be able to do much."

"What do you mean?"

"Think about it. What really happened here? A woman tries to take a dog out for a walk. Not exactly a felony."

"But they were trying to kidnap him."

"Even if you could prove it, it's still just a dog."

Hey, who are you calling just a dog?

"It's not just a dog, it's Cody. What about extortion?"

"No proof."

"Damn. Now what?"

"I think the police will still try to track these people down. At least they'll know we're on to them and they may not try again."

"All right. I'll give them a phone call. In the mean time I'll speak to all the staff and inform them of the situation. We'll have to be extra vigilant until this situation is under control."

****

"Sorry, Cody," Jennifer apologized. "I'm busy, so I can't let you out."

Aah, it just takes a second to open the door!

"I'll call Carter."

If you've got time to call Carter, you've got time to open the door.

"He'll be here in a minute."

"Hi, Cody," Carter said. "Do you have to go out?"

No, I'm sitting by the drafty door because it's so comfortable.

"Sorry to keep you waiting but you're not allowed out by yourself any more since the incident this morning."

Perfect. Just because a woman wanted to take me for a walk, I can't go out alone? I suppose you have to watch me do my business. This should be fun.

****

"Any news from the police?" Carter asked Michael.

"Yeah, guess who rented the car?"

"I don't know. Who?"

"Our friend Paul Jennings."

"No way. That son of a B!"

I hate bees. One bit me on the nose once. It hurt.

"He hasn't returned it yet, so he's still in the city somewhere."

"What are we going to do? They could try again."

"I know. I've put a full-time observer on the surveillance cameras. Everyone has a picture of the woman, and we're not letting Cody out of our sight. I don't know what else we can do. We can't lock him in the suite."

No you can't.

"How about keeping him on a lead with either you or me?"

I don't think so.

"I hate to do that to him. Keeping him tied up might really upset him."

Yeah, it would.

"There's no way we can make him leery of strangers. His whole world is dealing with new people."

"That's the truth. At least we know he would alert us if Jennings himself shows up. Remember how he shied away from him. I just hope he'll let us know if this woman comes back."

"I think he might."

"Let's hope so."

****

I like being the center of attention, but this is ridiculous. Everybody is always looking at me.

"Anything new, Michael?" Carter asked.

"No, it's been three days, and the car still hasn't been returned. Poor Cody hasn't been on a walk for days. I'm a little worried about taking him out alone."

"I can go with you. The two of us should be able to handle anything."

"Thanks, Carter. I think I'll take you up on that. I'm getting a little squirrelly myself."

Oh no, not the squirrels. Lock up the food.

****

That was a good walk. Michael and Carter seemed awfully nervous, but I had a good time. All this tension is wearing me down. I'm going to sleep. Great, what does this old lady want?

"Hi, little dog. Want a cookie?"

"*Grr...grr...grr.*"

"Cody, no." Michael rushed over. "Sorry, ma'am, he's never acted like this before. He's been a little edgy lately."

Mike, it's her!

"I was just trying to give him a piece of my cookie."

"Yes, ma'am. I'm sorry. Are you a guest here?"

"No, I just dropped in for lunch. But if this is the way you treat your guests, I'm glad I'm not staying here." The old lady turned away and slowly started for the front door.

Mike, stop her.

"Cody, look what you've done. You can't treat people like that."

Right, one day she tries to steal me and then because she dresses like a little old lady, it's okay. Make up your mind.

"What's wrong?" Michael demanded as Rollie went running by.

"That was her. I'm sure of it."

"Who?"

"Our woman, the old lady."

"No, it wasn't. I was talking to her."

"I saw you. I thought she was an old lady too, but as she approached the door she straightened up and her walk became brisker. I'm sure it was her."

"I'm so stupid. Cody was growling at her. He was trying to tell me, but it didn't click. Now what?"

"I guess we just wait for the next attempt. Everyone entering the hotel has to be a suspect."

"What a way to live."

****

"Good news, guys. I think our problem might be over," Michael declared. "The Jennings returned their car yesterday afternoon, and the rental company delayed them long enough for the police to pick them up."

"Are they being charged?" Carter asked.

"No. Here's their story. They came to town to celebrate their anniversary. That checks out. Jennings had told his wife about Cody, she wanted to see him, so she came into the hotel. That's when she decided to take him out to see her husband."

"Oh sure," Mitchell sneered, "and she just happen to sneak in the back door and have a lead with her."

"She said she found the lead lying on one of the chairs—which you know could happen; we are careless at times."

"What about her coming back a second time?" Rollie asked.

"She swears she never did. Anyway, the police don't feel they have a solid case to charge them, so they let them go. They flew out about an hour ago."

"What now?" Carter asked.

"We'll try to get back to normal. I've got workmen coming this afternoon to improve Cody's run. It will have a higher fence with a lean out at top. If Cody is going out with anyone other than Carter or myself, then Mitchell has to hear it directly from me. You can inform the rest of the staff. At least nothing bad happened, and now we've got better safeguards for Cody. Thanks for all your help."

Yeah, thanks.

Chapter Twenty-Five

Laura slumped down into the chair beside Michael's desk. "I hate November. It's all rain and chilliness. I can't even get home for Thanksgiving this year."

"Cheer up, Christmas is coming." Michael opened his arms expansively. "We'll be decorating the lobby before you know it. Do we have a guest for Cody yet?"

"Yes, Miss Melanie Cooper. She's in town for a couple of days on business. I liked her, and she was thrilled to stay with Cody. She left a couple of dogs at home and really misses them. Cody took to her right away. It should be a good match."

"You know, Laura, when you think about it, we've been pretty lucky with the people we've chosen. We only had that one problem with Jennings, and Cody spotted him right away. How many guests do you think he's had?"

"Jeez, I don't know. Let's say on average four per week, sixteen per month. I guess about one hundred and sixty. That is a lot when you think about it."

"Sure is," Michael agreed. "Makes you think, doesn't it, about all the good people we see everyday? If you only watched the news and read the papers, you'd be scared to death to leave your home. I wish good news sold as well as bad news."

"I couldn't agree more. Thanks, Michael. I feel a little better. I'm going to start looking for the good things about November."

"Where is Miss Cooper now?"

"She had a business dinner to attend. She expected to be in around nine."

"All right, leave a note for Krista. They can make sure Cody is ready by then. He can go right up with her when she comes in."

"Will do. Have a good evening."

"Thanks. Bye, Cody."

Bye, Mike. I sure wish he'd take me home more often.

****

"Good evening, Miss Cooper. How was your evening?" Krista asked.

"Fine, thank you, but I'm feeling a little under the weather."

"Would you like us to keep Cody down here tonight?"

"No, of course not. He'll be a comfort. It's probably just a touch of the flu or something. I'll be fine after a good night's sleep. Can I take him with me now?"

"Yes. He's just come in, so he should be set for the night. If there's any problem, just phone down."

"Thank you. Come on, Cody."

I'm coming.

"I'm really glad to be staying with you, Cody. I really miss my dogs, Polo and Buffy. I hope they'll be all right while I'm gone."

I'm sure they'll be fine. Let's go to bed.

"Man, I feel awful. I might have to throw up."

Throw up what? Is that a new game?

"Uh oh!" Melanie ran to the bathroom.

What are you doing in there? I've never heard those noises before.

"Aah," Melanie moaned as she came out of the bathroom. "I feel awful."

You don't smell too good either.

"I've got to lie down."

I know, it's called going to bed.

"Not again!" She rushed into the bathroom, barely making it before the noises started again.

I don't like this.

"I couldn't get the flu this quickly," Melanie said as she crawled into bed.

Try to get some sleep. That should help.

"Oh, no!"

She must be really sick; this isn't normal.

"I've got to get a bowl from the dining room. I can't keep running to the bathroom. I almost didn't make it last time."

Please don't cry.

"You're so sweet, Cody. I'm sorry to worry you."

It's okay. I think you need a vet.

"I'm freezing. Can you snuggle in?"

Wow, you're hot!

"I've never been this sick before."

There she goes again.

"I'm sorry, Cody. Look, it's already two. I've got to get some sleep. I can't go again; there's nothing left to come out."

I hope not.

"Good night."

Good night.

Melanie mumbled as she rolled over. "Hi, Sammy. What are you doing here?"

Great, she caught Alzheimer's.

"If Dad catches you, he'll whoop your butt."

She must be dreaming out loud.

"Just a minute, I'll come with you."

I'm not going anywhere. Hey, where are you going? You can't go out like that. Melanie, get up. You can't sleep on the floor.

"Mmmmm."

Wake up.

"*Bark, bark, bark.*"

Something's really wrong here. Wake up. I've got to push her over. She's too heavy. I think she might be dead! No, I can hear her breathing. What's wrong with you? Somebody, help!

"*Bark! Bark!*"

Nobody will hear me up here. Wait. Krista said, "If there's any problem, just phone down." That's it, the phone. Krista will help. Knock that top off and speak.

"*Bark!*"

Hello? Is anybody there? Just a buzz. I wonder if the phone is trying to talk to me. Hello, phone. Can you get Krista?

No, I know, I have to push some buttons.

There.

"*Bark! Bark!*"

Hello, is anybody there? I need help.

Just that stupid buzz again. Come on, buttons, work.

"*Bark! Bark! Bark!*"

Wake up, Melanie. Help me push the buttons.

Now what can I do? That's it! The panic button. I'm so stupid. How many times have I heard my guests being told about it? "If you ever need help in a hurry, push the panic button. We'll be here before you know it."

Rats! I can't reach it. I've got to. I've just got to. I can't jump that high. Maybe I could jump off the bed and reach it.

Wait a minute. I never did try to run up a tree like the squirrels did. Maybe that would work. I don't have to go far. Here goes!

Ow! My nose!

Maybe I could jump off the bed and reach it? Almost. I've got to try harder.

Ow! Now it's my leg. Maybe if I run across the bed and jump.

Yes! I did it! Ow, ow! My leg! I can't stand on it.

Great, now we're both down. Hold on, Melanie.

"Hello?" Gordon called out from the door.

"*Bark!*"

"Damn, what happened?" Gordon grabbed his cell phone.

Help us.

"Krista, it's Gord. I'm in Cody's suite. Get me an ambulance quick. Miss Cooper is unconscious on the floor. There's vomit all over the place."

"No, he seems fine. Cody, come here."

I can't, I hurt my leg.

"Maybe he's not. He's not moving. Call the ambulance, and I'll check him over."

Don't touch my leg. It hurts.

"It's okay, Cody. I'm not going to hurt you."

You don't have to. I'm already hurt.

"I'm just going to touch you gently. That's a good boy."

Ouch!

"Is your leg sore?"

Yes.

"Hello?"

"We're in here," Gordon replied.

No, not them! It's the men in the blue pants who took Mrs. Haney away. Get out! She's not dead. I hear her breathing.

"Is this how she was when you found her?"

"Yes. I just checked her airway to make sure it wasn't blocked, and then I tilted her head back a bit."

"Do you have any other information?"

"I might," Krista suggested as she entered the room. "She was out at a business dinner tonight. When she came in around nine, she said she wasn't feeling well. Then she came up here."

"Probably food poisoning to have struck so quickly. She must have pushed the panic button and then collapsed."

"I don't think so," Gordon commented. "I was here within thirty seconds. She was already unconscious over there by the door. The panic button is way over there on the other side of the bed. It doesn't make sense."

"We can't worry about it now," replied one of the men. "We've got to get her to the hospital."

Don't let them take her. She's not dead. We'll never see her again. I've got to help. Ow!

Krista rubbed my side. "It's okay, Cody, Michael's on his way. You just lie still, and I'll sit with you. That's a good boy. Gordon, you better get back to the front desk. I'll wait here for Michael."

"Okay. Krista, I think Cody pushed the panic button and that's how he hurt his leg."

"How could he? Look how high it is."

"I don't know how he did it, but I know he did," Gordon declared as he left the suite.

****

Mike, can you help me? I hurt my leg.

"It's okay, Cody. Don't get up. What the heck went on here?"

"We're not sure. The panic alarm went off at 4:32. Gordon was here thirty seconds later and found Miss Cooper unconscious on the floor with Cody lying beside her head. The ambulance drivers think she might have food poisoning. They arrived at 4:50 and left about ten minutes ago."

"So how did Cody get hurt?"

"Gord thinks he got hurt by pushing the panic button."

"He couldn't reach that. Look how high it is."

"I know, but all the evidence points in that direction. Michael, look—the phone's off the hook. Do you think he tried to call first?"

"Krista, really."

"Michael, listen! If Miss Cooper had knocked the phone off trying to use it but couldn't, she would have collapsed beside it. But she was way over there by the door. We all know about Cody's exploits, and I think he's capable of figuring out that the phone could get help."

"You're probably right," Michael conceded. "People use the phone to order food and it arrives; they call to have their luggage picked up and someone comes to get it. He's probably heard lots of conversations taking place over the phone."

Will you guys stop talking and get me out of here? It smells awful.

"He probably figured if he barked into the phone, someone would come," Michael continued.

Yeah, except the stupid phone couldn't understand me.

"The problem is he couldn't get an answer, so he had to use the panic button."

"And how do you think he knew that?" Michael smiled at Krista's analysis.

"I bet he's heard a lot of guests being told about it. I know I've said it a thousand times—'In an emergency if you need help, just push this button.'"

"I concede all that, but how did he reach the button?"

"I've got two answers for that, but I don't like either," Krista said as she walked to the panic button. "He either jumped higher than we think he can or he took a run and ran part way up the wall."

Hey, what do you think I am a squirrel?

Krista turned around with a big grin on her face. "Wait a minute! Maybe he ran across the bed and took a flying leap. It looks impossible, but he might have been able to do it in a panic. That looks like the most likely way he'd hurt his front leg."

"Man, Krista, you're good at this."

"I read lots of mysteries, and I love those brain teasers. I'm pretty good at them."

"I bet you are. Enough speculation. I'm going to take Cody downstairs and call the vet's."

No!

"You call housekeeping and get this place cleaned up."

"You don't have to tell me twice."

****

"Are you still here?" Krista asked when she returned to the front desk.

"Yes. I called the vet's and got their answering service. Another clinic is on duty right now. I don't particularly want to take him to someone he doesn't know."

I don't even want to go to someone I do know.

"They suggested if Cody wasn't in too much pain, I could wait until 7:30. Our vet comes in around that time for early morning surgery. I decided I'd rather wait and have him in familiar surroundings. He's been up a bit, even though he can't put any weight on his leg."

"Has he had a drink?"

"No, I was afraid he might need surgery."

I need something.

"I also called the hospital. Miss Cooper is in critical condition. She's extremely dehydrated and while she's not totally unconscious, she's delirious. They are sure it's food poisoning but have to wait for cultures to come back. They'll know more in a few hours."

"It was so sudden and so severe."

"I asked about that. They said it's not common, but it's also not unheard of. I'll check again when I get back with Cody."

****

"What's wrong, big fella? Can't you walk?"

"No, I hurt my leg."

"What did you trip over?"

"Funny."

"That's me, Boots the comedian cat."

"Hi, Michael. What happened here?" Dr. Cameron asked.

"I think Cody may have broken his leg."

"How?"

"We're not sure exactly, but our best guess is he took a flying leap off the bed to hit the panic button in the suite."

"What?"

"His guest was lying unconscious on the floor and needed help. I guess he figured out that was the best way to get it."

"And the guest?"

"In critical condition, probably food poisoning."

"Okay, bring him in. I'll check him over."

"Hey, Cody, you're a hero. I'm glad to be your friend."

"Friend? You hate me."

"Weelll...I might have been a little quick to judge. Good luck."

"Thanks."

"Let me see." Dr. Cameron started running his hands gently over the leg. "I don't feel any deformities, but there is a little swelling just above the paw. He may just have a severe sprain, but we'll take him in for an x-ray to be sure. Why don't you come and hold him steady?"

No, not the back room. Don't cut me open.

"Cody, be still. Everything is all right," Michael whispered. "I'm right here."

"Okay, lay him here and put this lead apron on. Can you hold the leg like this? Good, don't move."

"Good boy, Cody. Stay."

"Good. One more from a different angle. That's it. Hold it...good. You can take him back to the examining room, and I'll develop these."

****

"Looks like we've got a break." Dr. Cameron returned with something in his hand.

Ow! Ow! I broke my leg.

"See this light line right here? It's a hairline fracture of the ulna. It's not too serious, and we can treat it with a splint."

"How long will he need that?" Michael asked with concern.

"Five or six weeks probably. We'll x-ray again in four weeks and see how it's coming along."

"Will he have to stay off it?"

"No, but he probably will for a while until he gets used to it."

Gets used to what? What are you going to do to me?

"Is it like a cast?"

"No, not a plaster cast. We'll pad it well, then use a plastic strip to immobilize it and then wrap it again. It should be fairly comfortable. I'll go get the stuff and someone to help me. I'll be right back."

"Cody. I feel so sorry for you," Michael sighed as he hugged me.

"So you broke it." Boots jumped down from the counter for a better look.

"Yes, what have they put on me?"

"That's a splint. It will keep your leg still until it gets better. You're lucky; it can't be too bad. I've seen dogs have to be cut open and have wires and pins put in. You'll be all right."

"Thanks, Boots."

"You're welcome."

"Thanks, Doctor. We'll be back in four weeks."

"Bye, Cody."

"Bye, Boots."

****

When we got back to the hotel, Carter came over with a concerned look on his face. "Is it broken?"

"Yes. Just a hairline fracture, but he'll need this splint on for about six weeks."

What do you mean just a fracture? I broke my leg.

"Can he walk on it?"

"The doctor said he should be able to, but he hasn't tried yet. Let's find out."

No! Don't put me down. I've got a broken leg.

I'm not moving.

"Come on, Cody. Do you want your breakfast?"

I never thought of that. You better carry me.

"He hasn't peed all morning. You'd better take him out first,"
Michael said.

"Okay. Come on, Cody."

I can't. Pick me up.

"I'd better carry him 'til he gets used to it."

Yeah! You've got it. You better hurry. I've just realized I do have to
go out.

"Here we are, Cody. I'll take you down to your favorite bush."

Thanks, Carter. How do I do this?

Darn.

What are you laughing at? Didn't you ever see anyone fall over
before?

"Sorry, Cody. I didn't mean to laugh. If you put the splint down, it
might help your balance."

It's broken. I can't wait much longer. I'll just have to swallow some
macho pride and squat. How embarrassing! Pick me up and let's get out
of here.

"Poor little Cody." Laura dropped to her knees. "Come here,
sweetheart."

You come here. I broke my leg.

"I feel so sorry for you."

I do too.

"Did he pee?" Michael asked.

"Yes," Carter chuckled, "you should have seen him. He fell over
twice before he decided to squat."

I don't think it's nice to laugh at the disabled. I'd like to see you try
to do it on one leg. I bet you'd sit down too.

"I talked to the hospital while you were out. Miss Cooper is about
the same. They've diagnosed Salmonella poisoning. They said she was
lucky we found her when we did. She might have died in a few more
hours."

"Cody, you're a hero," Laura declared. "You saved Melanie's life."

She's alive!

Yes! I am the Codyman!

****

"What are we going to do with Cody tonight?" Laura asked.

"Let's fix up that spot under the front desk for him. You can bring his dog pillow over from the window, and I'll get another bowl for some water."

Hey! I don't like the sound of this. It's sounding kind of permanent. What about my suite? All you have to do is find a guest who will carry me. Is that asking too much for a free suite?

"He can't go back to the suite until he's a lot more mobile. Besides, I want an eye kept on him. He'll be all right in the lobby for a while."

Aahh! The vacuum cleaner! I won't be able to run away. It's going to eat me. That's a great way for a hero to die. I can see it now—"Hero Dog Sucked into Vacuum Cleaner."

****

Hey, Laura put me over in the sun.

"What do you want, honey? You've already eaten and been out. I bet you want to sleep someplace more comfortable. I get it; this is the time you usually lie in the sun. I'll take you over."

Ah! What a life!

****

"Michael, Cody hasn't walked for three days," Carter said. "I think he's in pain."

"I think he's playing for all the sympathy he can get. I phoned the vet, and he thinks Cody is pulling our leg. After all, why would he hobble around if someone will carry him?"

Busted.

****

"Laura, I saw Melanie Cooper this afternoon."

"How's she doing?"

"Much better. She doesn't remember much of the first week and a half. This week she's a lot better. Her younger brother, Sammy, was there."

Aha, her brother.

"They are both very grateful to Cody. She calls him her guardian angel. She believes, had she been in any other room, she probably would have died. She'll be released next week and wants to come by to thank him."

"It's been a tough haul for her."

"Three weeks already. The doctors are pleased with her recovery. There won't be any permanent damage or long-lasting effects."

"That's good. Listen, Cody has been getting along fine on his leg. Can we put him back in the suite?"

"I don't think so. Look at him. His bandages are filthy, and he stinks from having to squat. Why don't we wait until next week? He goes back for x-rays then, and I'll see if they'll change the bandage and clean him up some."

I don't want to go back to the vet's unless he's taking this thing off. And I'm not standing around here listening to you two talking about my hygiene. I'll be sleeping under the chair if you need me.

"Cody! Michael! Come here quick." Scottie yelled across the lobby.

I'm coming.

"Hurry."

I've got a broken leg, you know.

"Look."

Oh my! Dusty and Janey are on TV.

"I was just flipping through the channels when I saw them."

Be quiet! I'm trying to listen.

"Scottie, what's going on?" Michael demanded.

"Dusty and his daughter are on Oprah! It's almost over."

"I want to thank you both for coming here today and sharing your amazing story. There aren't many businesses that would develop such a revolutionary product and keep the price low enough for everyone to benefit from it. Now are you sure you won't tell us more about this Cody?"

Hey, that's me. Tell her all about me.

"Sorry, Oprah, he lives in a very unique situation, and we don't want to invade his privacy," Jane replied.

"Thank God for that," declared Michael. "That's all we need, a big media frenzy. It might be impossible to keep Cody here if that happened."

That wouldn't be good. Thanks, Janey.

****

"Michael, Good news on Cody's leg. It looks like we can get rid of all the bandaging. See here, the break is completely healed. I don't think we need to do anything else with it. He shouldn't jump off anything too high, but I'd let him go about his regular routine."

"Can I take him back out for his walks?"

"Sure, but remember he hasn't used it for a month, so it will be a little weak. Maybe you should gradually work up to any type of long distance."

All right! Back to normal.

"I saw a father and daughter on Oprah last week talking about a dog named Cody. That wouldn't be this guy, would it?"

"I'm afraid so."

"So this broken leg wasn't his first act of heroism."

"I wouldn't go that far, but he has helped a lot of people."

"Cody, I'm proud to be your doctor."

"One more thing, Dr. Cameron: would it be all right to get him groomed today?"

No! Say no, doctor.

"I think that's a good idea. It might make him feel better."

Thanks a lot. I was starting to like you.

****

"Hi, Cody." Cathy picked me up to put me on the table. "I hear you broke your leg. Wow, you do need a bath."

"He had to squat for about a week. I'm afraid it got all over his belly."

"No problem, I'll have him looking and smelling great in about an hour. Are you going to wait for him?"

"I think I'd better. He just got his splint off, and the vet's and your shop aren't exactly his favorite places."

At least he knows that much.

"Did you see Oprah last week?" Cathy asked.

What? Does everyone stop work to watch this lady?

"I saw the end of it, and yes, they were talking about this Cody."

"Wow, way to go, Cody."

Thanks.

****

Laura ran over to meet us. "Cody, you look great!"

Thanks. I must admit, I do feel better.

"Look who's sitting over there waiting for you."

Hi, Melanie. You look better too.

"Hi, Cody. Can I pick you up?"

Sure, go for it. But don't drop me. I broke my leg.

"Cody," Melanie whispered as she started to cry, "I don't know how to thank you. You saved my life. I'm sorry you broke your leg."

So am I.

"I went up to the suite, and I don't know how you ever reached that panic alarm. It's unbelievable. I know I didn't push it because I hadn't even realized it was there. I still can't believe that a dog would know enough to push it in an emergency. You are so smart and so special."

I am the Codyman.

"Are you going to spend the night with us?" Michael asked.

"No, I just came to thank Cody and all the staff who helped me. I'm sorry I won't see Krista and Gordon. Please thank them again for me. I've spoken to both of them on the phone, but I was hoping to see them in person. I brought these flowers as a small token of my appreciation. Would you see that they get them?"

"Of course."

"I'd also like to buy Cody a hamburger if that's all right?"

Of course.

"I guess that would be all right."

What do you mean, "I guess"?

"I'm not the first person Cody has helped, am I?"

"No, but you're the first one with a situation so dramatic. Why do you ask?"

"I was watching Oprah last week…"

Here we go again.

Chapter Twenty-Six

Holy cow! A tree grew in the lobby overnight! It's beautiful. It's got colored lights and pretty balls all over it. I've got to check this out.

"Cody, come here. You have to go out."

Wait a minute, Carter.

Presents—I bet these are for me.

"What's Cody doing?" Michael asked.

"I just brought him down to put him out, and he went straight to the tree. He's smelling all the presents."

"It's the first big Christmas tree he's been around. Mrs. Haney just had a little one on the table."

"Come on, Cody. You have to go out."

I'm coming, hold your shirt.

None of these presents smell like they're for me. In fact they don't smell like anything.

"Cody, those aren't for you," Michael said.

I knew that. I like it under here. I think this will be my new sitting and sleeping spot. I like the cover over my head.

****

"Mother, look at the stuffed dog under the tree. I want one of those."

Hey, I'm not stuffed. I didn't eat that much.

"Mother, it moved."

"Honey, look, it's a real dog. Isn't it cute?"

"I still want one."

"Let's go talk to the concierge and find out about him."

I've got to hear this.

"Hello. I'm Mrs. Theodore Leadley. This is my daughter, Nicole. I was wondering if you could tell us what kind of dog that is under the tree?"

"Yes, ma'am. He's a West Highland White Terrier."

"Look, Mother, he followed us over here."

"His name is Cody."

"Hi, Cody." Nicole dropped to her knees and started rubbing my back. "Mother, can I have him? He's so sweet."

No, you can't.

"No, honey, he belongs to someone else."

Nicole stood up, put her hands on her hips, and stamped her foot. "But I want him. Buy him."

"Is he for sale?" the woman asked.

"No, I'm afraid not."

"Do you own him?"

"Not exactly."

"What do you mean, not exactly?"

"Well, it's complicated."

"Mummy, I want this dog," demanded the little girl.

Man! And people think I'm spoiled.

"I want to talk to the owner. I'll pay anything."

"I'm sorry. He's not for sale."

"Don't be silly. Everything is for sale. Get me the owner."

"Yes, ma'am. Come with me."

Mike! What are you doing?

"Laura, this is Mrs. Leadley. She'd like to buy your dog."

"My dog?"

"Yes, how much do you want for him? Money is no object."

"I'm sorry, he's not for sale."

"Mother, I want him. He can be my friend."

"Of course, he's for sale. I'll write you a check right now for two thousand dollars."

"I'm sorry."

"Five thousand."

"I couldn't part with—"

"Ten thousand."

"Weellll…"

"Laura!" Michael exclaimed.

"Mrs. Leadley, listen, that dog is my best friend. He goes everywhere with me. I'm all alone in life except for him. Last year he even saved my life. You can't just go around buying and selling friendship. It's something you have to earn. I don't think it's a very good example to set for your daughter that everything can be bought or sold."

Way to go, Laura.

"Humph!" Mrs. Leadley took her daughter's hand and marched off.

"Mother, I want that dog…"

"It's all right, honey. I'll buy you a new one."

"What was that all about?" Laura asked.

"She demanded to speak to Cody's owner. There's no way I was going to tell her the truth. Thank God you picked up on it right away. You handled it great, even if you got a little melodramatic. And what's with the hesitation at ten thousand?"

"I just wanted to see your reaction." Laura started to laugh.

"You scared me for a second."

Me too.

****

Laura called Michael over to the front desk. "Another bunch of cards came in for Cody today. What are we going to do with them all? That makes about fifty this week."

"I can't believe all those people would take the time to send him a Christmas card. Any more gifts?"

"Ten."

"All right, give me the cards, and I'll read any personal notes to him. You keep the gifts with the others. We'll decide what to do with them later."

Hey, they're my gifts, give them to me.

"Come on, Cody. Some more of your guests have sent you Christmas cards. Let's go see what they have to say."

I'm right behind you.

"This is from Jake and Elizabeth: *'Dear Cody, Merry Christmas. Just a short note to thank you again for sharing your suite. It meant a lot to us.'* No note on this next one, it's just signed Colleen."

I remember her; she had just gone through a divorce.

"Here's one from Andy: *Dear Cody, I'm so excited. Mom and Dad and I are going to Vermont to ski for Christmas. I'm getting pretty good at it. Dad says I'm a natural. He also said we might be able to come see you when we get back. That would be the best present. Love, Andy.*"

I can't wait.

"Michael, we've been opening Cody's presents, and I need to know what to do with them," Laura said.

Hey, you can't open my presents.

"Have you been cataloging everything?"

"Yes. There are about 20 boxes of dog bones, 10 chew bones, and 25 toys. There is no way Cody can use all this stuff."

I could try.

"All right. Let's let him choose a couple of the toys, then we'll pack everything up for the animal shelter."

"That's a good idea. I'm sure they'll really appreciate that. I've got the bag of toys right here. Come here, Cody. What would you like?"

Wow, look at all those toys.

"He's smelling them all. I wonder why?" Laura asked.

I'm seeing who they are from. I'll take this one and this one.

"I guess they're the two he wants." Michael said. "I'm curious, who are they from?"

"Let me see. Number 12 is from Rachel. Remember her? The little girl in the wheelchair. Number 18 is from, guess who?"

"Andy."

"That's right. It's amazing. The only toys from kids, and he chooses them."

Ah, it was easy. I could smell them. They'd be disappointed if I gave them away.

"Let's get a thank you note printed off to send to everyone. It will have to be generic; we can't send individual notes to everyone."

"Yes we can. We'll do one up in the computer and just change the name and gift before we print it."

"Can you do that?"

"Michael, when are you going to start using a computer?"

"Soon."

****

"Merry Christmas." Laura gave Jennifer a quick hug. "I thought you two were off today."

"We are, but we wanted to see Cody and bring him his gift."

"That's sweet."

Yeah, that's sweet. What is it, Mike?

"Here you go, Cody. Merry Christmas."

Thanks. I know what this is. Yup! A new chew stick. My favorite.

"You guys doing anything special today?" Laura asked.

"We're going over to Dusty and Jane's for dinner," Michael replied.

What? Take me with you. I haven't seen them for ages. Please, Mike. I want to see Bud. Come on. It's Christmas.

"Now you've done it," Jennifer said.

"Sorry. I didn't mean to say anything. It just slipped out."

Yeah, right. You were going to sneak over there without me. You blew it. I'm coming.

"Okay, okay. You can come with us."

****

"Merry Christmas." Janey smiled as she opened the door. "It's so good to see you."

Surprise! I came too.

"Cody. I'm so glad you came. Merry Christmas, sweetie."

Ah, I'm still in love.

"Come on in. Dad's just taking the turkey out of the oven. He'll be out in a second."

"Hi, Bud."

"Hi, Code. Whatcha doin' here?"

"I was invited for dinner."

"Good. Whatcha been up to?"

"Not much. I broke my leg saving a guest's life. Other than that it's been about the same. How about you?"

"Mmm, not much. I spend most days down in the workrooms. Dusty and Jane go away a lot, so I've spent a lot of nights with Kiki."

"This is a nice place. It's pretty big."

"It's all right."

"Merry Christmas, everyone," Dusty came in from the kitchen. "Hi, Cody. Come here, fella, I haven't seen you for a while. I hear you broke your leg."

That's right. How did you know? Do you guys talk when I'm not around?

"How's he doing?" Dusty asked.

"Good. You'd never know it was broken," replied Michael. "By the way, thanks for not revealing Cody's home on Oprah. It could have been disastrous."

"Hey, no problem. We're sorry his name even got out. It just kind of slipped. Did you see the show?" Jane asked.

"No, just the last five minutes. Scottie was flipping the channels when he saw it. He called us over to see it"

"We're sorry if it caused a problem," Dusty apologized.

"No harm done. But I'm sure everyone who knows Cody figures it was him."

"Bud, did you hear that?"

"What?"

"Did you hear that noise?"

"Nah, I was sleepin'."

"I see nothing has changed with you. I heard a noise downstairs."

"I don't think so. Nobody's workin' today."

"I'm telling you, I heard something break. Let's check it out."

"I'm tired."

"You're always tired. Now come on. How do we get down there?"

"Through that door over there. But it's closed."

"Grr...grr...grr..."

"Cody, what's wrong?" Jennifer asked.

"*Bark, bark, bark.*"

"What's behind that door, Dusty?" Michael came to stand beside me.

"It's the door that goes down to the offices and storerooms."

"*Bark, bark, bark.*"

"I think we'd better check it out."

Let me go first. I'll get them.

Get out of here. "*Bark, bark.*" Take that.

"Ow! Damn dog bit me. Let's get out of here."

You'd better run.

"Dusty, over here. Look, the back door's been jimmied open, and a van just took off."

"I'll be. Look at this. They were stacking our boxes of computer chips by the door. Can you imagine committing a robbery on Christmas Day? Thanks, Cody. Looks like you did us another favor."

No problem.

"What happened?" Jane asked as she came down the stairs.

"Someone was trying to steal our inventory. Cody scared them off. Thank goodness he was here."

"How can one little dog do so much for two people?" asked Jane.

It's easy. We're friends. Even if you didn't invite me to dinner.

"Can you help me fix this door, Michael? I've got some tools and wood over here. Janey, take Cody back upstairs."

"Sure. Come on, Cody, we'll go upstairs."

Okay. Wasn't that exciting?

"*Bud, didn't you come downstairs?*"

"*Nope, didn't want to get in the way.*"

"*You were scared.*"

"*Was not. What happened?*"

"*Two men broke the back door and were trying to steal something. I bit one of them on the leg. They ran away.*"

"*Good for you, Code. If I'da known anyone was down there, I woulda come and helped.*"

"*I know you would, Bud.*"

"*Sorry, Code.*"

"No problem."

****

"Ah, that was a great meal. Thank you," Michael said, getting up from the table.

"You're welcome. Dad and I are glad you could share it with us. We're extra glad Cody was here to stop the robbery. We're on a tight enough schedule without losing our inventory. How come you decided to bring him anyway?"

"It was just a fluke. We went into the hotel to give him a present. It slipped out where we were going. When he heard, he went crazy. We had to bring him."

"Are you two ready for your wedding?" Jane asked as she led the group into the living room.

"I hope so," Jennifer replied. "Will you two be able to make it?"

"We wouldn't miss it. It's the fourteenth of February, right?"

"That's right. The winter is the best time for both of us to get away. Besides, I think having it on Valentine's Day is romantic."

"I do too."

"Is everything set for the thirtieth, Michael?" Dusty asked.

"Yup, 1:30. Will you guys make it?"

"If we couldn't before, we will now."

"Good."

Now what am I being left out of?

****

"Hi, honey. Cody and I are home."

"I'm in the kitchen. I'll be right out."

"Come on, Cody. Let's catch the news."

Sure, if I can sit on your lap.

"Don't you two look comfy." Jennifer smiled as she entered the room. "Can I get you anything?"

"I'd love a beer."

I'll have a hamburger.

"What time are you going in tomorrow?" Michael asked.

"Ten. There's a lot to do to get ready."

Get ready for what?

"Okay, we'll be in around two."

Why so late? What's going on?

****

The lobby seems awfully quiet. Where's Mitchell and Carter? And Laura? Something is wrong. I can feel it.

"Come on, Cody. I have to go upstairs to the conference rooms. Do you want to come with me?"

You never take me there. What's going on?

"Here, I'll carry you up the escalator."

No need. I do this all the time. You might as well find out the truth.

"Cody! Have you done this before?"

Yup.

Stop! Something's going on in that room.

"Come here, Cody. I want to pick you up."

Okay. But don't go in that room. I said no. Don't open that door.

"Surprise!"

Wow, it's my birthday again!

"Merry Christmas, Cody. We had so many of your guests writing to see if they could stay with you at Christmas, we decided to have a party."

What a great surprise!

Michael carried me to the front of the room. "Ladies and gentlemen, thank you all for coming. I know you all want a word with Cody, but I don't want him swarmed and frightened. I'm going to put him on one of these chairs. As you came in today, you received a number. That is the order in which you will visit Cody. I'm afraid we'll have to limit everyone to five minutes if you're all going to get a turn. I'm sorry if it sounds a little tacky and callous, but it's the best way we could figure it all out."

Why is everyone clapping?

"I guess they think it's a good idea," Michael said. "Okay, Cody, you sit right here and everyone will come visit you."

Sounds good.

"Number one."

"Hi, Cody. I hope you got our card. I just wanted to say thank you and let you know that since we stayed with you, our marriage has been a lot better. So thank you and let me give you a kiss."

"Number two."

"Cody!"

Andy!

"Hi, Cody."

Hi, Bruce. Hi, Kim.

"Cody, I missed you. I think about you all the time. I'm always saying I bet Cody would like this. Aren't I, Dad?"

"Yes, you are."

"You should have seen me skiing. It was awesome. I went right to the top all by myself. Didn't I, Dad?"

"Yes, you did."

"Guess what? I can swim ten lengths of the pool without stopping. You'd be proud of me, Cody. No life jacket."

I am.

"In school I got all As first semester. I take advanced math classes two days a week after school. I have to be good at math if I want to study astronomy." Andy leaned over to whisper, "Don't worry, I'm still going to be a doctor, but stars will be my hobby. I'm just going to be really good at it.

"I have lots of friends. My best friend is Joey. Not better than you, but my best people friend. He's good in school too. But I read better. We do everything together."

I'm glad you've got a good person friend.

"He takes swimming lessons too. He's a little bit better than me, but I'll get better."

Michael interrupted. "I'm sorry, Andy, your time is up."

"But I'm not finished."

"I'm sorry, Andy, but all these other people want to see him too."

"But he's my friend."

"I know, Andy. You are special, but everyone needs their turn."

"Bye, Cody." Andy hugged me hard and started to cry. "I love you."

I love you, too.

"Bye, Cody," Kim said with tears in her eyes. "You've given us the greatest gift in the world."

I didn't give him, God did.

"Number ten."

"Hi, Sammy."

Hi, Bert.

"Number seventeen."

"Hi, Cody."

Hi, Daniel. Hi, Danny.

"We just wanted to drop by to say thanks. I owe you so much. Danny and I are having a great life. Thanks."

"Number nineteen."

"Hi, Cody."

Hi, Peter.

"I know I live right here in the city, and I could have dropped by anytime. I just wanted to let you know I've had two bonuses and a promotion, and I've done it all clean. Thank you."

Well, I would hope you wouldn't go to work dirty.

"Number twenty-three."

Andy, you're back.

"Andy, you've already had your turn," Michael said.

"That nice lady gave me her turn. See—I've got her number."

Thanks, Janey. See why I love her?

"Anyway, like I was saying, my school is great. I've got lots of friends besides Joey. We play together and have sleepovers."

"We went down to see Mrs. MacNeil this morning. She was glad to see me and very happy for me. She still has Tommy and Mark. Jason got sent to another home. This year I'm going to have a real birthday party with kids and everything, but no birthday will ever be like the one I had with you and Michael. That will always be the best. Just like you'll always be the best."

"Sorry, Andy. Time again."

"I know. Bye, Cody. Is it all right if I kiss you? I know boys don't kiss but sometimes you just have to."

Sure.

"Bye, Michael. Thanks."

"Bye, Andy."

"Number twenty-eight."

"Rachel, how are you?"

"Good. You sure know a lot of people."

"Most of them were my guests."

"Did you help them all as much as you helped me?"

"Nah. Mostly I just listened."

"What did you do for that little boy that was up here twice?"

"I helped him find a mother and father."

"Wow, you must be really good. Can you talk to him?"

"No, you're the only one who's ever been able to communicate with me."

"I'm glad. Sorry. That sounds selfish, but I just want to be special to you."

"You'll always be special, Rachel."

"Thanks. You should see my Cody. He's great!"

"Where is he?"

"Mom said we had to leave him up in the room. I don't know why. I wanted him to meet you. He goes to school with me every day. All the kids wish they had a dog like him. He's pretty smart, but not half as smart as you. I've talked to a lot of dogs, and I think you're a lot smarter than all of them. I don't think dogs are supposed to be as smart as you."

"What can I say? I'm just lucky I guess."

"No, everyone who knows you is lucky."

"Time, Rachel."

"Okay. Bye, Cody. Thanks again. I'll keep writing. Does Michael read my letters to you?"

"Of course. I enjoy them."

"Goodbye."

"Bye, Rachel."

Phew! Is that the end? I'm exhausted.

"Man, Cody, you sure had a lot of people thanking you for things I never heard of."

You don't know the half of it.

"Come on and get your supper. I bet you have to go out, too."

I sure do. I wish I could have seen Andy longer. That was so sweet of Jane, giving up her time to him.

****

Hey, where are we going? I didn't choose a guest for tonight. Uh, Mike, hello! Remember I have to choose a guest? What a waste of time. All the way up here to remember that you forgot. Hurry up. Open the door, so we can get out of here.

Andy!

Chapter Twenty-Seven

"I can't believe it, three more days and I'll be a married man."

Don't tell me your problems.

"Jen's parents and sister arrive today. They are going to be staying with you. My mother flies in at three. Do you want to go with me to pick her up?"

Sure. I'd like to meet your mother. She must be a nice woman to make a son as sweet as you.

"Do you think we need any more practice for the wedding?"

No! At least I don't; you might. We walk in, you stop, I sit, you take the rings off my neck, then we all walk down the middle of the room. What part do you need practice with?

"It's just that I'm getting nervous. This is a big step."

If it's a big step, why didn't you practice that too?

"Come on, let's go for a walk. I've got to put in some time."

****

"Michael, I can't believe you picked me up in a limousine," Mrs. Goodwin exclaimed, as she climbed in.

"You can thank Cody for that. He owns it."

"So, you're the famous Cody."

That's right. And you're Michael's mother. I like you already.

"He's so cute, Michael. Look at that face."

"He's more than just a cute face. You wouldn't believe half the things he's done."

Thanks, Mike.

"Sounds like you're very taken with him."

"I am."

"So, what's going on for the next couple of days?"

"Tomorrow night the guys are having a bachelor party for me, and Friday night Cody is going to spend the night with us. We'll all go to the church together on Saturday. Jen's parents and sister are staying with Cody. We're all having dinner at the hotel tonight, if that's all right?"

"Of course, honey. It's about time I meet Jennifer's parents. Tell me about Saturday. The wedding is at two, right?"

"Yes, and the reception is at the hotel from three to seven. Our plane leaves at ten for Miami, and the next morning we leave for Cozumel. I've booked a room at the hotel for you for Saturday night, and Jeffrey will take you to the airport on Sunday."

"You didn't have to do that, honey."

"I know, but I didn't want you going back to my place all alone."

"That's very thoughtful of you."

Yeah, it was. But what's this about going on a plane? I wonder if I'm going.

****

"Hello, Mrs. Goodwin." Jennifer gave her a hug and kissed her on the cheek.

"Hello, dear."

"I'd like you to meet my parents, Len and Etta Paff. Mom, Dad, this is Michael's mother, Mrs. Goodwin."

"Please, call me Susan. I'm very pleased to meet you."

Len stepped forward to shake her hand. "Same here. I can't believe my little girl is getting married, but I must admit I'm very happy with her choice. It's going to be nice to have another male in the family."

"Mrs. Goodwin, this is my sister, Shelley. She's my maid of honor."

"Hello, Shelley. I see you have your own big event coming up."

"Yes, I'm due in May."

"I guess everyone's been introduced," Michael said.

Hey, what about me?

"Sorry, Cody. Everyone, this is Cody, your host."

"He's so cute," Mrs. Paff said. "Thank you for giving us your suite. It's lovely."

Ah, I didn't give it. I'm sharing it. I hope you know that.

"Let's go in to eat," Michael suggested.

****

"Man, Cody. I feel so awful."

What's wrong, Mike?

"I made a fool of myself last night. Why are men such barbarians? I vowed I wouldn't fall into the trap of all bachelor parties and what did I do? Became an animal like everyone else."

What kind did you become? I never heard of this before. I should have gone to the party—maybe I would have become a human.

"I've been sick all day. I'm just starting to feel human again."

You look human.

"Are you ready to come to my place?"

I'm always ready to go to your place.

****

"Hi, Cody," Mrs. Goodwin said. "Did my growly-bear son pick you up already?"

So he turned into a bear.

"I'm sorry, mom. I apologize for my behavior today. I felt rotten."

"Serves you right. I never saw the point of having a party to act the fool one more time when you never acted that way before."

"You're right. It is kind of stupid. Especially when you can't remember half of what went on. Never again!"

"Why don't you go have a nap? Cody and I will cook a nice roast beef dinner for you."

Sounds good.
"Thanks, Mom."

****

"Are you all ready for tomorrow, dear?" asked Mrs. Goodwin.
"Yes, everything's laid out."
"What about the rings?"
"I had the seamstress at the hotel sew a little hook on Cody's bowtie. I'll put them on at the church."
Bowtie. Wow, I'm going to get dressed up too.
"In the meantime, they're in my pants pocket. That way I shouldn't forget them."
"Have you got the license?"
"Thanks for reminding me. It's in the buffet. I'm glad you mentioned it."
"And how are we getting to the church?"
"We'll take my car. Carter's going to drive you and the car back to the hotel after the ceremony. He'll bring our luggage up to the front desk."
"Sounds like you thought of everything."
"I hope so."
"Michael, honey, I want you to know how proud I am of you. You've become a wonderful man. You're kind and gentle and at the same time still very manly. It's a wonderful combination. I'm proud to be your mother."
"Thank you, Mom." Michael took her into his arms. "I've only become what you taught me to be. I've been blessed to have a mother as wonderful as you, and I'm proud to be your son."
I think I'm going to cry.
"Come on, Cody. Let's get to bed. We have a big day ahead of us."
This is going to be a wonderful night. Just Mike and me.

****

Mr. Paff put his hand on Michael's shoulder. "You know, son, I had my reservations about having a dog in the wedding, but this little guy was terrific. He's better behaved than most kids I've seen. Heck, he's better behaved than all the kids I've seen."

"I don't think you'd be so amazed if you knew him better. He's very smart, sometimes too smart."

How can you be too smart? See—I can't be too smart or I'd know the answer to that.

"What are we going to do with Cody during the reception?" Jennifer asked.

"He'll be fine. He can just wander around. Carter said he'd keep an eye on him. We better get in and form the receiving line."

I bet they're going to receive a bunch of presents.

"Hi, Cody."

Hi, Janey. Hi, Dusty.

"You're so handsome in your little bowtie."

Yeah! That's the word, handsome.

"I didn't expect anything less," Dusty said, "but you were wonderful at the wedding."

Thanks.

"Hi, Cody."

Hi, Andy! I didn't know you were here.

"Mom and Dad wanted to come to Michael's wedding because of what he did for us. I wanted to come to see you. They said I can't talk to you long because you're in the wedding party and you have to mingle. I like your bowtie, you look good. I was proud of you at the church. You did good, I mean well."

"Andy, it's time to sit down," Kim called.

"See ya later, Cody."

Sure.

"Ladies and gentlemen, I'd like to make a toast to the bride…"

Toast? I thought this was a high-class meal. How come we're having breakfast food?

****

"We'd better go get changed, Jen, or we're going to miss our flight," Michael suggested.

"All right. I'll be down in about twenty minutes. I love you."

"I love you, too. Now hurry. Cody, why don't you come with me?"

Sure, Mike.

"This is my mother's room, I'm just going to change, then I want to talk to you for a minute."

No wonder people are so happy to get into my suite. This place is little.

"Come here, Cody. Sit up beside me."

You bet.

"Cody, we're going away for a week."

Yippee! Where are we going?

"Don't get excited. I didn't mean us. I meant Jen and me. It's called a honeymoon. When you get married, you go away together to get to know each other better."

So? I won't get in the way.

"We can't take you because we're going in a plane."

So what.

"Also the place we are going to would require you to have a whole bunch of needles from the vet."

No thanks! Have a good time.

"I just wanted to let you know, so you wouldn't go off your food or anything. I'll be back in a week."

Thanks for the warning.

"Carter will take you out for a walk every day, and you can go with Jeffrey when he picks us up at the airport.

All right!

"There's something else I wanted to say. In a couple of days it will be one year since you became a ward of the hotel. I wanted you to know how proud I am of you. It can't be easy not really belonging to anyone and always having different people staying in your suite.

"I've talked to Adam a couple of times about you becoming my dog, but he says we can't disregard the terms of Mrs. Haney's will. I'm sorry."

It's okay, Mike. It's nice to know you wanted me.

"I feel bad because you give so much to others and I'm not sure how much you get back. I love you, Cody. I never thought a person could feel so strongly for a dog, but I do."

It's okay, Mike, don't be sad. I wish I could talk. Listen to me. I wouldn't change my life for anything. Everyone in the hotel is so nice to me. A day is never boring, there's always something going on. I'm fed well, even better than you know. I like having all those people stay in my suite. Look at how many people I've helped. That's the best part. It makes me feel good. I've made so many wonderful friends who all love me.

Best of all, I've got you. I know how you feel about me, and I feel the same way about you. You're my favorite of everyone. Here, let me give you a kiss.

"Thanks, Cody."

No problem. Besides I can't stop helping people or I wouldn't be the Codyman.

Acknowledgments

I would like to thank Jane Danielson for her insistence, persistence, and extraordinary help throughout this process.

Also thank you to Debbie LeClair and Bonnie Arthur for their enthusiasm and assistance.

Special thanks to my editor, Abigail Mieko Vargus, whose encouragement and support have been invaluable.

I would also like to thank American Book Publishing for taking a chance on a first-time author.

And finally, my love and appreciation to my own Cody, who makes me laugh everyday. He has been an inspiration for many of "Codyman's" antics.

About the Author

Linda Stubbs is a first-time author who resides in Nova Scotia. For many years she has taught school, where a sense of humor has served her well.

She is a lifelong dog-owner and at one time bred Old English Sheepdogs and Westies.

Readers can contact Linda or Cody through their Web site, www.thecodyman.com.